HIDDEN FALLS

a novel

KEVIN MYERS

BEAUFORT
BOOKS

Hidden Falls is a work of fiction. All incidents and dialogue, and all characters with
the exception of some well-known historical figures, are products of the author's
imagination and are not to be construed as real. Where real-life historical figures
appear, the situations, incidents, and dialogues concerning those persons are entirely
fictional and are not intended to depict actual events or to change the entirely
fictional nature of the work. In all other respects, any resemblance to actual persons,
living or dead, events, or locales is entirely coincidental.

For inquiries about volume orders, please contact:
Beaufort Books, 27 West 20th Street, Suite 1102, New York, NY 10011
sales@beaufortbooks.com

Published in the United States by Beaufort Books www.beaufortbooks.com

Distributed by Midpoint Trade Books, a division of Independent Publishers Group
www.midpointtrade.com www.ipgbook.com

Hardcover ISBN: 9780825309335 Ebook ISBN: 978082530816

Library of Congress Cataloging-in-Publication Data
Names: Myers, Kevin, 1967- author.
Title: Hidden falls : a novel / Kevin Myers.
Description: First edition. | New York, NY : Beaufort Books, [2020] |
Summary: "Michael Quinn is not well equipped for his odyssey through New
England's dangerous underworld. In fact, he isn't well equipped for much. Michael's
only goal was to become an editorial writer at the Portland Daily, a milestone he
achieved just the paper was picking up momentum toward irrelevance. Middle-aged,
romantically unattached, distant from his only child, and in search of love through the
missed connections classifieds, Michael thinks these are his only problems. Returning
to Boston after his father dies unexpectedly, Michael's journey home forces him into
conflict with unresolved family issues, denial, and the revelation that his father had
ties to organized crime. Michael inherits some unfinished family business that places
him as the unwitting linchpin in a major criminal conspiracy. His journey brings
danger and betrayal, but also self-discovery and the possibility of a windfall of cash"--
Provided by publisher.
Identifiers: LCCN 2019050952 | ISBN 9780825309335 (cloth) | ISBN
9780825308161 (ebook)
Classification: LCC PS3613.E984 H53 2020 | DDC 813/.6--dc23
LC record available at https://lccn.loc.gov/2019050952

For Zoe, Joe, and Niya

I

#1 BOBBY DOERR, SECOND BASE, BOSTON RED SOX

Even after his death, my father found ways to show his disapproval. He never told me the truth about his life, but he'd saved his biggest lie until he was dead.

I stormed out of First Citizens' Credit Union, straining the hinges of its glass and steel doors. I headed up Front Street toward Eugenia, where I'd parked my rental SUV amid the valley of triple-decker homes. My thoughts felt like a thousand screaming voices echoing though my head. My mind was stuck in a loop of unanswered questions.

I wanted to know who stole the money from the safety deposit box.

I wanted to know why my father lied to me about his entire life.

As I turned the corner, I collided with an enormous man who'd been leaning against the stop sign at the corner. He thrust his massive arm toward my throat and grabbed the collar of my undershirt, knocking me on my heels and slamming me against the wall of the bank. My shirt seam dug into the back of my neck. The man pulled me forward, then sideways, then tossed me back against the wall two or three times, just to prove how easily he could.

I know this guy, I thought. His doughy features seemed familiar, but my focus quickly shifted to the handgun in his right hand. He was twisting it and slapping the barrel against his massive stomach to make sure I saw it. He didn't need to put in that much effort.

"Give me the fuckin' money," he said.

Adrenaline straightened my spine and steeled my words. "There is no fucking money. It was all a myth." I showed him my empty palms and he tightened his grip.

"Don't fuck with me!"

"I'm not fucking with you! The box was empty!"

"'Ah you in on this?"

I had no idea how to respond.

"Did you moth'ahfuck'ahs double-cross me?!" He suddenly noticed the group of people gathered in the bank parking lot staring at us. His anger became anxiety. His pupils dilated, then rapidly constricted as he stretched his eyes wide open. His head swiveled this way and that way, looking for threats as if he'd heard sirens. Eventually, he let me go, his next words resolute.

"I hate ya whole fuckin' family," he growled as he released the safety on his gun.

I had only one card left to play, but it was a good one. "We're not who you need to be worrying about. Walk away and I'll tell my dad's boss to let you live."

He paused for a second. I felt a tinge of hope.

"You 'ah as dead as I am," the massive man scoffed and then convulsed with anger.

I'd just convinced a desperate man with a gun that he was out of options. I could almost hear my farther whispering in my ear, "Nev'ah mistake bein' smah't with bein' right."

"*Fuck!* Fuck! Fuck! *Fuck!*" His face turned red and the veins at his temples began to throb and bulge.

I've made my last mistake, I thought. *I'm going to die right here on the streets of New Bedford. It was a terrible place to live, but it's a worse place to die.*

Time slowed. I became acutely aware of my senses. My vision was so clear it was like I was seeing things before they happened. I decided in that moment that I was not going to die, but I didn't know how I was going to live.

Then out of nowhere, I heard yelling, roaring car engines, sirens, and screeching tires. All my attention stayed on the man in front of me. His eyes squeezed shut. He jutted the gun toward me and I reacted too late. I saw fire and smoke blast from the gun's barrel. I felt a sharp pain in my chest that spread like a fireball. I looked down and watched my shirt turn red with blood. "Fuck me," were the last words to gurgle from between my lips as I fell to the ground. I couldn't breathe. My lungs were filling with blood. I was drowning. I knew I was dying. I saw strangers, body armor, men in blue, and more guns. There was so much screaming. I saw cops rushing the shooter and heard a flurry of gunfire.

A voice I knew told me I would be okay. I smiled. I felt fingers press against my neck, seeking my carotid artery.

The last thing I remember hearing before going unconscious was the sound of a gunshot. The noise from the street faded to total silence. I felt light and free. *I should get shot more often,* I thought, and then it occurred to me that I had, in fact, just been shot, and that I might be dead. Having never been dead before, I had no way of really knowing.

All I could think about was my son.

It's an odd place to begin a story—the moment before I died. It is a pretty important moment, however, compared to all the others. As I lay dying, I yearned to look into my son's eyes one last time and tell him I loved him. Everything else that had seemed so important before faded away. I thought of my mother, my brother, my father, and I thought of my new love. Time lost its meaning. Love lost its need for an object. *Love isn't a thing—it's the only thing,* I thought as my body lay bleeding in the street.

But time is linear, so it probably makes sense to go back

and begin this story a few weeks before I was lying in a pool of my own blood on the streets of New Beige.

I'll begin on the other side of the country at the University of Oregon in Eugene, where I dropped off my son, Ben, for his first year of college. Eugene is the go-to trope for liberal Portlanders when they need an example of a whacky liberal place. Ben chose it, however, in part because it's only two hours from his mom and stepdad's house. Hopefully I factored into that decision, too, but I wasn't certain of that at the time.

Dropping Ben off at college was the second most traumatic thing to happen to me that month.

2

#2 ARNOLD "RED" AUERBACH, COACH, GENERAL MANAGER, BOSTON CELTICS

Ben sat between his mom and stepdad atop his newly purchased Oregon Ducks yellow and green comforter. His dorm room smelled of plastic from all the freshly unwrapped college-living paraphernalia. Every shelf, desktop, and inch of floor space was littered with packaging, gadgets, snack foods, toiletries, and neatly folded clothes. The room looked like Bed Bath & Beyond had Target's baby.

We had reached that point during the move-in process when the grownups had clearly overstayed our welcome, but the kids were too polite to kick us out. We ran out of advice and warnings to share, and none of us were sure what to do to delay the inevitable. Ben's roommate and his four parents dawdled on one side of the room. Ben, Sarah (my ex), and her husband—who by some evil deity's whim resembled my son and shared his name—occupied the other side of the room. I stood alone in no-man's land among the move-in day refuse. Either I looked like I had something to say, or everyone else intuitively knew it was the job of the least popular parent to decide when it was "time to go."

As I looked between the extended families, I found myself wishing Ben was small again and that he would run into my arms and say, "Daddy, don't go!" I would hold him and tousle his hair while our cheeks rubbed together and his pudgy little arms reached around my neck. "It's okay, little man," I'd say and gently bounce him in my arms until his world felt right again. But he was actually taller than me now, and sitting next to his stepdad, who was also taller than me.

"Well, buddy, I love you," I finally said to my son. This was greeted by a chorus of "*awwws*" from Ben's roommate's dad and his three moms. The cooing made us all giggle and gave me time to think of what to say next, but nothing came. As a writer and a father, my lack of words made me feel like a failure.

I thought back to the prenatal visit when the nurse pointed to Ben-the-fetus's penis on the sonogram monitor and told us we were having a boy. Sarah giggled cruelly and said, "And he takes after his dad." From that moment on I was determined to have a better relationship with my son than my dad did with me. Nineteen years later I was still questioning if I had succeeded.

The fear that in that moment, Ben and I were as close as we'd ever be caused my breath to shorten and my knees to weaken. My head felt so precariously balanced on my neck that I thought it might fall off. The only other time I felt like this was when Ben had appendicitis and I watched his gurney roll toward the operating room. It was a routine procedure and it was the most afraid I'd ever been, my worst memory as a parent, until I thought too long about leaving Ben alone in Eugene.

There are only a few moments in life that don't feel temporary. Saying goodbye to my son when I didn't know what our relationship really was felt agonizingly permanent. The only certainty I felt in that moment was that it was time for me to go.

3

#3 DENNIS JOHNSON, GUARD, BOSTON CELTICS

Until Ben matriculated at the University of Oregon, I was the only person on my side of the family who had ever attended college.

My younger brother, Derrick, had made plans to go Dean College that never materialized. He was invited to play Division III basketball, but the summer before his freshman year—or as he called it, his rookie season—he tore the ACL and MCL of his right knee while running from a cop. Our mother had given him money and sent him to the store for cigarettes. While he was in line, he chatted with an off-duty cop that he knew from playing city league basketball. They talked about college and Derrick told him he was thinking of majoring in criminal justice.

The clerk put the cigarettes on the counter. Derrick just grabbed them and sprinted out the door. Within a matter of seconds, the cop went from wishing him luck at college to chasing him down for petty larceny. As Derrick ran out the door, he had to take a sharp turn along Orchard Street to avoid traffic. His foot slid between a sewer grate and the curb and his knee bent in the wrong direction. The coach rescinded Derrick's invitation to play basketball and my brother lost his motivation to attend college.

When I asked him why he stole the cigarettes when he had the money for them, all he said was "I knew I was fast'ah than him." He didn't think beyond that. My mother, being a devout Catholic, blamed herself, and quit smoking as her penance. The charges were dropped when Derrick agreed to do volunteer work at a city-run basketball clinic. He later became a cop himself, and eventually worked alongside the guy who'd chased him.

Derrick and I were not close, but as I drove north from Eugene, I wished we were. I wanted to talk through feeling like a shitty dad with someone who knew what it was like to have a shitty dad. I wondered if I did enough, or was enough, for Ben. I worried that I worked too much and maybe sometimes drank too much as he grew up.

I also wanted to talk with someone about the modern weirdness of standing in a dorm room with Ben, Sarah, Other Ben, and Ben's roommate's many parents. One of whom, within three minutes of meeting me, mentioned she was in a polyamorous relationship. I wanted to have the kind of brother with whom I could process things like this, but I didn't. We had a relationship filled with arguing and avoidance, and almost nothing beyond that.

To be completely honest, I wanted to talk about Ben with someone who would feel the need to tell me only the things I wanted to hear—and that was definitely not Derrick.

Despite the student services staff feeding me a bunch of pablum on emotional intelligence during New Parent Orientation, I wasn't prepared to cope with how alone I was feeling on the 111-mile slog home. As I thought back on the hours of presentations saturated with the words *thriving, wellness, well-being, holistic,* and *success,* I imagined how my father would have responded to them. My father was not emotionally intelligent in the least—in fact, both my parents would likely have been expelled from remedial emotion school.

My father was stoic and aspired to be nothing more than dependable. One night in the '90s while we were drinking at Sully's, his neighborhood bar, my dad was introduced to a man I didn't know by another man I'd seen around. The familiar man said, "This is Jake, he's a good guy, friend of ours, you can depend on him." It was an introduction that clearly made my father very proud. His obvious pride in that everyday moment was so rare that it stuck with me. Every other emotion shown by my father was attached to exceptional feats by professional athletes—Boston athletes, like Pedro Martinez, Big Papi, Bobby Orr, Larry Bird, and Tom Brady. Emotions were largely reserved for wins and losses rather than friends and family.

The first time I witnessed my father express an emotion that was not engendered by a New England sports team was in 1978. I subsequently watched him implode out of pure disappointment later that year after the Red Sox blew a 19-game lead in the American League East pennant race and then a one-game playoff, and then again when they caved to the Mets in the World Series in '86. I experienced his eruptions of uninhibited pride after the '01, '03, and '04 seasons when the Patriots won their first Super Bowls and "officially" became a football dynasty, and then his utter despair after their shuttered perfect season at the hands of the New York Football Giants in Super Bowl XLII. I was also with him in October of 2004 for his single greatest emotional outpouring yet. I stood next to him in Sully's Tab and Bite after the Red Sox won their first World Series in his lifetime, and I watched him cry real salt-and-water tears of joy.

But, back to the summer of 1978, when I was 12. We were on a camping trip to the White Mountains of New Hampshire. The great promise of the trip was a visit to Hidden Falls. The brochure described it as "a hidden oasis carved by the forces of nature into the landscape of the White Mountains." It sounded magical. As we departed from New Bedford, I imagined standing beneath the cascading water that I pictured, somehow, as being turquoise and tropical. I'm sure my mental image was inspired by the *Love Boat* episode with Kristy McNichol, as my pubescent mind populated the scene with Kristy look-a-likes in halter tops and cutoff jeans. Their bodies glistened in the sun as they beckoned me to the water's edge.

My fantasy was interrupted by a stop at a rest area. Even though I had to pee, there was a burgeoning reason to stay seated, so I opened the *Rand McNally* across my lap and convinced my father I could wait.

"I'll see how far we have left to go," I told him as I fidgeted in my seat and thumbed through the map.

Whenever we traveled to the north country, my dad followed the old routes to Boston rather than taking the quicker less inspiring 495 to 93 North through the southern suburbs. We'd wind our way through the old-moneyed towns that stretch west from the Hub of the Universe. As we got close to the city, he'd make so many twists and turns that it felt like we were evading a tail. He'd bring us through Jamaica Plain and Chestnut Hill to a section of Soldiers Field Road where the Charles River became so narrow you could skip a stone from Boston to Cambridge. The route through Boston was carefully designed to pass the campuses of Boston College, BU, Emerson (which he never pointed out), MIT, and of course, Harvard.

"The smah'test people in the world 'ah right he'ah in about a two-mile block in Cambridge," he'd say. Then his eyes would narrow as he'd pat me on the head. "And that's whe'ah you belong, Mikey, right he'ah with those people."

To me, however, they were "those people," not "our people." Our people didn't go to college—we found jobs and got by. We tracked the seasons by the type of ball that was in play: baseball, basketball, football, and hockey. The idea that I could go to Harvard felt as possible as riding my bike to the moon. I would just smile, nod my head, and sit quietly for a few minutes until we reached the Citgo sign, which to a Red Sox fan was like seeing the Star of Bethlehem. It marked the entrance to the Holy Land, Fenway Park, where every spring the region threw its faith into a band of saviors who always found a way to break our hearts in the fall.

"But this is the year!" my dad exclaimed as we drove past in July of 1978. "Freddie Lynn, Yaz, Remy, Burleson, Rice, Fisk, Dwight Evans, the Boomer, Bill Lee, Dennis Eckersley, Bill Campbell, this is the best team since '75 or '67!" Those were years when World Series losses made for longer, colder winters.

Even though the Sox held a 14-game lead in the American League East as we drove past Kenmore Square, they ended the season tied with the dreaded New York Yankees and lost the pennant in a one-game playoff. It was such an epic failure that the local press dubbed it the "Boston Massacre."

We camped like British explorers (which is to say, not lightly) in the National Forest off the Kancamagus Highway.

The campground was beyond a covered bridge with a red tin roof that was supported by giant crisscrossed timbers. The water beneath it carried the tannins of decomposed foliage, which gave it the color of weak tea. The air felt clean like after a heavy rain, and smelled like my grandmother's embroidered pine-needle pillow.

It took our combined strength to remove the canvas tent from the back of the Country Squire station wagon. The tent stood eight feet tall and was supported by wooden poles. It had three compartments: a bedroom for each of us and a living room between them. It took the better part of an hour to set the thing up. We had a six-burner Coleman stove, and a metal ice chest that was so heavy when loaded it could only be moved in a succession of short bursts. Our army surplus cots probably weighed 25 pounds each, but they needed to be sturdy to hold our musty wool insulated sleeping bags.

But the important moment came the morning after we arrived: the long-awaited trip to Hidden Falls. As we got in the car, my father placed three things on the seat between us: a canteen, a basketball ref's whistle, and a small box wrapped in butcher-block paper. The wrapping was held to the box with twine—pretty anachronistic. My father didn't have the type of personality that invited questions. "If I wanted you to know what was in the box," I knew he'd say, "I'd have told you." So, I waited and wondered.

My imagination ran wild trying to concoct a situation

in which a canteen, a whistle, and something the size of two stacked decks of playing cards would become necessities. A gin rummy marathon was as close as I got.

After about 30 minutes of winding through narrow backroads, we turned onto an even narrower dirt road. The Country Squire wasn't really made for country driving, and we bounced so vigorously over swells and potholes that we joked about putting on our seat belts. We came to a stop where the road widened enough for my father to make a three-point turn. He shifted the car into park. His face became so serious that it frightened me, it was tight with an urgency reserved for illness, divorce, and death. My heart skipped as he reached across me and opened my door.

"Straight out the'ah, Michael, is ya future." He handed me the canteen and I almost shat myself.

Is he sending me off into the woods to survive on my own?
"Dad—" I started.

"Listen," he interrupted, his eyes softening a bit. He placed the box and the canteen on my lap. "The wat'ah you need to survive, but in this box is the most important thing I'll ev'ah give you. It's the most important thing any fath'ah can give a son, mo'ah than money or the keys to a family business—it's direction. The swimming hole is about a mile due north. In that box is a compass. The needle always points north. Follow the needle, and I'll be waiting fah you." And with that he pushed me out of the car and drove only a few yards before slamming on the brakes. The car slid to a halt on the rocky dirt road. I thought, this is where he'd say "Just kidding!" out his window, but instead he tossed me the whistle and shouted, "And if you get lost, blow this every few minutes until someone finds you!" before he drove off again.

The whistle was attached to a hockey lace that my father had balled in his hand. He had a good throwing arm, but it didn't reach me. The lace uncoiled and fluttered behind the hard-plastic casing like the vapor trail of a sputtering plane. I didn't move to catch it. I just watched it hit the ground as the car bounced and bobbed away from me.

I was dumbfounded.

I stood by the side of the road like an expectant dog tied to a pole waiting for its owner to return. Anger slowly burned away my initial fog of disbelief. I wanted to get to the swimming hole so I could yell at my father—maybe even punch him. My palms sweated through the wrapping of the package before I got around to opening it. It took me a few minutes to untie the string and clear away the damp paper. The compass looked like a pocket watch. On the front of it was engraved: "Always move toward your goals."

"Okay, I get it!" I said aloud. "It's good to have a goal. You can come back and get me now."

After a few minutes, I decided there was no sense in standing around. *It's only a mile,* I thought. *I can beat him there. I can run a mile in under 10 minutes. That'll show him. When he gets there, my hair will be wet and I'll be relaxing on*

the rocks, spinning the compass on its chain, and the whistle
will be at the bottom of the lake.

I popped open the compass's lid and used the red needle
to get my bearings. The forest was second growth, so there
were lots of shrubs and ground cover to get around. There
was an outcropping of rocks due north about 400 yards away,
at the top of a bluff. I'd work my way there as quickly as
possible, find my bearings again, and then set the next mark.

The first stretch was pretty easy—deer trails crisscrossed
the hillside and I was able to scamper to the outcropping in
a matter of minutes. The rocks were surrounded by enough
unripe blueberries to make my stomach hurt for days.

Down the other side of the bluff was a ravine with a
gently running stream. There was an eddy just a few degrees
east of due north—it was the widest crossing point, but also
the most obvious landmark. Thick brush made the trek slow.
I was so determined to get there quickly that I didn't even
consider the possibility of poison sumac, oak, or ivy until I
was a hundred yards down the slope. Imagining my father's
face when he saw me standing at the swimming hole waiting
for him diminished my concern. His brow would furrow.
His head would cock slightly to the side and the corner of
his lips would bend upward until a dimple formed.

"How the hell did you get here so fast?" he'd ask.

I worked my way to the eddy, then followed a path that
ran parallel to the water while I looked for a shallow or rocky
crossing. The path brought me far off course, which made

me nervous, but I also became curious about the increasing force of the water. The calm jabber of the gentle current was being overcome by the sound of powerful rapids downstream. Mist filled the air, and rays of sun shone through the evergreen canopy, illuminating patches of wildflowers along the ravine. Dots of purple, white, and yellow flashed brilliantly against an endless palette of greens and browns. The forest was a kaleidoscope of sensations: scents of lavender and pine, the chill of the mist mixed with the warmth of the sun, light sparkling and refracting in every drop of morning dew. The forest seemed to exhale and stretch itself awake.

I've gone too far east, I thought as I turned from the sun and headed back toward the eddy, running twice as fast to make up for lost time. I swam across the stream holding the compass above the water and floating the canteen between my chin and shoulder. The opposite shore was rocky and steep, but it was as easy to climb as a staircase. It was also a perfect hiding place for water snakes, my least favorite thing in the world. Swimming snakes are an evil evolutionary invention.

I scurried up the cliff. It seemed higher looking down from the top than it did while looking up at it from the below. Goosebumps covered my body as a breeze blew through my soaked cotton shirt and cutoff jeans. I moved out from the shadows of the birch trees that lined the cliff. To the north stretched an open field. Bugs and butterflies hovered just above the bending stalks of wheat grass, and the sunlight hit the field at such an extreme angle that all I could see to my east were silhouettes of grass and trees.

I looked for a landmark at the north end of the field, but nothing stood out against the wall of pines and maples. Before I could identify what was rustling by my foot, I was startled by a high-pitched screeching and a blur of feathers around my head. I had stepped on a pheasant hole, and said pheasant was letting me know visitors were not welcome. I was already five yards north before my brain could completely confirm it was a pheasant and not a phantom that had scared my nut-sack into my stomach. My pace had been fueled by adrenaline and it couldn't be sustained for very long.

There was a giant oak tree 200 yards away, but it was too far east to be a landmark. I was determined to maintain my pace until I crossed its long shadow. *The shadow,* I thought, *goes east and west. If I cross the shadow, perpendicular to it, I should be heading exactly north.*

I concentrated on the area immediately before me, searching for anything like that pheasant that might trip me up. As I neared the oak, my approach was slightly caddywhompus, and I adjusted my course accordingly. I slowed as I crossed the shadow to check my logic against the compass. The needle pointed north, but it occurred to me for the first time on my journey that without a map (and unless my father had exactly calculated my departure point, which I was very certain he had not), I was more or less flying blind.

Suddenly, doubt and fear gripped me. *What the hell?!* I thought as I slowed to a walk. I stopped in the middle of the field, my vigor gone, and looked in every direction for something manmade, somewhere to walk to where another human might happen across me and help me find my way—a road, a building, something, anything—but I saw nothing.

I contemplated turning back. I knew I could find the Forest Service road again, and that would lead me back to the highway. It would take half a day, but I'd be safe and easy to find. I was probably closer to the swimming hole, but I had no real way of knowing if I was on track.

I decided to continue north.

What a jerk. Leaving me out here to die.

My concern was no longer getting there first—I was now concerned about getting there at all. As I walked, I scanned the horizon about 90 degrees in front of me, hoping to find some sign that I was heading toward Hidden Falls. With the compass open, I followed the needle diligently toward the wall of pines and maples. As I got maybe 175 yards from the end of the field, I noticed a road just inside the tree line.

I shut the compass and broke into a sprint. Within fifteen seconds, I'd covered half the ground to the road. The compass was clammy against my palm and the whistle, which I'd strung around my neck, was bouncing off my chest, then cheek, then chest, then chin, then chest, then eye, until I batted it like a tetherball around my neck. Through the trees I saw the outline of a trail sign. I focused on that sign like a hungry lion hunting its prey.

As I got close, I slowed and took several deep breaths. "Hidden Falls .3 miles," read the bright yellow lettering carved into the brown sign—an arrow pointed toward a footpath. I sipped from the canteen and caught my breath as I walked in the direction of the arrow. My wet shirt clung to my skin. A drop of sweat fell into my eye. I ignored the stinging as I focused on covering the last three-tenths of a mile as quickly as possible.

Confident now, I began to run as fast as I could. My thoughts again drifted to my father's face when he saw me climbing out of the majestic waters surrounded by all those glistening Kristy McNichol look-a-likes. The forest's canopy opened before me. *This must be it,* I thought as I slowed to savor the moment. The path took a ninety-degree turn and followed along a rocky face that had been excavated to make room for a parking lot. I stood at the path's elbow and looked across an expanse of asphalt to find the empty promise of a marketing brochure.

"What the hell?"

I desperately surveyed the area, looking for something redeeming, but there was nothing. The "falls" were a concrete ledge over which water dripped from a 12-inch corrugated-steel pipe. The catch basin was also constructed of poured concrete with a spill drain downriver to ensure the water level would always be sufficient for swimming, and probably most often stagnant. The wooden picnic tables were all missing slats, the swing set had no swings, and the bottom third of the lone fifty-five-gallon steel trashcan was completely obscured by overflowing refuse.

Tucked in the far end of the parking lot was a '73 Oldsmobile Cutlass Supreme resting on cinderblocks with all its windows smashed out. The recession took its toll on many aspects of life in the United States, but this place seemed earmarked for aggressive neglect. Hidden Falls wasn't hidden: it was abandoned. I walked to the end of the path, sat on the curb, sighed, and waited for my father to show up.

The sun rose above the trees and its warmth chased the goosebumps from my arms and legs. Heat bugs screeched as the humidity increased, but still there was no sign of the Country Squire. I looked at the engraving on the compass once more (*always move toward your goals*), and passed the time by thinking of more fitting alternatives (*think things through, have a plan, bring a map*).

I didn't think of anything as motivational or affirming as the saying on the compass, but my phrases all certainly seemed more pragmatic. Having a goal is important, and moving toward it is important, but how you experience the journey is also important. Missing from the lesson on the compass was how to reach your goals without feeling lost, alone, and afraid for your life.

I sat and waited. I skipped stones. I sat and waited some more.

The sun was high above the trees by the time the station wagon jounced into the parking lot and screeched to a stop just a few feet from where I was sitting. My father sprung from his seat and ran to me before the car had rocked itself still. His expression was nothing like the one I had imagined. His eyes were wide and bloodshot. His chin trembled and his clinched lips had turned white around the edges. He was so unrecognizable that I felt a tinge of fear race along my spine as he rushed toward me—I relived that exact moment in anxiety dreams for the rest of my life. No words escaped as he opened his mouth to talk. Then he reached down and hugged me. His cotton and polyester shirt felt like burlap against my sun-reddened face.

I tried to say something, but I was distracted by the sound of his heart. It thumped so loudly that I could still hear it as I pulled back from his chest to see if his face had regained its stoic detachment. His expression had changed, but it was still unfamiliar.

He kissed me on the head and said, "I love you," as he wiped a tear from his cheek.

It was twenty seconds, probably less, but that moment stayed with me for reasons I never completely under-stood—just like the compass that I still sometimes carried in my pocket. Maybe I kept it for the message inscribed on the lid (*always move toward your goals*) or maybe I kept it to feel closer to my dad.

Either way, it was in my pocket when I contemplated calling my dad after leaving my son in Eugene.

I was a cocktail of emotions: anxiety, fear, doubt, and deep awareness of my own mortality. During moments like this in my past, I'd often reached for a drink. Had there been a place to stop, I probably would have bellied up to a bar rather than picked up the phone.

I had no reasonable expectation that my father and I would talk about anything other than the Red Sox's awful mid-relievers and the struggling bullpen, but I wanted him to tell me everything would be okay. I wanted him to assure me that Ben and I would grow closer. And if I was being totally honest, I wanted him to apologize for being a cold-hearted bastard and admit that he'd always favored Derrick. But I was ready to settle for a few reassuring words.

As I drove north on I-5, I couldn't shake my chills. *I've lost my son*, I thought. I felt myself sinking into a familiar, concerning melancholy. A sad little gremlin, poking at me, telling me one drink would set everything straight. I always thought the first drink would fix my problems, and then the second, but that would typically lead to the eighth or tenth, and these tended to cause my problems.

I looked east past the lush emerald fields populated with flocks of domesticated sheep, to the rocky foothills just beyond. I wanted to feel solid and secure like the bases of those mountains, or even to feel the contentment of the sheep and what I imagined was their certainty that grazing and breeding were the complete fulfillment of their potential. *Lucky bastards*, I thought as I scanned my contacts for my parents' phone number. I doubted my decision to call my father for at least a third time, then inexplicably determined it was my best course of action and dialed the number. I wished beyond reason that by some kind of magic, he was going to make me feel like less of a failure.

My mother answered the phone after having just watched a *60 Minutes* segment about sexual assaults on college campuses. She gushed warnings for Ben about not getting in with the "wrong crowd," subject to the whims of "women who lie about such things for attention." I asked her if that was the focus of the segment. "No," she said, "but you have to read between the lines with the mainstream media these days."

Being a member of the "mainstream media" myself, I took a deep breath to maintain my composure. I paused to feel grateful that I did not live in the world that existed in my mother's mind. Her world was filled with constant threats from forces she could not see or understand—all of them from non-Catholic foreigners and atheist liberals who hated "American values."

"Is Dad around?" I asked.

She tried to drag me deeper into her delusion—I didn't take the bait. It was easier to let her think I was offended by her jab at my profession than to try to convince her that

Title IX enforcement was intended to gain equality for victims of sexual crimes and not to emasculate boys. I was going to tell her that Ben and I had had many conversations about drinking, consent, and sex, but instead I chose to stick with my family's hereditary strength: avoiding directness and confrontation.

"I didn't mean you," she suddenly clarified.

"I know, Mum, I know," I said, with no conviction.

My father got on the phone and immediately asked what was wrong with my mother. "Oh, you know, Dad, it was just Mum being Mum. Nothing serious," I said.

"Well, take it easy on the old lady," he said. "Ya know she's not as tough as she used to be."

"Is everything okay?" I asked. He was usually the guy who piled on rather than coming to anyone's defense.

"Nothin' time can't fix," he said wryly. It was a reference to a joke he told on his seventy-fifth birthday and had been repeating in some form ever since. "I've lived a good life and learned everythin' I'm gonna learn—only time will fix the rest of my faults," he'd said before blowing out the candles. That he is not a funny man by nature or practice made his repetitive joke more endearing than it was tedious.

I tried to think of the best way to broach my fears about Ben, but we had no entry point for that kind of talk. The most personal thing my father and I generally talked about was the Red Sox injury report. They were off to a slow start, so instead of trying to break new ground, I chickened out and goaded him to call for the manager's job. To my surprise, he didn't bite.

"Who c'ah's about the problems of the rich?" he asked.

For last forty years, I can't think of much else you have cared about, I thought. But I said, "Yeah, I guess you're right."

"You know, Mike, what really matt'ahs is your relationship with Bennie." His voice cracked. I couldn't have been more surprised if the sheep in the pasture formed a chorus line and danced the cancan.

"He grew up quick," I said, shocked. "He's becoming his own man."

"Time nev'ah slows down, Mike," he said, and took a pause that felt like an eternity.

Even though this was exactly why I called, the conversation was way outside our wheelhouse. It felt too foreign. My chest tightened and I began to sweat a little. New Bedford men don't fix our problems by talking about them—we pat each other on the back and drink them away. Whatever was bothering my dad, I assumed, had to be more serious than my concerns about my relationship with Ben.

"Is everything okay, Dad?"

"You know, Mike, the'ah so many things I wish I did different." His voice was so distant, it felt like he was talking from the future into the past.

"Dad, are you and Mom doing okay? Is there something you want to tell me?"

"I wish I told you a lot of things, Mike," he said. "But,

I don't know. I'm just getting' to be an old man lookin' back …"

"You're a good father, Dad," I said, quickly realizing I commented on what I was thinking, not what he was saying.

"I wasn't a bad fath'ah, Mike, but that's not the same thing as bein' good," he said with an ironic laugh.

"Dad, where's this coming from?" I asked. "You were always there for me and Derrick."

"I'm becomin' a sap in my old age, Mike, that's all." He started to sound more like himself. "And everythin' else good?"

The pause lingered. It's how our conversations always ended. "Everythin' else good?" he'd say. My response changed with the season: "Everything but our mid-relievers," or "offensive line," or whatever ailed the team we had been talking about. This time was different. There was only one thing to be said that could match the weight of the silence. The words "I love you" pushed their way toward my mouth and got stuck like a popcorn kernel on my tonsil. I cleared my throat.

"Alright then, Mike. Be well, okay, kid?" and that was that. Those were the last words he said to me while he was alive. Maybe that's where my story actually begins.

4

#4 BOBBY ORR, DEFENSEMAN, BOSTON BRUINS

I was a journalist, or to be precise (as a good journalist aspires to be) I was a columnist for the *Portland Daily*. Since I'd been a paperboy for the *Boston Globe* and *Herald*, I wanted to follow in the tradition of Mike Barnicle (the '70s and early '80s version), or Jimmy Breslin from New York. When I was fifteen, I found Breslin's Watergate book, *How the Good Guys Finally Won*, at a yard sale and bought it for fifty cents. Reading it gave me a deeper appreciation for the legendary Massachusetts Congressman and Speaker of the House, Tip O'Neill, but I came away from that book wanting to be Jimmy Breslin. Even as a kid, I felt like telling the story could be just as important as doing the deed. To poorly paraphrase Foucault, the institutions that are reinforced are capable of enacting power. Tip helped save the country from the corruption of the Nixon White House, but in telling Tip's story, Breslin reinforced the institutions of democracy as people were losing their faith in them. Both men have their place in history.

I have always believed that a robust press is a key component to a robust democracy. This is one of the reasons I loved teaching Intro to Journalism at Portland Community College, something I started to do for extra money after my divorce but continued to do out of passion. The class satisfied an elective requirement in the communications track and could count as an English course within certain vocational majors. Enrollment was usually somewhere between 20 to 30 students, usually with little to no interest in becoming reporters. Huzzah! But there was always one student with a burning desire to be a journalist, sometimes more. Those were the students who kept me coming back.

I taught at the Sylvania campus, which is tucked into the hills of Southwest Portland, on the border of the moneyed plutocracy of Lake Oswego. The grounds were dotted with remarkable hemlocks and Sitka spruce that were five to six feet in diameter. There were a few weeks during the spring and fall when the sunset coincided with my arrival to campus. Those glorious evenings, I would admire the golden light warming the ticky tacky suburbs that sprawled west toward mountains of Tillamook State Forest. The sun seemed to dawdle above the horizon, admiring the splendor of all creation until it touched the mountain's ridge and hurried off to its next destination. The streetlamps, storefronts, and trails of brake lights and headlights lost their import in the dim haze. They became part of a landscape of distant glowing objects stretching infinitely into the impending nighttime sky.

My classroom was next door to the ceramics studio and around the corner from the auto shop. I suspect the architects copied that layout from the Columbia Graduate School of Journalism. The ceramics instructor, Mary Russell, was an old classmate from Emerson College—we worked together on the student newspaper, the *Berkeley Beacon*. We knew each other then, but not that well. She worked in layout—I was an editor, and took my work, and myself, pretty seriously. Had she not recognized my name from the course schedule, I'm not so sure we would have gotten reacquainted. She had transformed from a quirky '80s pre-grunge John-Hughes-movie character to something of a modern free spirit, like one of those people I'd see in the fancy grocery who seemed to always be coming from hot yoga or massage therapy. She belonged to the tribe of people who were always centered, breathing peaceful breaths, and comfortable in their perfectly exfoliated, glowing skin. I envied those people as they moved through the store with a sense of direction but no urgency. Once, while standing next to the bulk food dispensers, I was so enamored by the presence of one such goddess that I uttered the phrase, "I can't believe I forgot my reusable rice satchel," as I filled up a paper bag with brown rice for myself. This did not evoke the desired response. I was not recognized as part of the tribe and in addition to my embarrassment, I had to eat brown rice for weeks: lose-lose.

What I'm trying to say is Mary had a natural ease, but I would never feel judged by her for buying white rice in a plastic bag. We were the same age and both grew up in Massachusetts separated by Buzzards Bay and a couple of social strata. We shared a lot of the same cultural reference points, which made for fun and comforting chats. We had a special kinship for being New England ex-pats. We got together a few times a month to reminisce, talk about politics, and bitch about our passionless students. Time with Mary always passed quickly.

On gorgeous days, like the Tuesday after dropping off Ben in Eugene, we would sit on the deck of Walter Mitty's and talk over the sounds of city buses and obnoxiously loud motorcycles passing on SW Capitol Highway.

"I meant to return the book you lent me," said Mary, "but I must have left it on the kitchen counter. If you need it back, we could stop by my place and grab it after we're done here."

"*Victory Lab*?" I asked.

She nodded.

"I'm in no hurry to get that back," I said. "Whenever you get it to me is fine. What did you think?"

"It was a little creepy," she replied, snickering. "I didn't get all the way through it."

"*1984* creepy?"

"Sort of. I know it's ridiculous of me to be so naive, but I want to be." She had this delightfully odd mannerism when she was being funny. It started with a crinkling of her nose, then she'd tilt her neck slightly, then look down. When she lifted her gaze, she'd smile the warmest smile. There was something very pleasant about it all.

"I saw it more as a way to rally the support of those who are already committed," I said, more defensively than I intended.

There was a pause, and she smiled.

"Do you miss him?" She'd jerked the wheel on our conversation, steering it in precisely the direction I'd hoped it would go. I enjoyed that about her.

"Ben? Yeah, I miss him a lot," I said with a polite chuckle. "I'm sorry, was I that distracted?"

"Don't be silly," she said. "No. You weren't, really. I was just thinking ahead a few years to when Esme leaves the nest."

"It's strange, you know? I mean, he wasn't with me all the time, and on a normal week I wouldn't even see him for a few days, but now that he's gone off to college, I miss him all the time."

"Weren't we just freshmen at Emerson?" She smiled. "How is it possible that so much time has passed?"

"One day at a time, I suppose," I said, trying to be amusing.

"Are you being profound or are we at an AA meeting?" She succeeded at being amusing. "Do you remember the first time we hung out?"

"Was it at that place in Allston, Arbuckle's?"

"No, but close. It was across Comm Ave at Uno's."

"It must have been a special occasion if we went to Uno's," I said.

"That's kind of what I remembered about it—how excited you were to be at Uno's."

"That was orientation, right? The journalism wannabes went off and did their own thing?"

"Yeah, the wannabe *Beacon* staff. I remember you were wearing Gap corduroys, a Celtic's t-shirt, and those green Converse All-Stars—your accent was thick as mud in those days, but everyone listened when you talked."

"All I remember is that I was so nervous ..."

"You're lying."

"I'm not! You know I was the first one in my family to go to college. Besides, I only had like fifteen dollars in my pocket and I was horrified I wouldn't have enough to cover my part of the bill. In those first few weeks, I contemplated going home about twelve times a day. I felt so out of place. I remember feeling silently judged by all you rich kids, especially the private school kids with their fancy clothes and BMWs. I felt like Emerson was such a reach for me, but for everyone else it was their safety school."

"I did not have a BMW! And Emerson was my second choice, well, third …"

"Maybe that's why I was so intimidated by you," I posed.

"You were not."

"Stop doing that. And besides, why would that surprise you?"

"I don't know. I guess I assumed that you saw yourself as I saw you, and you saw me as I saw me: awkward and searching for my identity."

"And how did you see me? The kid with the ugly sneakers and the thick accent?"

She chuckled. "The confident kid who was sure of his direction in life—unflappable. The rest of us were just like, 'Whatever, let's get drunk for a few years and then find a job.'"

"Except Paul," I clarified, remembering my best friend from college through to that day, and who helped me get my job at the *Portland Daily*. "Paul was unflappable—I felt very flappable. I was just like every other guy from New Bedford, but you had your own thing going on. You were unique. You knew all these bands that I'd never even heard of, and you were so well read, and well traveled, and you had your own sense of style. You had it goin' on, Russell!"

"Paul was a year ahead of us and already had the system wired when we got there. It's surprising to me how uncomfortable you felt."

"U of O had all these orientation sessions for first

generation kids. I'm glad for them, you know? I would have benefited from that. I always just felt kind of lucky to be at Emerson, but never really like I belonged."

"That's terrible," she said. "That makes me feel awful."

"Good! Because it's mostly your fault. I've blamed you all these years. In fact, I'm going to send you my therapist bills." My attempt at humor was met with a blank stare. "I don't think it's a bad thing to feel lucky, and to get a great education."

"Why are you always so infuriatingly affable? Sometimes I just want you to be angrier about things."

"Are you paraphrasing the Buddha right now?"

"Yes, that's precisely what I'm doing," she said, and altered course again. "So, what was the funny story about Ben's roommate?"

"Oh, right, yes, oh my God, you're going to love this. So, Ben's roommate has a dad and three moms, which, you know, whatever. Who cares?" Mary's raised eyebrow made me realize I was leaving out too much information, but I was excited to get to the punchline. "Um, two couples, not sister wives," I clarified. "But his step-mom, who's married to his dad, says, 'Hi, my name's Meredith, and Steve and I are in a polyamorous relationship. He's my primary, but we're thinking of adding a co-.'"

That amusing, if not remarkable, news was met with almost no reaction from Mary, who had been divorced and part of the Portland dating scene for several more years than me. I was still getting used to all the open marriages I encountered on OK Cupid. It seemed like half of the dating pool in their forties had "amazing partners" who were willing to share them with others—usually alone but sometimes as part of a group. I am not making a moral judgement—it's really not any of my business what consenting adults do while strapped to their bed posts and wearing rubber clothing—but the idea of monogamy had always been so appealing to me that the alternatives became something of a fascination. Mary always had insightful, and often hilarious, observations about various subcultures and I hoped, in vain, she would explore this one with me.

"What did you say?" she asked like a prosecuting attorney.

"I'm an Aquarius," I laughed.

"You did not!" She broke with a small chuckle.

"No. I said something like, 'Oh, is that working out for you guys?'"

Mary shook her head. We just looked at each other for a few beats as a sport bike accelerated through the yellow traffic light with a high-pitched mechanical whine. I had no idea what she was thinking. Then, her neck tilted in the way it does before she starts in on me. One side of her lips quirked and made her dimple appear. She had that sparkle in her eye.

"Okay, what?" I sighed.

"Where was her husband when she said this?" She did the thing with her nose again.

"It wasn't like that," I said. "Why can't I ever just tell a funny story, you know, without it becoming a therapy session?"

"How is this becoming a therapy session?"

"Well, you know, I tell a funny story, then you point out why it's not funny but is really a sign of some deficiency in my character."

"What are you talking about?"

"It's true! You and Paul do it to me all the time. You were about to tell me that she wanted to make sweet, sweet polyamorous love to me and that I just couldn't see it. Well, that's what Paul would have said, for sure, but you were either going to say that or that I should stop being so small town, or that I should have kicked everyone else out and put a sock on the door handle and had sex with one of Ben's roommate's mothers then and there."

"I see your point, but I wouldn't call it therapy as much as me calling you a dumbass. And I wouldn't recommend that you have poly-sex, but I will point out that the only reason someone tells you they're polyamorous is because they want to open the door to sweet, sweet polyamorous lovemaking—um, your term—which is, absolutely, a blind spot of yours, and you're right, that Paul and I have both identified this weakness in you."

She delighted in this sort of banter and, frankly, so did I. It playfully pushed us to see ourselves better—but mostly me, I suspect.

"You're alright, Russell," I said, suddenly noticing that our beers were mostly gone and that the waiter had just come out on the deck. "So, what are we doing here?" She got quiet, slumped in her chair, and gently bit her bottom lip. I wasn't sure what happened. I thought things were about to become fun, but suddenly they felt a little weird. The waiter came and asked if we'd like another round.

"So, what are we doing here, Russell? Are we getting another round or not?" I asked again.

She laughed and smiled at me. It was like we had an inside joke that I wasn't in on. "I'll have another," she finally said.

"What just happened?" I whispered to her as the waiter left.

"We're having another beer," she whispered back, and she did the nose thing.

5

#5 NOMAR GARCIAPARRA, SHORTSTOP, BOSTON RED SOX

My brother Derrick called while I was driving to work. His *modus operandi* when discussing family business was to call during my morning commute. This gave him a built-in reason to cut short our conversation and make it seem like it was my fault. I wanted to ask what was bugging my dad, but Derrick was terse from the get-go. He had an agenda and he was sticking to it.

Derrick saw our parents almost every day and was resentful that I only saw them a few times a year. To me, it felt like proper recompense for his being my parents' favorite son. That statement was not born of sibling rivalry, but rather of cold hard immutable fact. My relationship with my parents was divided in two phases: being their *only child*, and then their *other child*. Derrick had God-given athletic ability, which my father greatly admired. He also believed that a Catholic God in Catholic Heaven gave him his athletic abilities, which commanded my mother's limited supply of affection. She was an old school Irish Catholic, descending from potato famine emigrants and was raised during World War II in the wake of the Great Depression. She believed that life was a hopeless struggle against sin and misery from the time of conception. She also quietly wished for a Rose Kennedy level of suffering that she could endure gracefully, and publicly. Being her eldest son, I was raised to produce her first grand tragedy.

The day she sent me off to kindergarten, she draped a pendant of St. Jude around my neck, tousled my hair, handed me a sack lunch, and sent me across the street to the Murphys' house to walk to school with Teddy, Julia, and Irene Murphy. Mrs. Murphy took one look at the pendant and burst into laughter. "St. Jude!" she gasped, amazed. "The saint of lost causes! Michael, ya only five f'ah God's sake. Let's at least get you to the third grade befo'ah we give up on you, my love."

She kissed me on the head and sent me off with her children. I never wore that pendant again, but my mother held on to it and mailed it to me as the ink was drying on my divorce papers. For my mother, the only thing worse than marrying a non-Catholic was leaving one. She was pretty sure that God could forgive me for marrying a Jewish woman but was unequivocal in her belief that there was no redemption for divorcing one. Breaking the bonds of holy matrimony guaranteed me an extended stay in purgatory amid unbaptized babies, masturbators, and tattooed utterers of profanity. It's like the old joke goes: they call you a practicing Catholic because no one ever gets it right. She had me as living proof of that.

All this to say, whenever Derrick called during the week, it was because my parents were complaining about me or he needed money. So, when I saw his ID on my phone, I sighed. He wouldn't tell me my parents' complaint about me, which was not that unusual. "What you said ain't impo'tant," he insisted. "What I'm tellin' you is what ya need to know, kid? Just focus. Just be nice to them. They 'ah fuckin' old, and you ain't gonna change them! But that ain't even why I'm callin'."

That got my attention. "Look, this is impo'tant. Dad's havin' trouble remberin' things and he's sayin' crazy shit. It's gettin' really bad. I think he's got dementia and Ma doesn't know how to do anythin' without him. I'm worried about them and I need you to help me become thei'ah legal custodian, even if they fight it."

"Derrick, this is a lot to drop on me first thing in the morning." My father seemed off, but he didn't seem that off. "Did something happen? I mean, it seems like we're jumping over a lot of steps here. He seemed a bit depressed when I last talked to him, but he also seemed to be in control of his faculties."

"Why can't you just talk like a no'mal fuckin' person, *'in control of his faculties!'* 'Ah you he'ah?" Derrick flipped the switch to the level of pissed off that couldn't be penetrated by logic. "Do you see the things that I see? You and ya fuckin' college bullshit always thinkin' ya so much bett'ah than the rest of us. Why don't you write a fuckin' column about Dad's dementia and make it all bett'ah? You 'ah savin' the world one fuckin' sentence at a time!"

"Derrick, look, we don't need to go through this every time I ask a question," I said. "You called for my help. So, tell me why you believe we have to take this dramatic step right now."

"Great, don't listen to me. I can't talk to you when ya like this—just leave everythin' up to me, like you always do. Okay! And don't you fuckin' tell them we talked about this." And he hung up.

When Derrick talked to me that way, it made me think he was a really bad cop. He was callous and expedient. I couldn't imagine having to deal with him in a life-or-death situation. I worked hard to keep a relationship with him, but he was resistant. I didn't know a lot about him anymore.

6

#6 BILL RUSSELL, CENTER, COACH, BOSTON CELTICS

After talking with my brother, I stopped at Blue Star Donuts to buy some happy feelings. The tourists go to Voodoo and get penis-shaped Bavarian creams, or whatever, but the locals go to Blue Star. God created the world in six days, and on the seventh she decided she deserved a treat and created Blue Star Donuts. They are divine.

The *Daily's* foyer looked like every lobby in Manhattan, lacking all the character of Portland—it was constructed of glass and marble and had towering ceilings—but architecturally it felt like empty space. I stopped at the security desk and opened the Blue Star box for Zeke. He was a former Portland State defensive lineman and the only person in my life who still told jokes. He took one of the three maple bacon doughnuts. I was keeping inventory, as my happiness that morning relied on having a Blue Star maple bacon doughnut. He was about to tell me a joke, but his smile got a bit brighter as he looked past me to the door. It was political reporter Katherine Hunza.

"Hey, Hunza, look what this guy did!" said Zeke.

"Blue Star," she gushed, and she took the second maple bacon as we headed to the elevator.

"Everything, okay?" she asked me, concerned.

"Yeah," I said. "Why do you ask?"

"No reason."

Katherine Hunza was a climber, which is not a compliment in Portland, but I mean it as one. She had sharp teeth and an old soul. After I became a columnist, she took over my old beat covering statewide politics. She was better at it than me. I tried to cultivate sources through relationships. Hunza just knew what she needed for a story and found a way to get it. In addition to being a top notch journalist, I also found her stunning. She was not a universal beauty, but *holy shit* there was something about her that appealed directly to the teenaged James Bond fan in me. She was determined, powerful, and had a smoldering Eastern-European-black-widow-spider sensuality that I had only encountered in Cold War thrillers. But she was also young, and distant admiration was the only reasonable expectation for our relationship.

"Oh my God, I keep forgetting to return the book you

lent me!" she exclaimed as we exited the elevator.

"The A.G.'s book? No worries. What did you think?"

"That 40-year-olds shouldn't write autobiographies," she said with an ironic smile.

"Yeah, I guess I hadn't really thought of it like that. But you're right—there's a lot of story missing," I replied.

"The good stuff. The scandals," she joked, referring to a non-scandal regarding his sudden resignation for reasons that were never revealed.

"Well, that book's for you to write," I said. "And I'm looking forward to reading it."

I didn't plan to offer anyone else doughnuts until the last maple bacon was securely in my possession. My long-time friend and colleague Paul Pierce (not the former Celtic) and I had neighboring cubes by a bank of windows that overlooked the Willamette River and Mt. Hood. I put the box on Paul's desk. I got him a blueberry glazed because it was his favorite.

"Hi, Kate," Paul greeted as he looked to me with a Cheshire Cat grin. It's a cliché, but Paul knew me better than I knew myself. He glanced at the doughnut box, then back at me, concerned. "Everything okay?"

"Why is everyone asking me that?"

"No reason," he insisted as he grabbed the last maple bacon and took a bite. "I haven't had one of these in a while. God, they're delicious."

It was going to be one of those days.

"We should grab lunch, or maybe a happy hour, and talk about the book," Katherine said as she left.

I was a little shocked at the invitation and took too long to respond, trying figure out if I should say something witty, flirtatious, or fatherly. "That sounds great. I'm happy to help brainstorm ideas," I finally said, deciding on collegial.

"Maybe we'll write it together," she said with a smile and a raised eyebrow as she walked back to her desk.

Paul waited for her to be out of earshot. "Well, that's going to be a Missed Connection," he commented, looking slightly envious.

"What does that mean?"

"Craigslist? The personals? This means nothing to you? 'Today you brought in doughnuts, but all I wanted was your cruller.' Nothing?"

"I still don't know what you're talking about."

"Seriously?" Paul shook his head. "C'mon. What just happened could not have been more flirtatious if Barry White was singing over your shoulder."

I could feel my heart begin to race. I turned beet red and attempted to laugh it off. "You're misreading that. Dude, she's like ten years younger than me. I don't want to be *that* guy."

"Closer to fifteen, my old friend, but that makes you the silverback ape," Paul said as he turned back to his computer screen. "You know, they have pills now that can help you keep up."

"Oh, ha ha," I said, and then thought about how long it had been since I'd had sex. "But, I guess that's comforting to know."

We laughed.

"So, when you check Missed Connections later, which we both know you're going to do, search for 'silverback ape.'"

I laughed, but of course, he was right. I was curious.

I loved my fellow reporters, and my job, but I'd come to hate the business. Paul and I survived newsroom purge after newsroom purge by the Suits from Staten Island—the corporate overlords from New York that owned the paper. The largest news source in Oregon was corporate-owned, publicly traded, and run like a widget factory. When the Suits didn't want to show stagnation or another quarterly loss to shareholders, they would cull the payroll by eliminating the most senior reporters except for the names the reading public looked for and trusted (ours), but soon even that wouldn't matter.

At some point, the Suits stopped hiring reporters and started hiring "content generators" to write surface-level stories, shoot video or snap photos for slideshows with their smartphones, and push their content through social media streams. The "more efficient use of human assets to create multimedia will maximize the delivery options for paid content"—that was the justification for what they called a title change but was really a mission change. The Suits cared more about the shareholders than they did about democracy.

They didn't care about our role as the fourth estate—they cared about our ability to more efficiently produce widgets. They conveniently blamed our dwindling readership on a lack of production rather than the reduced quality of our product. I suspect they will ride the efficiency train to its logical conclusion and eventually the *Daily's* output will consist only of tweets.

Since I didn't get the last maple bacon donut, I was still in search of comfort food. There was a food cart over by the Portland State campus named East Coast Oscar's. The proprietor, Oscar Casale, was from East Boston. He met an Oregon girl while they were attending U Mass Amherst and as his story goes, "followed his heart from one end of Route 20, in Kenmore Square, to Portland." Oscar left East Boston, but Eastie never left him. He was an unapologetic Bostonian, refusing to assimilate into the laid-back Pacific Northwest culture. He was just over five feet tall and almost as wide. His forearms were almost bigger than his impressive biceps. Every day, no matter how cold it was, Oscar rolled up his selves to his elbows to expose his four-leaf-clover tattoo—each leaf contained one of the logos of the Boston Four: the Celtics, Patriots, Red Sox, and Bruins. In the stem was written his mother's maiden name, Margaret Fitzpatrick. Oscar was a lot of personality stuffed into a compact body, but his defining feature was that he made the best steak subs west of the Connecticut River. He was the nicest guy on the planet as long as you never make the mistake of calling his delicacy a Philly Cheesesteak. You can call them subs, sandwiches, heroes, bombs, hoagies, or cheesesteaks, but don't sully his food with the same qualifier as the Sixers, Phillies, Eagles, or Flyers.

"Those mutts in Philly think it's okay to mix steak and Cheese Wiz. 'Ah you effin' kiddin' me? Cheese Wiz? That's like mixin' lobst'ah and peanut butt'ah for Christ sake! It screws with their brains. That's why Philly fans are all a bunch of A-holes!"

That was the answer I got after knowing Oscar well enough to ask about his aversion to the modifier "Philly" without fear of losing my steak sub privileges. To recap, Philly equals Cheese Wiz, which creates overzealous sports fans (seemingly unlike those in Boston).

An invitation to Oscar's was something neither Paul nor I possessed the will to resist. So, I lured Paul out of the office with an 11:30 proposal so we could beat the crowd. Paul had been my closest friend since college and I really needed advice on what to do about Derrick's insistence on taking over my parents' estate. We walked past the oodles of other food cart patrons, and around the tourists, who always block the sidewalk, to find a place to sit. I ate as we walked.

"So, what's up?" asked Paul as I was mid-bite.

My brow furrowed as I tore into the pointy end of the sub. The first bite is always transformative. The steam, which softens the bread to a perfect chewy texture, is still rising and carrying the harmonious aroma of steak, cheese, and onions. The melted provolone and cheddar blanket the thinly sliced and chopped top round that was cooked until its edges were crisp. It creates a cacophony of sweet and savory, succulent and crispy, creamy and chewy perfection. My first bite is always like a portal to a parallel state of existence where life was beautiful and effortless. As I've gotten older, I feel exponentially happier with every first bite, as if that sensation accumulates in some sort of cold storage inside my mind. Each time I tear into that chewy, crusty bread, it deepens my sense that benevolence rules the universe.

In reality I recognize this feeling probably has something to do with the level of cholesterol in my bloodstream or plaque coating my arteries, but I don't care. Oscar's subs reassure me that perfection is attainable. A string of provolone clung to the corner of my mouth as I remembered time and space existed outside of Oscar's steak bomb.

"What do you mean, 'what's up?'"

"Really? Boston comfort food, getting me out of the office, being quiet as we walked here. You don't see a trend?"

"Am I really that predictable?" I laughed.

"Yes," said Paul. "To me, anyway. Let me guess. Hunza realized you were impervious to flirtation and said something like, 'Michael, can't you see that I'm willing to lower my standards to make this thing happen between us?'"

"Um, no. Not even close," I said, but Paul had dragged me down a path that held more interest for me in that moment. "But, let's table my issues for a minute. Tell me how serious you're being right now, or are you just totally fucking with me?"

"For someone who's so insightful about politics and understanding what people want to read and whatever, you are as dumb as a lead swimsuit when it comes to reading women." Paul had not yet bitten into his steak bomb. "She's been begging you—*begging you*—to make a move!"

"She has not."

"I'm being serious right now," scolded Paul with a frown. "You're so deaf, dumb, and blind when it comes to women that you don't even have a type. You never make a move. You just go with the woman who hits you over the head and drags you away."

"I am not deaf, dumb, and blind when it comes to women," I retorted.

"You have no idea when women are coming on to you. None! Zero!"

"I got game," I said slyly.

"Michael, please. Stop it. You don't. You. Do. Not. Have. Game. If you have a game, it's Pokémon." Paul was overreacting a bit. "I'm going to give you one example *from this morning!* When we went for coffee. There was a brunette who was just milling around by the cream, standing there for like ten minutes with the lid off her coffee, and she told you to use the cream first, and then she was chatting you up—"

"She was just being nice," I said, but I began to wonder.

"I've seen her there before is all."

"Exactly! She's seen you there before, too, and she was being nice *to you*. She wasn't being nice to me, or anybody else. She was locked and loaded *on you*. She kept gesturing with her left hand, which didn't have a ring on it. She could not have been more obvious if she were holding a sign that read 'ask me out!' It was like Chip Kelly was standing in front of you two holding up those giant poster-boards telling you what play to run, and somehow you missed it. 'Oh, thanks for the cream.'" Paul made a dumb-looking face to mock me as he opened his sandwich bag and sat on a bench. "Now tell me what the fuck's going on with you before you make me lose all my patience."

"Well, you've clearly already lost your patience, but okay. But actually, first, for real, you feel one hundred percent positive that Hunza wants me to ask her out?" I wanted to be absolutely sure that I wasn't misunderstanding what he was saying.

"Yes! Jesus, God, help this boy!" Paul said, almost spitting out his food.

"So, on a scale from one to ten …" I smiled to let Paul know I was joking, and he glared at me. So, I got to the point. I explained Derrick's proposal to take control of my parents' estate. I let him know that I was concerned about my father, but thought that he might be depressed, not suffering from dementia. Paul was not exactly an unbiased judge when it came to my brother. He never liked Derrick.

When we were in college, I invited Paul to come stay at the house in New Bedford for a long weekend, which he cut short after "suddenly remembering" he had a psychology paper due. He later told me that Derrick made him feel unwelcome and uncomfortable with racially tainted "jokes" and warnings that sounded like threats about the places where "black people shouldn't go" in New Bedford.

"You know what I'm going tell you about your brother," Paul said. "So, why wouldn't you ask someone else about this?"

"I know," I said. "I think I just needed to say it out loud. I needed a second source."

"Now that you have one, what are you going to do?" Paul asked.

I looked down at my steak bomb getting cold in my lap and allowed the idea that Derrick had untoward motives to settle in my brain. I wondered about what those motives could be—was it addiction problems, was it greed, was it gambling? I didn't want to confront Derrick. Time and distance had allowed me to construct a fragile apriorism in which my family ties were bound by galvanized cable and sweet as ZaRex syrup. I dreaded having to abandon the warm comfort of my denial. I didn't want to accept that Derrick was probably trying to siphon money away from my mother and father.

"Well, I'm not sure yet what my options are," I said. "But the most attractive one at the moment is to ignore it and hope it goes away."

We laughed.

"I wish I knew you were joking," said Paul.

"Me, too. I wish I could ignore it. This is not going to be pleasant."

Paul just nodded. There was nothing left to say.

"So, for real. Hunza's into me?"

"Eat your fuckin' sandwich," Paul said with a chuckle. We spent the next few minutes eating and not talking. I took a deep breath, closed my eyes and turned my face to the sun. The MAX train rattled to a stop nearby. I turned from the sun as the doors opened with a loud sigh. A throng of PSU students, city workers, and tourists ambled off the train at a Pacific Northwest pace. Tattooed flesh, unusual piercings, and hair dye once shocking to many was now just a standard uniform among Portland's youth—the look inspired no more attention than the tourists with their golf polos tucked into their kakis or the city workers wearing their keycard lanyards and defeated expressions. Some people paused and looked to the unusually clear sky before continuing their journeys. A young woman wearing combat boots, what seemed to be a kilt, and a tank top that was several sizes too large, turned her face to the sun and twirled with her arms extended to the world. She seemed to be untangling herself from the knots and strings that bound and guided the others to their destinations. She clearly had arrived at hers. I knew nothing about this woman other than I envied her unfiltered exuberance. Her traveling companion extended her arms toward her friend. The wind caught the twirling girl's shirt like a sail and expanded it to its full capacity. It doubled the space she occupied. With each rotation, the twirling girl's friend tried to deflate the shirt, laughing harder with each failed attempt. They were intoxicated with joy and probably some mondo strain of weed. After several turns she noticed that her friend was attempting to cover her exposed breast. Dizzy and weak with laughter, they embraced and fell to the ground. We were one day closer to the end of summer, and nobody was in a rush to let it go.

7

#7 PHIL ESPOSITO, CENTER, BOSTON BRUINS

I spent a lot of time wondering why the men in my family weren't closer. It's like we were cursed to speak only in sports jargon and bond by proxy of New England sports teams. In fact, my most enduring memory with my brother and father came in October of 2004, when the Sox swept the St. Louis Cardinals to win the World Series. I flew back east after Boston went up three games to none to sit by my dad and Derrick to witness what I was certain would be another soul-crushing playoff collapse. For 86 years, the Red Sox had found extraordinary ways to steal defeat from the jaws of victory, and I prepared myself to experience their magnum opus.

The Quinn men went to Sully's Tap & Bite, where my dad sometimes tended bar. There were two open stools waiting for my dad and Derrick. I'd grown just up a few blocks from those barstools, but I felt like an interloper amid the faithful. During the American League playoffs, the Sox were down three games to none against the dreaded New York Yankees and pulled off the greatest comeback in sports history to get to The Series. Sully's regulars occupied the same chairs since the night the Sox won game four and began their epic comeback. For the first three games of the World Series, the superstitious crowd arrived at Sully's wearing the same lucky clothes—they drank the same drinks and ate the same foods. Before the National Anthem, Sully Jr. poured a Budweiser down the drain as an offering to Babe Ruth so his spirit would reverse the Curse of the Bambino and allow the Sox to hoist the trophy for the first time since he was traded to the Yankees for a pile of cash.

Sully Jr. would quiet the bar and shout, "To the Babe!" Everybody would lift a glass and shout it back. In the middle of the eighth inning, every vocal cord was stretched to its breaking point belting out "Sweet Caroline." This went on through game four as I stood next to my dad and Derrick and watched the crowd cheer every pitch in the bottom of the ninth. And then the impossible happened—the Sox won the 100th World Series—and the crowd at Sully's felt part of it. They believed their actions helped guide the Sox to victory. They rode on every pitch, anticipated and debated Francona's every decision, and argued every call that went against the Sox. They were elated. I only felt relief.

My presence was the only change to their routine, and if the Sox had lost, I certainly would have been blamed using the same 1690s scientific method that got people hung as witches in Salem.

My dad cried and hugged Derrick, and his buddies Joe Staid and Bill and Sandy Kocher, and then, his face damp with tears, he turned to me, patted me on the shoulder and said, "I'm glad you could make it, kid," and that was that. The most affection my dad managed to show me since he thought I was lost in the woods.

* * *

It was Saturday afternoon. Ben was in Eugene not responding to my texts, and the rest of my family was 3,000 miles away ignoring me in other ways. I sat on the balcony of my West Hills apartment drinking iced coffee that I'd made from the morning's stale leftover pot. I looked across the valley past the mishmash of a city to Mt. Hood. The mountain was mesmerizing. It dominated the horizon, a thing of absolute beauty, power, and wonder.

Since I last talked to my dad, I'd been carrying the compass he gave me. I took it out of my pocket and read the inscription: "Always move toward your goals." I pressed the stem and popped it open. During the most difficult times of my life, the compass has been a cross between a religious icon and a set of worry beads to me. I'd hold it, spin it, obsessively open and close it, and rub my thumb across the inscription, which had become something like my mantra. I had read it over and over, meditated on it, repeated it again and again in my mind until the words lost their meaning.

I turned to the mountain and looked at the compass's red needle. It was due east. *The Great Creator in the clouds has placed Mt. Hood to the east of my apartment so I will always look toward Fenway Park with awe*, I thought before shutting the compass and reading the inscription again.

What does it really mean? I wondered. *"Always," assumes you never get there; "move toward," seems to assume your goals are not within you. Am I moving toward my goals?* I wondered. *Do I even have goals anymore?*

The truth I didn't want to face, as I sat there staring at my compass, was that I had lost my way. Being a columnist was the only goal I ever had, but after doing the job for years, it seemed like a feral cat begging for food and offering no affection in return.

But what do I want to do? I had no answer, so I ordered Chinese food from a place in Old Town and grabbed a six-pack of Rogue Dead Guy ale, the putty knife and spackle I needed to patch the cracks in my soul.

I couldn't stop thinking about my dad. I envied the simplicity of his life. After dinner with my mother, he'd go to Sully's, sit on his barstool, and talk with the Kochers about the Red Sox. They'd share hopes about the Celtics, gossip about trade rumors they picked up on WEEI sports talk radio, and pray that Tom Brady and Bill Belichick would lead the Patriots longer than the trio planned to live. At some point during the conversation, Bill would say "These 'ah the good old days, my friend! We 'ah livin' in the Golden Age of Boston sports. We've been spoiled in our lifetimes." Then, if there was nothing worthy of their attention on the TV, he'd launch into the legends talk: Orr, Russell, Pedro, Bird, Brady, Cousy, and Teddy Ballgame.

They would reminisce about plays they saw in person at Fenway, Foxborough, or in the Garden, and then they'd talk about the turning points of big games and playoff series. My dad would likely end the night talking about Red Sox pitcher Pedro Martinez with a reverence my mother saved for saints and martyrs. Meanwhile, on the opposite coast, I sat alone in my rented apartment eating second-rate Chinese takeout and watching Netflix while I searched Missed Connections on my iPad.

I clicked through each vague headline: "Hey, Where'd You Go?" and "My Middle Aged Crush" and "Handsome Guy on Belmont." I was so smug while I was sitting in my cube after learning about these posts, thinking, *What a bunch of poor lost souls.* But, of course, I was now one of them. I desperately wanted to find myself in a post. *Is this how I'm going to spend my mid-life crisis?*

I anticipated the posts would all be crude booty calls, and there was some of that, but mostly they were irresistible vignettes of humanity. People at their most vulnerable, anonymously exposing their deepest fears and longings. Post after post came the overtures of hopeless romantics, seekers of reconciliation, unrequited lovers, fearers of rejection, and those who were certain they'd briefly veered off the path of their destiny and missed a chance meeting with their soulmate. Their allure was obvious: we all want to believe there's someone out there waiting to complete us. When life accelerates faster than fate, Missed Connections gives destiny a second chance.

The biggest downside of this for me was that I was a helper by nature, and I felt an overwhelming desire to intervene in situations that were obviously careening toward catastrophic dysfunction. I could have spent all day writing "Dear Abby"-type advice to people who didn't ask for it, but this was no place for rational thought—in fact, reason belied its very existence. Missed Connections existed outside the reality of missed opportunities and unrealized dreams. It was a place to store your most private thoughts and irrational hopes—to express desires that were too intimate to share with friends and too radical to ask for in prayers.

Some posts were so universal that it was easy to see yourself in them. Calls to former lovers and secret crushes were so prevalent that it seemed like the whole world was crying out. "I was in that restaurant where we stopped on our way back from the mountains. I thought back to when we were "us" during that perfect summer day. I was so certain I was with the perfect guy. We were so in love. I miss that. I miss you. I saw a figure silhouetted by the sun, and for a moment,

I thought it was you. It must have been wishful thinking. Maybe I wanted to will you back into my life. I know you'll never see this, but if by some chance you do, send me an email and let me know there's still hope for us."

I wanted to find that woman so I could wrap her in grandma's hand-crocheted afghan and give her a cup of chamomile tea and hold her until she cried that man out of her system. It seemed like the humane thing to do.

Then, I came across this: "My delightfully delusional political idealist. You seem to have no idea how much I want to be with you, which makes you all the more attractive. You are a cause for optimism. It gives me chills when you talk with passion. It makes your eyes light up and my heart flutter like a fangirl's. I imagined your face today as I read your column and wondered if you're the last good man on Earth. All I know for sure is that you are the only man for me. Ask me to return your book and I'll know you've seen this."

I read it three times to be sure I wasn't missing something. *Political idealist, read your column, return your book, holy shit! It's got to be Hunza!* Rather than responding immediately, I became paralyzed with doubt and fear. I'd found a needle of hope in a haystack of despair and I didn't know whether to use it to darn the hole in my heart or poke my stupid eye out.

I was intrigued by Hunza. I had tremendous admiration for her work, but I really knew nothing about her.

Relationships tend to exist on a continuum. At one end are people who are like the sun, generating power from within and providing warmth and light to others. On the other end are the Great Chicago Fires: their flames burn brightest as they consume everything in their paths and leave destruction in their wakes. I didn't know if Hunza was a life-giving star or Mrs. O'Leary's cow and I didn't trust myself to know the difference. But I also didn't care. *I'll answer now and sort the rest out later,* I thought, opening another beer. I created a Missed Connections account using a new email under the name of Sonny Icarus and spent the remainder of my night eating too much Chinese food, drinking too much ale, and writing and rewriting a post in response to Hunza's.

Finally, I posted under the heading Political Idealist: "I didn't see this coming and I'm still not sure it's real. But what can we ever know for sure. I know I'm attracted to you. I know my heart skipped a beat when I read your post and I'd be lying if I said I'd never thought about the possibility of us being together. I know this could be a remarkable coincidence and you're reaching out to some other political idealist who lent you a book, but the next time I see you, I will ask for it back and we'll know we found each other."

I thought I would click "post" and go to bed, but of course I couldn't sleep. I checked the listings several times, and my email a dozen. There was nothing—well actually, there was an auto-reply with a picture of a naked woman with fake breasts and a phone number photoshopped across her midsection. I took that sight in for a short while before eventually nodding off.

* * *

On Monday, the book I lent Hunza was sitting on my desk with a sticky note that read, "Let's write the rest of this story together!"

Is this the sign? I wondered. *She told me to ask for the book back. I agreed. This can't be a coincidence, can it? I hate how my brain works! The post was obviously for me. I told her I would ask for the book. She returned the book. Of course it's her!*

I felt like a tween with an erection during health class. I contemplated asking Paul for his opinion, but I knew he'd just yell at me for not listening to the advice he already gave me. The anonymity of the whole thing somehow made it more exciting. I got caught up in the intrigue. I checked the Icarus email on my phone. There were no new messages, so I peeked at the email with the naked lady and the fake boobs. My phone rang, startling me. It was my mother. A shock of Catholic guilt hit me like a nun's ruler across my knuckles. She never called me at work. I yanked my thoughts out of the gutter, closing the Icarus email.

She called to tell me that my father had a heart attack while getting the *Globe* off the front porch. "I called the ambulance, but they said he was probably dead before I made the call. I'm all alone now, Michael," she said. "He's all I had."

I didn't know what to do with that comment. Derrick was her favorite and lived a mile away. *She's probably just in shock,* I thought. I assured her that she was not alone and that Derrick and I would take care of her. I promised her I would get on the next plane and help her with the funeral arrangements and whatever else she needed.

"I don't care about that, Michael," she said. There was nothing but fear in her voice. "I can't let you end up like them."

"Like who, Mum?" I could hear someone call to her.

"It's Derrick. I'm going to go," she said. "But promise me you'll pray for him, and you, and fah all of us. Say it Michael. Tell me you'll pray."

I didn't want to lie to her. "It will be okay, Mum," I said.

"Promise me, Michael!" Her fear turned to anger.

"I will, Mum," I lied. I knew it. She knew it. But it still made her feel better.

I called Sarah first. She always loved my dad, and I was hoping she'd have some advice on how to tell Ben. I hated the idea of sharing this kind of news with him over the phone. Sarah seemed confused as to why I called her, which made what was already an uncomfortable call even more painfully awkward. Maybe it's weird to call your ex-wife with bad news, but I didn't know who else to call. I thought she'd care more, or at least be nicer. I thought of our current relationship as that of old friends, but I guess she just thought of it as over. I'm not sure how some people can just turn that off. She asked me why I didn't call my brother first. It was a reasonable question if you didn't know me, but from her it felt vindictive and heartless. There was no care in her voice, no concern, no empathy. It made my father's death feel like gossip.

Our divorce never felt like it completely ended our relationship to me until that moment.

* * *

I got a window seat on a redeye. The seat next to me was empty, which was a godsend.

My father was almost 80-years old, but his death was still a shock. I was glad for him that he went quickly. Planning and contemplation were not his strengths. I, on the other hand, could have used more time to adjust to the finality of it. There was so much left unsaid—a lifetime of words, really. Forever is too long to wonder how someone felt about you, but I'm not certain knowing would have been more comforting. Maybe his silence was an act of kindness.

My call with Ben was easier than I imagined. Sarah texted him as soon as I hung up with her, which, well, what the fuck. He was crushed by the news and annoyed he'd learned it via text but was empathetic and comforting on the phone. I bought him a ticket to fly back at the end of the week so he wouldn't miss too much school.

I reclined my chair the full inch and tried to nestle into

the space between my seat and the fuselage. It was like trying to cuddle with a turtle. I needed rest. I needed strength. I was already feeling depressed and guilty. I knew Derrick, Bill Kocher, and the other shanty Irish mugs from the neighborhood would be making lace curtain jokes behind my back, or more likely, slightly to the side of my face. I'd committed the unforgivable sin of getting out of New Bedford, and even worse, I'd lost my accent. "I'm su'prised he came back at all, the fuckin' lace-cu'tain prick," I imagined them saying as they walked up the steps to Saint Anthony's. The whole neighborhood would pour out of Sully's and walk down the street to McMahon's Funeral Parlor. They'd make sure they were seen paying their respects and they'd talk shit about all those who didn't. They would come to honor my father and judge me for "puttin' on airs."

None of us is owed anything, I thought as I steeled myself for the turbulent days to come. I popped my ears and looked out the airplane window into the darkness and let my mind wander. I tried to imagine what my dad thought about me. I'd spent my whole life measuring my worth against his vision of the perfect son. The Harvard graduate. The something after that. I still don't know what that would have been. I'll never know. I just feel like whatever he envisioned for me was always outside of my reach. And then there's my brother. Derrick had so much God-given ability and none of the discipline needed to take advantage of it. He took the things that fell in his lap, made a life out of them, and then went to Sully's at the end of the day. *Maybe all my dad ever wanted was a drinking buddy.*

I pulled the compass out of my pocket and stared at the inscription again. This time it made me chuckle. *Maybe my father was trying to get me to move away so he could have more time with Derrick. I should have thrown this fucking compass in those hideous falls when I had the chance.*

"The arrow always points north. Follow it, and I'll be waiting there," he told me. "Direction is the most important thing a father can give a son."

Well, I could use some direction now.

I retreated to my laptop, the place where I could turn an entire universe of infinite possibilities, problems, and fears into a finite 750-word capsule of consumable comfort. All I had to do was write it down so that others could read it on Wednesdays, Fridays, and Sundays in the *Portland Daily*. This is where I would make sense of my relationship with my father.

I spent the rest of the flight writing about the meaning of home when you live 3,000 miles from the place where you grew up. I wrote about the things we hold on to—the stories, the landmarks, the comfort foods, and the people. "Home," I wrote, "is a feeling that comes without explanation, apology, or invitation." These were things I wanted to be true. I wrote that I missed my father, and that "I knew I would feel most at home when I got to Sully's." In reality, I felt certain nobody there would remember me. "I will be able to feel his presence in the laughter and warmth of those with whom he shared seasons of hope and joy," I concluded, shutting my laptop and feeling sure of my place in the universe as a person who provides comfort by imagining what it could possibly feel like.

8

#8 CARL "YAZ" YASTRZEMSKI, OUTFIELD, BOSTON RED SOX

All the economy cars were gone by the time I got to the rental counter, so instead of the modest compact car I chose online, the eager and delightful clerk gave me a fancy SUV for the same price. I could think of only two circumstances when the free luxury upgrade would feel like a burden: driving to a climate change protest and visiting my hometown. Rolling up to my mother's house in a car with a sticker price higher than the neighborhood's median income was going to make the lace curtain Irish jokes even lacier.

While on the shuttle from the rental headquarters to the car pickup, I checked the Sonny Icarus email. As the inbox loaded on my phone, I pushed past the guilt of engaging in such a base endeavor while I was on my way to my father's funeral. No matter how innocent my intentions, there was something about looking at Craigslist that made me want to sheathe my eyeballs with condoms. Regardless, my heart raced when I saw a response to my post.

"I've hoped for so long that it is hard to tell if this is real. It's like I've walked into someone else's dream. I so cherish our friendship that I have hidden my true feelings for fear it might jeopardize what we already have. Our circumstances always kept us apart, but close enough for me to know that you are all I've ever wanted. Even if it's not you, it feels so good to write those words, read them, and know that it feels true in every cell of my being. I want us to share our thoughts and hopes and to hold your hand as we walk together through life. When you look into my eyes and smile, I feel as if I've known you for a thousand lifetimes— like I've been waiting that long for us to be together. I'm glad the waiting is finally over."

A tear welled in my eye as I read the response. *Holy shit. That was beautiful,* I thought, hit with the realization of how truly alone I'd been feeling.

I never imagined Hunza capable of words like those. It surprised me to no end. It made me reconsider my disbelief in fate. *Paul was right.* There's no doubt that I was physically attracted to her, but maybe there was more to it, to us, than I imagined. My heart quickened and my face warmed. The rush made me feel even more guilty. I was on my way to my father's funeral, but my thoughts dwelt on earthly pleasures. *There's a special place in hell for thinking this sort of thing under these circumstances,* I thought as I imagined my father sitting on the shuttle next to me, watching me blush like a schoolboy who just got caught passing love notes.

Being raised Catholic, it's hard to know which day-to-day thoughts are normal and which were planted by nuns. I was torn. *He'd want me to be happy, wouldn't he?* I wondered. I decided not to judge my emotions, but just try to experience them as they came. It was going to be a hard week, and no amount of second-guessing myself was going to make it easier.

* * *

I took my father's old winding route to New Bedford. I drove through the patchwork of suburbs that sprawled south toward Cape Cod. There was something reassuring about the resilience of all the mom-and-pop roadside taverns, clam shacks, and roast beef sandwich shops that marked the way—even the ubiquitous Friendly's ice cream parlors and Dunkin' Donuts felt like greetings from old friends. The expressway would have been quicker, and would have taken me past the *Boston Globe* building—my Mecca—but it lacked the nostalgia I was craving. On the backroads, I could drive slowly and keep the windows rolled down in the land yacht. There was a magic quality to the cool damp New England summer morning air.

Being up and out that early reminded me of being a

paperboy when I delivered the *Globe* and *Herald*. The papers were both broadsheets back then. They were dropped in stacks on the sidewalk in front of my house, bound by wire, and they always smelled of fresh ink. I was supposed to count them out, fold them into thirds, and fasten them with rubber bands before starting my route, but I always began by throwing the stacks in my bag where I kept my wire cutters. I would cut the wire, then fold them as I approached each house. At first, the bag took all my effort to lift, but it got lighter quickly as I ran through the rows of small capes and the rows of double-decker homes. The Pulaskis wanted their *Globe* on the front porch—the Mookas had a special holder under their mailbox and always gave me cookies when I came to collect their bill. When dogs still roamed freely throughout the neighborhood, the Houldens' mutt, Hondo, used to run alongside me, wagging his tail. I could still remember the sound of his nails clicking rhythmically against the pavement. I loved that dog.

I stopped in Abington and got a medium regular at the Dunkin Donuts across from the used car lot. "Regular" meant the "normal" amount of cream and sugar, which was almost enough cream to stop your heart and enough sugar to give you diabetes. It was tastier than I remembered. I had to check the navigation on my iPhone to make sure I was still heading the right way. I was at a junction where my father would have taken a serpentine "short cut" to avoid a few extra traffic lights. I was getting close enough to home that my nostalgia began to wane—it was being replaced by the foreboding of my adult obligations. I got jittery. It was hard to tell if my tremors were a response to the caffeine and sugar or my proximity to my family. As I drove closer to my old neighborhood, I could feel myself regressing. Each click of the odometer stripped another layer of veneer from my denial until all that was left were the raw emotions of an insecure child.

Welcome home, I thought.

I cringed as I turned onto my mother's street. The SUV seemed to grow bigger and fancier against the modest cape style houses that marked the edge of my old neighborhood. I felt pangs of Catholic guilt. I imagined the nuns who taught my Confraternity of Christian Doctrine classes shaking their heads and making "tsk tsk" noises as I drove. Had I bought the extra insurance, I would likely have just driven this ostentatious display of gluttony and pride straight into the ocean. *Always buy the extra insurance,* I reminded myself as I took a deep breath and accepted my fate.

Basketball shoes dangled from the telephone wires that hung across the last intersection before my parents' block. They brought back wonderful memories of playing basketball with great friends during summer days that stretched into long summer nights. "Raising your sneakers to the rafters" was a tradition that went back to at least the late '50s. In my day, we couldn't retire our sneakers—almost exclusively Converse All-Stars, also known as Chuck

Taylors—until we could poke a finger through the soles. The shoes that dangled above me as I passed the intersection were at least $150 new and still looked like they had $90 of life in them. They were in better shape than Murphys' double-decker house, whose porch had begun to sag from age and neglect. I had arrived.

I parked across the street and sat for a few minutes to collect my thoughts and admire the old house. My dad always kept it looking good, right up to the end. It was a little weathered, but it was still the best-looking house on the block. I saw the living room curtains move. I'd been spotted and knew I couldn't sit long.

The front door was propped open, which meant my mother was getting a lot of random visitors. No one who knew us ever came through the front door—it was old and swollen, hard to open and harder still to close. It was the original door from when the house was built in the late 1800s and it still had the original hardware. The key looked like something out of a Dickens novel: a long rod with teeth that looked like, well, actual teeth. The key was needed to lock the door from either side, so it remained propped in the inside keyhole at all times. That door would likely remain cracked open until the mourners stopped visiting.

I grabbed my bag and walked along the driveway to the back porch. The Kochers and Staids were in the kitchen with Derrick, making room for all the food brought by well-wishers. Mrs. Costello brought by a pan of her eggplant parmesan. The Cronins brought a shepherd's pie. The Figueroas brought a cold cut platter, bulkie rolls, and some Portuguese sweet bread from their deli. Boxes and bottles of wine, cases of beer, and two-liter bottles of soda lined the Formica countertops. Before I even got through the door, I was greeted by the smell of cinnamon buns warming in the oven and coffee percolating on the stovetop.

I placed my bag in the sunporch and stood by the door in the kitchen. Nobody noticed me as I stood by the threshold for a second or two and watched Mr. Staid and Mr. Kocher pack beer into our ancient metal ice chest as their wives portioned shepherd's pie and eggplant parm into Tupperware containers.

"We should probably just freeze this whole thing," said Mrs. Staid as she turned to look toward the freezer in the back hallway. She gasped when she saw me. She put her hands to her cheeks, then they moved to her lips as her eyes welled. "My God, Mikey, you looked just like ya fath'ah standin' the'ah."

Everyone stopped. There was a pause as Derrick and the family friends adjusted their social filters to account for the outsider. Their shit talk would now be strained though passivity or cloaked in humor. The adjustment was slow. I nodded to Derrick, but he just leaned against the countertop and looked as if he was sizing me up for a fight. His eyes were dull and faded against his ruddy skin. I wondered how long he'd been drinking heavily again—weeks, months, or longer.

Since my freshman year at college, my return home always felt like a social experiment on how long it takes to assimilate back into New Bedford life. My dad always helped with the transition. He was the center of our universe. He was the guy we all had in common, but now he was gone, and we were standing around in his kitchen.

"Get ov'ah he'ah and give me a hug," Mrs. Staid finally said as she opened her arms. "I'm so sorry about ya fath'ah, sweetie."

"I knew it wasn't Jake, because his ghost would'a wanted to be clos'ah to the booze," said Mr. Kocher as he offered his catcher's-mitt-sized hand and squeezed my knuckles like they were marbles in a sack. He was a massive human being and kept himself in great shape for his age, for any age, honestly. Him and my dad were friends from the neighborhood. They went to school together since first grade, were co-captains of their high school basketball team, and were best men at each other's weddings. Bill and his wife Sandy were Derrick's godparents, which in the Catholic Church is a pretty big deal. When I was a kid, my mother confided, with the aid of quite a bit of alcohol, that "God chooses ya pa'ah'ents and gives them the wisdom to choose ya godpa'ah'ents. For Derrick, your fath'ah chose Sandy Kosher and her drunken pet orangutan." My mother never liked Bill.

"True enough," I said with a laugh, trying not to wince as my knuckles popped and stung with pain. "It looks like the neighbors brought enough food for the next six months."

"You won't go hungry, that's for sure," said Joe Staid, who moved to New Bedford from Connecticut in the '70s and never adopted the accent.

"Where's my mother?" I asked.

"She went to take a show'ah a little bit ago," said Sandy Kocher. "I haven't seen h'ah since. She may have gone to lay down for a bit. I'll go check. And Bill, get the kid some coffee f'ah Christ's sake. He just flew across the freakin' country. He must be ready to fall down—and take those cinnamon rolls outa the oven. Derrick, get ov'ah he'ah and hug ya broth'ah! What the hell's a' matt'ah with you two!"

Bill took orders from Sandy like an Army private from a general. He slapped me on the shoulder on his way to the coffee pot. It felt like I'd been hit with a side of beef. "Hey, it was a blow for us all, Mikey. They don't come any bett'ah than ya fath'ah. Ya handlin' it, okay?"

It was an odd way to describe the mourning process, and before I could think of a decent response, Bill had moved on. Derrick walked over, switched his coffee mug to his left hand, then threw his right arm around my shoulders. "Ya home now," he said and went back to his place against the counter. It felt more like a threat than a greeting. The Staids were warm and welcoming, as they always were. They were sweet people. Bill handed me a mug of watery coffee. "How do ya take it? Black? Well, you know whe'ah everything is." He went back to loading the cooler. "Ya probably used to bett'ah coffee out whe'ah ya from now. Anyway, that's what we drink he'ah."

And so it began: the first not-so-subtle snob jab was thrown in less than three minutes and came before I even got to say hello to my mother. "Black is great," I said as I walked toward the dining room. "Thanks, Bill."

"Good to see ya, kid," Joe said in his reassuring way. "Wish it was under better circumstances. When's the last time you were back? It's been a while."

"It *has* been a while. Too long." I smiled and nodded. "Thanks, Mr. Staid, for being here and helping my mother out like this."

As I passed the threshold between the kitchen and dining room, the floorboard creaked so loud it made me look under my foot to make sure I hadn't killed an animal. My mother sat undisturbed at the dining room table. Her eyes were closed, her head was bowed, and her chin rested atop her knuckles. A crucifix dangled in the triangle created by her elbows, the table, and her folded hands. Her right thumb dutifully rubbed against a rosary bead as she worked her way from prayer to prayer—the Apostles' Creed, Our Fathers, Hail Marys, Fatimas, Hail Holy Queens—recited silently, repeated, and supposedly counted by Jesus, Mary, and the saints. Her lips moved as she rocked forward and backward ever so slightly. Sandy Kocher stopped rubbing my mother's back to bring her index finger to her lips, as if a decade of marriage to a Jewish woman undid forty-four years of being my mother's son. I knew better than to interrupt my mother while she was praying. There was nothing short of a manifestation of the Blessed Virgin sitting criss-cross applesauce on the dining room table that could distract her from completing the Rosary.

I headed back toward the sunporch to collect my bag and bring it to my old bedroom. I took an extra long step as I passed back into the kitchen. The floorboards creaked slightly less. When I got back to the kitchen, the men were cracking their first beers of the day. They were admiring the results of their tidying and organization, and they had decided to celebrate their successful efforts. Their Budweiser cans were embellished with the colors of the American flag, adding a dose of patriotic zeal to the scene that would have made Norman Rockwell blush.

"Cold one?" Bill asked without bending toward the cooler. He thought he already knew my answer.

"But they ain't so cold," joked Joe Staid.

"Absolutely," I said, to his surprise. The last thing I wanted was a beer, but it couldn't be worse than the coffee I poured down the sink. It had been years since I drank a Bud, and longer since I wanted one. But if this week was going to be tolerable, I needed to expedite the assimilation process.

Bill handed me a beer. The can was wet from the ice, but not cold. I popped the top and sipped off the foam. "Mum doing alright? Considering?" I asked Derrick as I leaned against the counter next to him. It took all my concentration to keep from wincing as the taste of warm beer washed across my palate. Derrick responded with a shrug and a grunt. He may have been about to say something, but Bill chimed in, as he was prone to do.

"Well, ya know, we 'ah all takin' it pretty hah'd," Bill said. "Ya moth'ah's got the church and that's keepin' h'ah steady. But aside from that, it's been a tough couple of days. They don't make them like ya dad anymore. Ya know?"

I nodded and waited for someone else to talk.

"How was ya flight?" asked Maryanne, who stood by Joe's side.

"Ah, not too bad," I said. "I was hoping to sleep more, but we all know how that goes."

"I've nev'ah been on a plane befo'ah," Maryanne said, and blushed. "Can you believe that? A woman my age. Well …"

"Well," said Joe, stiffening a bit as he put his beer on the counter. "We should probably let you get settled in. You must be exhausted."

"Oh, no, I'm fine, really." I was concerned that I had inadvertently offended the Staids, possibly the single nicest couple in the world, and my only immediate allies. My mother had started her marathon prayer session as soon as she saw me through the living room curtains, Bill Kosher already knocked me for liking decent coffee, and my own brother greeted me with all the warmth of an iguana. I walked through the door feeling like I had nothing but enemies—I couldn't afford to insult my only friends. "I find it's better to stay awake until my normal bedtime, you know, ignoring the time change—it helps me fall back into my natural rhythms. It helps prevent jet lag."

"Well, we wouldn't want to get in the way of that," said Maryanne. "Ya rhythms and whatev'ah."

"I don't think my dad would approve of you leaving before you finished your beer," I said to Joe as I raised mine for a toast in a last-ditch effort. "I think he'd call that alcohol abuse."

Bill raised his can with a chuckle. Joe recovered his and joined us.

"To Jake!" said Bill.

"To Jake!" we echoed. And we drank from our patriotic cans.

"Will you join us, Maryanne?" I asked, to her surprise.

"Oh, I know whe'ah ya moth'ah keeps the Bailey's— maybe I'll put a little in my coffee," she said as she hurried to the pantry.

"My father would approve. I'm certain of it," I acknowledged.

My father once told me that he could never fully trust someone until he shared a drink with them. He'd followed up that statement with a racist diatribe about Muslims, which I shan't repeat, but I assumed that Bill, Joe, and Derrick held similar beliefs about drinking and trust, and unfortunately, probably, also about Muslims.

It was confusing to feel responsible for being a gracious

host in a home where the guests felt more comfortable than I did. We drank warm, weak beer and I pondered things to say that would help me gain their approval. I wanted to be one of the guys, to feel like I belonged in the life my father left behind. I loved my father deeply, but I couldn't help questioning if I was mourning him or the loss of a relationship we'd never had. I would miss our talks about baseball, sure, but what tore my heart out was thinking that he never really knew me. I was worried that Ben and I were heading in the same direction. That thought caused a lump to swell in my throat and tears to well in my eyes. Bill patted me on the back and told me things would be okay.

I smiled and nodded.

In that moment, my mother launched herself from the living room like she'd been possessed by the spirit of Babe Zaharias. She took my beer can from me and in a fluid motion shoved it into Bill Kocher's chest, showering him with Budweiser. Joe slid out of the way just in time to avoid the beechwood-aged fallout. Maryanne instantly looked guilty and poured her Bailey's and coffee down the kitchen sink before it ever reached her lips. My mother took my wrist, pulled me toward the sunporch, and grabbed her keys that hung from a hook screwed into the doorframe. "We've got a few things to do," she said without looking at anybody. "See ya'selves out. Derrick, we'll be back in a while. Don't fo'get to push the front do'ah closed when you leave, and we'll see you tonight for dinn'ah."

"Where are we going, Mum?" I asked.

"It's not too late f'ah you," she muttered under her breath. "I'm not going to just sit by and watch you go down the wrong path."

"Oh Jesus," I said, and continued to follow her out the door. She had a distant look on her face that my father referred to as "drifting." It was relatively common during stressful times, but could also be triggered by something as trivial as learning I'd bought Ben a skateboard, or that I'd gotten a speeding ticket. When she got like this, it was hard to know if she was looking *at* you or if she was looking *through* you. At times, she believed she heard voices answering her prayers. The voices came in the form of assurances that Ben would do well in school or not fall and break his neck at the skatepark. She'd always tell me when her prayers were answered so that I wouldn't worry.

Not worry that my mother's hearing voices? Definitely not. Nope, I'd think.

On very rare occasions, the voices came as warnings, like when I got married to a Jewish woman in a civil ceremony, or when she caught me masturbating to the 1983 *Sports Illustrated* Swimsuit Edition with Cheryl Tiegs on the cover. These offenses demanded severe and immediate intervention to spare my soul from eternal damnation. There was nothing but the passage of time that could help her drift back to reality. Fighting her would only make it worse, so I just went with it and wondered from which mortal sin I was being saved from now.

Bill watched though the kitchen window as we walked up the driveway. He was giddy as a schoolboy watching the principal pull a bully down the hallway by his earlobe. "You go beat some God into him, Adeline. Take 'em behind the woodshed and beat some Jesus into that boy!"

Bill and Derrick doubled over with laughter as my mother dragged me to her car. Bill looked to Sandy for approval, which he did not find.

"Grow up." Sandy slapped him across this shoulder. "I swea'ah to God, it's like I'm mah'ried to an 80-year-old toddl'ah."

* * *

Neither of us said a word as my mother pointed her Plymouth Sundance in the direction of St. Anthony's church. *She's bringing me to see Father Francis,* I thought. She had been encouraging me to call him since the divorce. We never really talked about what happened between Sarah and me. She just told me to pray, call her priest, and wear the St. Jude pendant she sent. "He'll be able to help you," she kept saying, until one day I finally lost my patience.

"With what?" I finally asked. "Is he a more powerful wizard than St. Jude?"

She yelled at me for making fun of her saint, her priest, and her religion. I'd said it out of frustration with what felt like automated responses from her, time and again. For ridiculous explanations of canonical law and mortal sins, press one. For a rundown of the various illnesses plaguing distant friends and relatives, press two. For small talk or other queries, stay on the line and someone else will get to you.

As she drove, her head bobbed and twisted the way it would when she silently pleaded with St. Jude or rehearsed a difficult conversation. I imagined she was running through her plan to force me to recite The Four Marks of the Church. If I'd just say, "I believe in the one, holy, catholic and apostolic church," in front of her, she'd know my soul was secure. There was no way for me to prove, or disprove, my mother's beliefs. I just didn't share them. My father always told me her faith brought her comfort, but all I ever saw in her was fear and insecurity.

We parked in front of the rectory hall. She opened her door before the motor had completely stopped running, then hesitated. I thought maybe she was coming out of her stupor.

"And don't you call Fath'ah Francis a wizard!" she snapped. "I don't want him thinking that I raised a heretic."

"I'm a heathen, Mum, not a heretic. I don't believe any of it. And if I get the sense that he put you up to this, I'll call him something much worse than a wizard," I replied as I opened my door. I was just as eager to talk with Father Frank as she seemed to be. I was willing to give him the benefit of the doubt. But if any of this was his idea, I was certainly going to let him know my feelings on the matter. I stormed up the stairs to the rectory hall and rang the bell.

The sense of purpose that radiated from her as she dragged me out of the kitchen dissipated as we stood waiting for someone to answer the bell.

We were escorted to a side room off the foyer and asked to wait. I sat in a cozy leather high-backed chair as my mother fidgeted, pacing in an erratic pattern on the oriental rug that stretched across the center of the room. The air was still and smelled like abandoned books. Dust floated and sparkled as it drifted through the streams of sunlight bordered by darkly stained window frames. The sun had risen above the church, cleaved by the steeple. I noticed the humidity for the first time since stepping off the plane. It made my shirt stick to the middle of my back. I adjusted my position in an attempt to free the damp patch of skin. A heat bug screeched, which startled my mother.

"It's getting hot," I said, realizing these were the first words my mother had actually heard me say. She had begun her transition back to the corporeal world. It was as if her body was reacting to the strain of becoming material. I stood from the cozy chair and went to her. She seemed as though she was brimming with shame and worry. All at once, I felt the gravity of our situation. My father was dead. My mother and I responded to this in very different ways. To my mother, his death was the beginning of a well-articulated sequence of events that would bring him either bliss, torment, or an indefinite stay in Purgatory. For me, his death ended my lifelong quest for paternal approval and unconditional love.

She felt responsible for his soul, and Derrick's, and mine. It's hard to fathom the enormity of concepts like eternity, permanence, and death until you feel you are personally answerable for a loved one's soul.

"I shouldn't have brought you h'ah, Michael," she said without looking at me. "This isn't right. Fath'ah Francis is going to be very upset with me. We should go. We should go, *now*."

"It's okay, Mum," I said as I moved close to her and took her arm. "He's a priest. It's his job to understand and forgive. If he's anything like you've explained, then that's what he'll do."

"Let's go," she said. Her words were intended for me, but they were not directed at anyone. Her eyes resembled those of a wild animal captured in a net. I put my hand on her shoulder and felt a wave of recognition wash over her. She finally seemed to notice that I had arrived at home and was standing before her, flesh and blood. She was confused. I knew I should feel compassion as she struggled to parse what was real from the intricate constructions of her mind. I tried, but mostly I pitied her for not being able to see the reality that I occupied, and I resented her for not seeing that I also struggled to find my place. The struggle is universal. As quickly as her eyes focused on me, they darted away.

Where were you? I wondered.

The blood drained from her face as the loose floorboards in the foyer squeaked, announcing the approach of Father

Francis. The humidity swelled the door snuggly against its frame and it brayed as he pushed it open. Each harbinger of his arrival caused my mother to enter into a deeper state of anxiety. It was confusing to see her turn gaunt as he stepped through the doorframe. *What purpose could all this fear serve?*

"You must be Father Francis," I said, with a tentative smile. He was pleasant looking, thin, with sandy blond hair, slightly pointy features, and sad eyes. He reminded me of Bing Crosby in *The Bells of St. Mary's.*

"And you must be Michael," he said as he extended his hand. "I'm sorry for the loss of your father."

"Thank you," I said. My mother was still fidgety. I put my hand on her shoulder once again. "My mother has told me a lot about you. I've been looking forward to meeting you. You've had a big impact on her life."

"A positive one, I hope." He smiled. He was listening carefully. "Your mother is one of our most faithful parishioners. Are you getting along alright, Adeline?"

She nodded and tried to talk, but had trouble getting out the words. He took her hands in his, preventing her fingers from winding in knots.

"He's in a better place now, Adeline," said Father Francis. "I've been praying for him. He feels no pain or want, only God's love."

And with that all the visible signs of fear in her were suddenly gone. The tension released from her body. Those were the words she needed to hear. It was like watching an addict get her fix. She wanted to know she'd see her family again in a place where we'd all be perfect. The place where her family would be together, safe, happy, and obedient. The blood returned to her face, and she glowed with the radiance of hope that we would all share a love that is without want, without need, without pain, and would come without effort.

He is a powerful wizard, I thought. My mother was torn to pieces, but with a few magic words, he put her back together. I envied the type of faith that could bring this kind of immediate comfort, comfort in an outcome for which there was no evidence.

Father Francis asked if I would speak at the funeral mass. I didn't think that would be allowed. I was forbidden to take Holy Communion since the divorce, yet he was willing to hand over the pulpit and turn me loose on his congregation?

Despite my cynicism, I liked Father Francis. He had lived his whole life since Vatican II and seemed to seriously believe that Earth was round. He was more like the black-and-white movie priests that I grew up watching in old movies than the distant, hungover ones who typically tended to the flock at St. Anthony's. Those ancient priests who resented the reforms of the Second Vatican Council and lamented that they had to face their parishioners and speak to them in a language they understood.

"Well, I'm glad you stopped by," said Father Francis. "If there's anything else you'd like to talk about or if you just want to get something off your chest while you're here in

New Bedford, Michael, please don't hesitate to be in touch. You can always find me here."

"Thank you, Father," I said. "I can see why my mother speaks so highly of you."

"Your mother's faith is a gift," he replied as he walked us to the door. "And it's parishioners like her that make me look good in front of the Archbishop."

My mother gave him I-bet-you-tell-that-to-all-the-girls eyes. I, on the other hand, wasn't sure if I had just made a new friend or if I'd been sold something. I guessed I wouldn't know for certain until I had a beer with him or received a bill.

9

#9 TED WILLIAMS, OUTFIELD, BOSTON RED SOX

It was the day before the wake. My father's body was at McMahon's funeral parlor being prepared and dressed in his best blue suit, which he bought to wear for Ben's Bar Mitzvah. There would be four viewings over two days, and then another the morning before the casket would be sealed and brought to St. Anthony's for the Requiem Mass. He would be laid to rest with four generations of Quinns in the family plot.

There was a constant crush of well-wishers dropping by the house. My mother's fellow parishioners at St. Anthony's knocked on the front door and waited to be invited in. My father's friends walked into the kitchen and called out until someone greeted them. Every visitor talked about my father's acts of kindness, his bottomless patience, and how he beamed with pride whenever he talked about me.

"He was so proud of you, Mike," I heard over and over again from close neighbors like Mr. Karolides, Mrs. Sanderson, and from people I'd never met like his favorite bank teller Alicia and Rob the newish bartender at Sully's who dropped in to introduce himself before his shift.

"I'm workin' doubles latt'ah in the week so the oth'ah guys can go to the wake. I just really wanted to meet ya," said Rob. "Ya dad talked so highly of ya. I really would'a regretted not sayin' how much I liked hearin' his stories, and readin' ya columns, especially this mornin's."

"Right! Thank you," I replied, remembering the article I wrote on the plane. "It wasn't too sentimental?"

"Well, I don't know 'bout that. I thought it was great," he said. "It made me wanna come say hello, and like I said befo'ah, tell ya how much ya dad meant to me and you meant to him. It's real good to meet you."

We shook hands and patted each other on the shoulder, like men do in New Bedford, and I walked him to the door. His eyes lit up. "Hey, I gotta ask. Do you still have the compass ya dad gave ya?"

"He told you that story?" I asked with a laugh.

"A couple times, yeah," he confirmed, smiling broadly. "It was one of his favorites. He said he'd nev'ah been mo'ah afraid, but he knew you'd be somethin' special aft'ah you found the place half a day befo'ah he did."

"So, he's told everybody that story," I said. Rob seemed slightly worried that he'd offended me. He hadn't. I reached into my pocket and handed him the compass. "I've probably told it a thousand times myself. The apple doesn't fall far from the tree, huh?"

"It's a great story," Rob commented as he read the inscription. "My dad died a while back, too, and ah, I wish we was as close as yous guys. Okay, well hey, I'll probably see you around Sully's, huh?"

I nodded and smiled, but I was honestly baffled. Everyone in my dad's world could recount details of my life that I thought he'd never paid attention to. It was disorienting to hear these anecdotes from the mouths of strangers, especially strangers who say 'yous guys.' *Did he really mean what he said to all those people, or did he feel like saying anything else would be admitting failure as a father? If he meant it, he would have thrown me a bone at some point, right?*

The secondhand admiration made me to want to fly back to the University of Oregon, throw my arms around Ben, and tell him how much I loved him and how proud I was of him. *I never want him to doubt how I feel.* He wouldn't be in New Bedford for another 48 hours, but it would feel like much longer to me.

There was too much to process. My dad had relied on strangers to share his most intimate thoughts with me after his death. Maybe that wasn't his plan, but it was my reality. I wanted to dig a hole in the backyard and stow myself in it until I could sort things out, but instead I went to the kitchen to make a sandwich.

On my way, I got a call from Patricia Bartlett, the paper's publisher. She wanted to let me know the column I'd written on the plane was resonating with the other Oregonian transplants—who at this point were a majority—and she "hoped I'd write a series of follow-ups if I was feeling up to it." By the time we hung up, it was pretty clear that I should find a way to "feel up to it" if I hadn't already.

I reached for the bag of bulkie rolls on the counter. They were hard. *Lucky rolls*, I thought. *They have no trouble getting stiff at their age.* I was pleased with my joke and wished I had someone to share it with. The sunporch doorknob jangled. *Careful what you wish for,* I thought. I needed time to process my emotions and to think about my next column. But a familiar voice called my name, a woman's voice that I couldn't exactly place, yet it filled me with a nostalgic warmth. She came in from the sunporch. The late morning sun streamed through the kitchen window and created a latticework of light that played across the contours of her face. The shadows made me second guess who I was seeing.

"Mary Russell?" I finally said, verging on giddy.

I was slightly disoriented, but she didn't give me time to recalibrate. She rushed to me with her arms open, she touched my cheek, running her fingers across my stubble, down my neck, and across my shoulder. I'd known Mary for twenty years and we had never touched each other like that. Her hands glided down my back, her heart beating against my chest. I wove my fingers through her hair. I felt grief, lust, love, friendship, warmth, relief, and mostly confusion. *What's happening?* I thought. I wanted to ask her how she found my mother's house, and why she was in New Bedford, but all of this felt inconsequential while she held me in her arms.

"Hey," she said.

"Hey," I responded, with less familiarity and more curiosity. "How …Where …What are you doing here?"

"I hope it's okay that I'm here?" There was a change in her eyes.

"Of course! I'm just surprised to see you."

"I'm visiting my parents in Bourne."

"Pocasset …" I said, remembering her origins.

"I feel less self-conscious calling it Bourne, but yes. Esme and I flew back a couple of days ago. I read your column about your dad, and anyway, I was so moved that I didn't want to wait to see you. I should have called. I just wanted to tell you how sorry I am. It was silly of me to come here unannounced at a time like this, and expect—"

"I hope you expected that I would be thrilled to see you, because I am. I was a bit thrown off, but I can't tell you how wonderful it is to see you. Your timing couldn't be better, announced or unannounced, or wearing a clown suit, or a Shriners' fez. I'm really, really, *really* glad you're here."

She laughed, but it was tentative, more reserved. I was

feeling so many conflicting emotions. "Have you eaten?" I blurted out. "I'm starving, and I can't eat one more cold cut or piece of eggplant parmesan."

"Have you been to Davy's Locker yet?" she asked.

"You remember everything I tell you." Fried clams at Davy's Locker was my one must-have meal in New Bedford. I definitely mentioned that to her once, likely while we were having drinks after class at Walter Mitty's. "Let me just leave a note for my mother. She's gone to St. Anthony's to pray for a better son."

* * *

Parked at the curb in front of my mother's house was Mary's red '73 VW Karmann Ghia coupe, a rare and welcome sight for anyone who liked old VWs. The car was waxed and shiny—it looked like it had just rolled off the Wolfsburg factory's assembly line. I remembered admiring it once before. "Oh my God," I exclaimed, enjoying Mary's embarrassed smile. "You let me drive this car twenty years ago."

"More like twenty-five," she corrected. "I thought maybe you'd forgotten. We took the long way back to Emerson."

"It took ten minutes for me to understand how to get it in reverse," I said with a laugh. "You were so patient. I would have kicked me out of the driver's seat."

"Do you still remember how?"

"Put it in neutral, push the gearstick down, slide it back under second and fourth, over toward me, and then backwards again," I answered as I shifted an imaginary gearstick with one hand. "Ah ... no. Not really."

"You're close enough," she said as she tossed me her keys. "But let's just go forward."

I noticed the doors were unlocked as I prepared for a long descent into the driver's seat. "I'm sure I looked more graceful getting in last time—I'm pretty sure the seats are lower now. Did you have the seats lowered since the last time I drove it?"

She laughed and easily slid into her seat, discreetly pushing a bag underneath it with her foot. "I don't think so. It's just that gravity has gotten stronger. Science," she giggled.

"That must be it," I said. "I never did well in science."

I turned the key and the car rumbled to life—it shook like a dog coming out of a pond. The engine hummed. The steering wheel and gearshift vibrated slightly. I felt like I was part of the car as it waited for me to engage the gears. There was the unmistakable smell of an old Volkswagen—one part musk to four parts melted crayons—and it brought me back to the '80s, the last time Mary and I sat in her sporty little coupe. I was still figuring out how to be a less awkward version of me, but she had figured out how to be the perfect Mary Russell. I envied that.

"We've known each other a long time," I said.

Mary cozied her back between the door and the seat. "Yes, we have," she said. "I'm going to enjoy this. I still remember how happy it made you, driving the backroads to Boston."

It struck me as being completely novel that someone could derive pleasure from my happiness. There was a bit of a clunk as I shifted into gear, but I eased off the clutch and pulled smoothly away from the curb. I felt like a young man. *Maybe there's something to this middle-aged guy sports car thing,* I thought as I shifted into second and accelerated past the telephone pole where in 1978, Dave Tully bolted a piece of hockey-net sized plywood and practiced his slap shot with such precision that the puck eventually bored four holes through the wood. I could almost hear the scraping of his stick and the slap of the puck as it ricocheted off the wood.

"You look intense," Mary joked. "Are you overwhelmed by her immense power?"

"I just got lost in a childhood memory," I explained, trying to ground myself in the present. "Everything was so predictable, but at the same time everything seemed possible."

"Something you want to share?" she asked.

"It's silly really, just random," I said with chuckle.

Mary laughed. "My favorite combination!"

"I was just thinking about how important sports were to my dad. When I was really young, he spent a lot of time teaching me how to throw a baseball and a football, and how to shoot a basketball, but it never really felt like time together. Do you know what I mean? It felt like something he was obligated to do until he knew whether or not I was a future big-leaguer. And then when Derrick got old enough, my dad paid the most attention to him. He had a lot more natural ability than me. He took to things right away. He was an all-star everything: short stop, point guard, wide receiver. At first, I felt really jealous, but as we got older, I just felt relieved. It allowed me to do what I wanted. I could play a sport for the enjoyment of the game, or I could choose to not play at all without disappointing him. My lack of size and skill had already taken care of that." I laughed because that's what I do, but Mary didn't. She gently caressed my hand that was atop the gearshift and rested her head against my shoulder. Mary's hair was more red than blonde, and her eyes were green, not blue as I thought before that moment.

Am I falling for Mary Russell? Or have I always been in love with her?

We drove for a while in silence.

"So! Change of subject. This is silly," I finally said, "but you didn't lock your doors when you parked in front of my house."

"Your family's lived in that neighborhood for generations," she said. "Nobody's going to mess with my car while I'm at your house paying my respects. There's a special place in hell for that kind of person."

"Exactly," I said. *So, the bag she slid under the seat, she was hiding it from me,* I thought.

"Or a spot at the bottom of Clark's Cove," she joked

with a wink that did not come naturally. The extra effort made the gesture extra adorable.

"And I thought all you Pocasset kids were soft," I teased.

"That's why I say I'm from Bourne," she shot back.

I'd known Mary for more than half my life, but the lead-up to our meal at Davy's Locker buzzed with the nervous energy of a first date. We sat outside under the awning and watched the ferries carry tourists to and from Nantucket. The air was dense, thick with the scent of the ocean and freshly fried seafood. The proud seagulls squawked over-head, their calls echoing across Buzzards Bay, while the brash ones hopped around the parking lot looking to steal a meal. I ordered my usual: a fried clam plate with french fries, onion rings, and coleslaw that I never ate. Mary got the clams casino.

Our conversation came as naturally as waves to the shore. We grew up just miles from each other, went to the same college, worked together on the school's newspaper, and now by kismet we lived in the same city on the other side of the country and taught at the same college. We lived a common history, but the details were painted from different perspectives, like Monet's Haystacks across the seasons. Her stories were more vivid and told with a quirky effervescence that made me want to see the world though her eyes. My own memories became richer as she infused them with details that had been lost on me. *There are no unimportant moments,* I thought as I listened to Mary's recollections of the regionally televised bowling show *Candlepins for Cash* with host Bob Gamere. I savored every detail, especially the delightful crinkle of her nose when she joked about Gamere's plaid suits, and the joy in her eyes when she learned that plumbers from both our towns competed on the show. She remembered how much her plumber won, but all I remembered was that mine stumbled over his wife's name during the introduction and he never lived it down.

Mary laughed and put her hand on my arm. The warmth of her touch became my entire universe. She invited me to talk about how I was coping with the loss of my dad, but she didn't push me. I wanted to convince her I was doing fine— that I was strong. But before the words even formed in my mind they were spilling out of my mouth. My insecurities escaped me in a wave that eventually, finally, ended with "I never knew if he loved me. He never told me once."

"Of course he loved you. But seriously, he never told you? Not even once?"

I dug deep into the ravines of my memory, and something came to me. "Well, I guess that's not true exactly. He told me one time when he thought I got lost in the woods, but it was actually him that got lost. Anyway, it's a long story, but after he found me he was completely rattled. It was the only time I ever saw him cry. Well, that and then after the Red Sox won the World Series. But it was definitely the only time he ever said he loved me."

I'd repeated that story often, but it never occurred to

me that the words "I love you" were what made it special to me. Sharing it with Mary made me realize why the compass meant so much. The needle didn't point me toward my goals—it connected me to my father.

"I don't think you need to diminish the emotion just because he didn't repeat the words," she said. "He loved you."

"Yeah, I guess if he said it twice it would have been more believable," I replied.

"I believe he loved you," she insisted. "I can feel it in the stories you tell about him."

"Might that just mean that I loved him?" I countered, not really knowing why I was continuing with this line of thought. "I *did* love him. Or at least, I *tried* to love him, but he always kept me at arm's length. All these people have been telling me stories about his admiration for me. I find it bizarre that he admitted that to them, but he never shared it with me."

"Sometimes things look differently than we think they should and so we miss them—we don't see them clearly. Communication is hard. Not everybody's good at it. After my grandfather died—he was a cold, distant man, affectionate as a stone—I asked my grandmother how they stayed together for all those years. She said, 'The snow never told me it was cold, and the water never told me it was wet, but in other ways I knew these things.'" Mary paused and took my hand. "He showed my grandmother he loved her in ways we never saw, in ways we didn't understand. Your father loved you. In the quiet of your mind, you know that's true."

"There is no quiet in my mind," I laughed, but it wasn't really a joke.

She gave my hand a little squeeze and it made the whole world feel right. I didn't want our time together to end. My heart yearned to stay in the warm safety of her presence where I felt protected from the cold realities that awaited me.

"You make everything seem so easy. You should stick around and make things easy for me—just for a week," I said with a chuckle.

"I'm glad it looks easy. It doesn't feel easy," she said with a smile. "I'd do it for you if I could."

"Where do you start?" I asked. "Is there like a cheat-sheet that could get me through the weekend?"

"Make peace with uncertainty," she said without hesitation and added a credulous smile. "Easy, huh?"

"What does that mean, really? Because, I believe you. But when other people say it, I usually interpret it as 'just give up!'"

"Yeah, it definitely doesn't mean 'just give up,'" she said. "But, gosh, I've never been asked to describe my life's philosophy in a fried fish restaurant—I'm searching for the short answer."

"I know I'm putting you in an impossible situation, but just help me attain enlightenment so I can get through this weekend. That's all I'm asking."

"Right? Let me grab my magic Buddha wand. It's in the trunk."

We both laughed.

"You're impossibly wonderful," Mary said, smiling. "You're going to be fine."

"Maybe I'm already enlightened, then," I posed with a comedic you-never-know expression.

Mary nodded playfully. "Maybe. Did you know that when Buddhists bow to each other they're bowing to the future Buddha that they believe is in each of us? So, in a way that might be true."

"Really? I didn't know that."

"The bowing part is true," she clarified. "I'm less sure about the other part, but the belief is that everyone who sets foot on the path eventually becomes a Buddha."

"But don't Buddhists also believe that we are all one?" I asked. "If that's true and there is one Buddha, then aren't we all Buddhas?"

"That's some next level Buddhist thinking right there," she conceded with a smirk.

"I think my work might be done here," I concluded. "Go in peace, but really, give me one thing to remember that will help me through the weekend."

"Okay. Are you ready to be impressed by my insight-fulness? All we can control is ourselves in this moment—nothing else. We can plant seeds, prepare the soil, and add water, but we can't control the sun, or the rain, or birds, or bugs, or natural disasters. If future circumstances don't cooperate with our plans, all we can do is whatever can be done in the moment as it arises. So, what I tell myself is, 'stay present in the only moment that matters.'"

"I like that," I said.

"I used to always get caught up trying to become 'someone,' some perfect person in a perfect life. Becoming an artist, dating certain guys, being the ideal wife and mother. But after my divorce, I realized none of that made me happy. I decided the feeling that I was looking for wasn't attached to anything like that."

"That seems sad," I murmured. "It does sound a little bit like giving up."

Her eyes were reassuring and kind, but the way she was looking at me made me feel certain she found that particular thought moronic. "That's the paradox," she explained. "If you're not happy on your way to your goal, then you're not very likely to be happy when you get there."

I let that sink in, then eventually nodded in agreement. We sat in a comfortable silence for longer than I normally would allow. What she said sounded like truth or wisdom, but there was something about it I couldn't fully embrace. It felt like she was saying that life hands out participation trophies and I just didn't believe that.

"Why haven't we talked like this before?" I asked.

"I don't know. I'm just glad we are now." She sighed. "I

hope I don't sound preachy or, I don't know, like I have all the answers, because I don't. I'm just sharing what works for me."

"You 'ah wicked smah't," I said in my best Boston accent. "I could listen to you all day. This has been very helpful."

We laughed, a nice catharsis. I steered the conversation back to safe topics: college memories, concerts at the Rat in Kenmore Square, the utter insanity of St. Patrick's Day in Boston after Billy Bulger declared Evacuation Day (which happens to fall on St. Paddy's day) a city holiday, eccentric professors, fashion trends, and the bizarre success of Sylvester Stallone movies. Time flowed, like clichés on a sports page. I told Mary I should probably check on my mother soon, which segued into Mary and I talking about being kids and having to be home when the streetlights came on. If your mother ever had to shout your name into darkness, you knew the next night you'd be stuck inside after dinner.

* * *

I pulled Mary's VW up to the curb. "You're good medicine, Russell," I said, not remembering where I'd heard that phrase but thinking it perfectly fit the situation.

"You too, Quinn," she replied as her smiling face turned serious.

I desperately searched for adequate ways to articulate my feelings, but found none. I didn't want to get out of the car.

The Karmann Ghia had become a magic bubble of warmth, kindness, and optimism. Mary was scheduled to fly back to Portland the next morning. Her daughter had music camp that weekend. I wished she were staying. I wished I knew what to say before she left, but all I managed to utter was a groan as I lifted myself out of the car. Mary got out and met me by the driver's door.

"I'll see you back in Portland," I said, each word steeped in longing, which probably sounded a bit desperate.

"I could change my flight if you'd like me to stay," she immediately offered. "If it would be helpful or comforting."

"It would be both of those things," I assured her, "but it wouldn't be fair to Esme. You need to get her back for music camp. I really want to be totally there for my mum through this, and Ben arrives the day after tomorrow, and I need to at least *try* to mend fences with Derrick, which may be impossible, but I have to try."

"You're a good guy, Quinn," she said as she touched my cheek.

I wanted to kiss her, but when she leaned toward me, I balked. I went in for a friendly hug instead, the kind where you pat each other on the back and make sure to let go before it gets awkward. But she didn't pat my back, and she didn't let go. I relaxed into her arms, took a deep breath in, and caught a pleasant scent from the past, something striking and iconic like Irish Spring soap or Charlie perfume, but I couldn't place it. We shifted in each other's arms so we could look into each other's eyes.

"You could kiss me if you'd like," Mary murmured. And she closed her eyes and parted her lips, and I leaned in to meet them, slow and sure. Like a first kiss.

"Wow," was the only response I could conjure from my vast journalist's vocabulary.

"Yeah," Mary agreed, amused. "Wow."

We admired each other for a moment.

Finally, I managed to speak. "Um, it's too weird."

"Weird?" She grinned and crinkled her nose.

"You're wearing something, perfume or something, that I can't place, but it smells really good," I babbled.

Mary laughed. "You're so wonderfully odd. My mother still uses Prell shampoo, so that was what she had for me to use. I've been self-conscious about it all day—I can smell it, too. It's garish and it's okay to say so."

"I like it!" I insisted, laughing with her. "I'm serious. It brought me back to my childhood. It was like I was experiencing my first kiss all over again."

"Now you're making fun of me," she said, putting on a fake pout.

"I'm falling for you," I replied, serious. "And I hope you're falling for me."

We kissed again, more passionately than before.

"I'm glad the waiting is finally over," she sighed as we pulled away. "I've been in love with you for a long time."

Holy shit, I thought. *You're Hunza, or it was you, not*

Hunza! I glanced into the car and saw the Baker's Bookstore bag sitting on the passenger's seat. She bought a new copy of *Victory Lab* to return to me. *Of course it was her you fucking idiot!* I froze as if she could read my thoughts, then noticed the curtains moving in the living room window. My mother had been spying on us.

"Are you okay?" Mary asked.

"There's just so much going on in my head right now, and my mother is definitely spying on us through the living room window," I said as we both turned to see the curtains move again.

"Now *I* feel like a teenager," Mary joked.

"Spying? I was not spying!" I mimicked what I assumed would be my mother's denial.

I felt conflicted about asking for the book, because I'd written my message thinking it was for Hunza, but I couldn't have been happier that I was wrong. I tried to gut up the courage to say something, anything, but my fear won out.

"Well, I should go," Mary said as she gently traced my jawline. "I'm here for you, though. Day or night, if you need me, just call me. Okay? Promise?"

"Promise." I felt a tear roll down my cheek. Mary dried it with her fingertip and kissed me three times along the path she traced. It was a simple gesture, one I'd never experienced, and I'd never felt more vulnerable.

We hugged one last time, and again I caught the scent of

the Prell shampoo. I wondered if this moment, her comfort, and that scent would forever be linked somewhere deep within my psyche. She didn't let go of my hand as she slid into the driver's seat of the VW.

"Mary," I said before she closed the door. "Thank you."

She smiled, pulled the door shut, and started the car. But as she tried to pull away from the curb, it stalled. She stuck her head out the window with an embarrassed smile. "That's the real reason I always let you drive!"

We both smiled at each other, then she was off with a rev of the engine and chirp of the tires.

* * *

I had dinner with my mother the night before the wake. We had frozen fish sticks, corn, and minute rice. We never talked about my father. We did, however, talk about the fish sticks that she bought at Costco, which she thought was better than the Super Stop and Shop for frozen bulk foods, even though some of the women in her rosary prayer group swore by Super Stop and Shop. *Are we that damaged, heartless, and distant from each other, or are we just that boring?* I wondered. I was trying to take Mary's advice and not question everything. *I'm just going to "be" for a while.*

Joe Staid asked me to go to Sully's for a few beers. An invitation from Joe was not in character for him. He was a homebody and an introvert who even after fifty years of marriage hated to be away from his wife. I suspected somebody had put him up to it—probably my mother trying to get Derrick and me in the same place at the same time. If that was the case, they should have chosen a location with less alcohol and testosterone. Sully's was a place to watch a game, not talk about feelings.

My mother practically pushed me out the door and said she was going to pray the Rosary. She told me it would be good for me to get out with Joe and the guys, "And don't feel the need to hurry back," she encouraged. But when Joe picked me up, she reflexively told him not to keep me out too late. It was what she used to say when the guys came for my dad. Joe and I walked the three memory-rich blocks to the bar. I silently recalled the family name of each house as we passed them and whether I'd delivered them a *Globe* or a *Herald*. I caught the scent of an ocean breeze as we walked across the cooling asphalt. It was the type of rare New England summer night that dominated my childhood memories. Warm with low humidity and cool air rolling in off the Atlantic. On a night like this thirty-five years ago, I'd have been playing basketball with my neighborhood friends or sitting in the sunporch with my dad and Derrick watching the Sox on the portable TV. "It's a great night for a ballgame," he'd say.

The green neon sign that once gave Sully's doorway a ghostly aura had been replaced with a carved wooden shamrock framing the words "Sully's Tap and Bite est. 1947," otherwise there was no discernible change to the place since I was there last.

Joe didn't say much as we walked, which was not unusual, but he put his hand on my shoulder as we got close to the door. He seemed concerned. My thoughts leapt to the scene in *Goodfellas* when Joe Pesci thinks he's about to become a "made man" but instead takes a bullet to the back of his head.

The door swung open and everyone turned to see who had arrived, just as they'd no doubt done many times before that night. This time, however, the chatter stopped, and no one turned away. Sully Jr. was standing on the workman's side of the bar in front of my father's regular seat. Joe gave me a reassuring smile and gestured for me to keep walking. Other patrons, most of whom I didn't know, patted me on the back and offered their condolences. As I made my way to the bar, the only sounds were chair and barstool legs scraping against the wooden floor as everyone stood—Sully Jr. had even turned the volume down on the TV. There was a Sam Adams in a frozen mug waiting for me on the bar next to a small rectangular brass plaque engraved with my dad's name: "John 'Jake' Quinn." Bill and Sandy Kocher were standing by their regular seats. Derrick stood next to them. They were already holding their beers in the air. As if it were all rehearsed, I grabbed my mug and stood in my dad's spot. Bill grabbed Derrick by the arm and pulled him next to me.

"F'ah those of you who don't know, this is Jake's oth'ah kid and Derrick's old'ah broth'ah, Mikey. Mike grew up just down the block, but now's a hot shit writ'ah in Portland, Oregon. He wrote in the newspap'ah today that he wouldn't be home until he was standin' in this b'ah drinkin' a toast to his dad," Bill said as his eyes filled with tears. His words struggled to find their way out. "No matt'ah wh'ah you 'ah—even in that weird freakin' town wh'ah you live now, wh'ah the ocean's on the wrong side and ya clos'ah to the Lak'ahs and the Yankees than the Celtics and the Sox and ya closest football team's named after a fuckin' seagull—this has always been ya home, and it always will be. This is wh'ah ya roots 'ah, wh'ah ya family is, and wh'ah people like ya f'ah who ya 'ah and not what ya do f'ah a livin'. Even if we wanted to fo'get about ya, ya dad wouldn't let us, because he nev'ah shut the fuck up about ya. Like ya dad and Derrick kept you close to us, we'll keep Jake's memory alive, because everybody gotta live someplace, but it's the people who ya choose to live with that makes it a home. Now raise ya goddamn glasses to my best friend, ya dad, and the greatest guy to ev'ah walk through those fuckin' do'ahs, Jake Quinn! And welcome home, kid!"

Everyone raised their glass and extolled my dad's name. "To Jake!" It was a great honor to my dad, but the bigger tribute was the silence that followed. It is only the truest friends who feel comfortable in such heavy silence. A word like "sorry" that we use every day—when we bump into someone on an elevator or don't hear part of a sentence—cannot possibly capture the depth of emotion experienced when we've lost someone. These moments are shared from a place that is older than language and deeper than wisdom; these feelings were expressed by the chill that rushed across my skin and the tears that returned the salt to the Earth.

There was nothing left to do but drink, which we did, and plenty of it. Things at the bar got back to normal quickly. There were bursts of laughter, salvos of F-bombs, and an indistinguishable tangle of sports and betting talk. It felt like home. "W'ah born, we die, and in between th'ah's the Sox to live f'ah," my dad used to joke. But as I looked around the room, I knew there was more to it than that. Sully's was a true neighborhood bar. These people were like family. Extended family maybe, but family none the less. The fact that I'd been gone wasn't important to them. What mattered was that I chose to come back. Generations before, the common denominator for everyone was fishing. On a night like this they'd share stories of George's Banks, Nor'easters, cod and whales, but now the thread that held us together was the local four: the Celtics, Bruins, Patriots, and Red Sox. It gave us a common vernacular. It wasn't about gleaning glory from the accomplishments of others—it was about sharing an experience. It was a place to start a conversation.

* * *

Derrick paced around the bar for much of the night. He didn't really talk to anyone, and when people talked to him, he either nodded or turned his back to them. He was a quiet guy, but not that quiet. When he sat, it was alone, hunched over his beer. There were no other cops there. I thought they stuck together. Not that I could identify every plainclothes cop necessarily, but the haircut, doubting eyes, and rigid demeanor usually were pretty reliable indicators. Each time the door opened, Derrick stiffened and checked to see who was coming or going. We all handle grief differently, but there was something going on with him that I didn't understand. He was so on edge that I wondered if he'd been doing coke, or meth, or whatever drug was moving through New Beige. The fact that I'd been home for more than twenty-four hours and we hadn't said more than ten words to each other was ridiculous. We were grown men, and brothers, who were here together to bury our father. It was time for us to talk.

I ordered another beer from Sully Jr. I didn't know how many I had drunk, but it was too many to start a difficult conversation yet not enough to know I was making a mistake. Joe Staid and the Koshers watched with what I assumed was morbid curiosity as I walked toward my brother. I put my hand on the middle of his back and could feel his heart pounding as I sat on the stool beside him. "You holdin' up?" I asked.

Derrick looked at my face but avoided my eyes. "Don't pretend you give a fuck about me. I'm not fooled by the bullshit you put in the fuckin' newspap'ah. Save it for somebody who gives a fuck. I'm the only guy in this fuckin' ba'ah that really knows what a fuckin' asshole you 'ah."

He swilled the rest of his beer and walked out of Sully's without looking back. *So that's what he's been waiting to say.* I thought about yelling "Fuck off!" or something equally erudite, but assumed that was the reaction he wanted to get out of me. Instead, I just shook my head, sipped my beer, and thought about the days to come.

Bill Kosher came over and slapped me on the shoulder. "Well, I was hopin' that would be mo'ah excitin'," he laughed. "Ya broth'ah's got a temp'ah, and uh, it's gonna take him time to figure his shit out."

With the promise of fisticuffs was off the table, Bill and Sandy decided to call it a night. Joe had been quiet and fidgety almost the entire time, but that wasn't strange at all. When he grabbed me by the elbow I expected him to say he was going home, too, but he took me to a quiet table away from the bar instead. He told me that Bill Kosher had always been jealous of me and Derrick. "Bill never had kids," Joe explained. "He's never known what it's like to care about someone else's life more than your own. So, always take what he says with a grain of salt."

I had no idea where this was going, but I was just drunk enough to hope it didn't end soon. *Keep the surprises coming,* I thought as Joe pulled an envelope from his rear pocket. "Your dad asked me to give this to you. He gave it to me a few years ago and asked me to keep it a secret, especially from Bill and Derrick. I never asked him what was in it and he never told me. So anyway, here you go, kid. And don't worry about Derrick. You guys will figure it out. It's a tough time right now and people deal with things in their own way. Ya know?"

He put the envelope on the table, looked into my eyes, nodded, and patted me on the shoulder as he stood. "Your dad really loved ya, kid."

And that was that.

I held the envelope like it was the Holy Grail. *Don't get your hopes up too high,* I thought as my mind wandered back to all the things I wished I'd heard from him throughout the years. My hands trembled slightly as I slid my thumb under the envelope's flap and gently tore through the fold. There were two pages. I unfolded them and stared at the first two words for a while before moving on. "Dear Son," it began. I don't know why those words hit me so hard, but they did.

> *Dear Son,*
>
> *I've spent a lifetime waiting for the right moments to do and say things. I made a life by taking what came to me and I was grateful to have it. I'll die having only left New England to visit you in Washington, DC and then again in Oregon. I always wanted to go to New York and look over the city from the Empire State Building, and to go South Bend and see Notre Dame play Navy, but those things will never happen for me. I've also been waiting for the right moment to tell you how much I love you and how proud I am to be your father. You are your own man and sought out the life*

you wanted. I took great pride in that and found great happiness in your achievements. It should be easy for me to tell you these things, but the words were always too hard to find.

My only goal was to give you a life that was better than mine. To provide you and Derrick with a stable home where you could focus on your studies and grow into the men I knew you could become. I wanted to shield you from the types of decisions I had to make to keep the lights on and put food on the table. If I seemed distant from you, it was only because I wanted to put distance between the choices I had to make in my life and your ambitions.

I stopped reading for a moment to sip my beer and brace myself for what was coming next. I wanted to savor those words I'd always wanted to hear (*how much I love you and how proud I am to be your father*), but I suspected the coming paragraphs were going to somehow make it easy for me to forget those words. I took a deep breath and read on.

After I got laid-off from the port in the '70s and couldn't find another union job, I decided to watch out for myself. Bartending a few nights a week at Sully's was not really where the extra money came from. Sully Sr. was a bookie, and he and I worked together until he died. We always kept it small and stayed under the radar from the guys in Providence and later when the Russians moved into Boston.

I reread that passage three times to be sure I wasn't hallucinating it. Nope. It said what I thought it said, in ink.

"Hey, Sully!" I called across the bar, which had mostly emptied out.

"Yeah, Mike? You need anoth'ah be'ah?"

"I *definitely* need another beer."

"Comin' right up," he said as he reached into the cooler beneath the bar, grabbed a frozen mug, opened the tap, and poured me a perfect beer. He walked it to the end of the bar where I was waiting for him.

"You know what my dad did for a living?" I asked.

"You mean bein' a butch'ah or the oth'ah thing?" he replied, as if I were deciding between types of frozen yogurt toppings—oh, did you want the crumbled Butterfinger or the shredded coconut?

I nodded thanks and grabbed my beer. "The other thing," I clarified as Sully Jr. went back to work.

"Don't worry about that, Mikey," he said as he turned away. "Ya know what I mean?"

I was horrified that I did know what he meant, and I went back to the letter.

> *I never told you these things because I didn't want to put you in a position where you'd have to lie about me. I wasn't proud of what I did, but I did it because I had to, because I never wanted you, or your mother and Derrick, to go without. It was all rainy day money. Sully and I used to say it was our pension.*

That money's hidden in the house and I want you to have it. You can make your own decisions about what you want to do with it. Your mother is set up and she'll be fine. When you're deciding what to do, remember that Derrick is a cop and that he also needs reminding of that from time to time.

Mike, whatever else you do in life, make sure your family comes first. Your mother and I felt like you sometimes put your job before your family. We understood, or at least tried to understand, but Ben should never feel like he comes second to anything else in your life. I made sacrifices so you wouldn't have to. I'm sorry my choices made it harder to be the father I wanted to be to you. I hope you always knew that I loved you.

The one thing I wish I taught you better is that you can be anything you want in this life and you proved that, Mike. But a job is what you do, it's not who you are. A title gets written down on a resume and when you leave a job someone else takes that title, but you take your family, your integrity, and your reputation with you. So, be sure those are the things that you work the hardest at. Don't go to your grave wishing you'd been a better father or a better man.

The money's in an old cracker tin in the cellar on my workbench. It's the same tin where Papa kept his money after the banks crashed during the Depression.

Finally, I know you still carry around that compass I gave you on our trip to the White Mountains. Bring Ben someplace special and when you get there, I want you to hug that boy with all your might and tell him how much you love him. Give him the compass and have him smash it into a million pieces. Tell him there's only one goal worth having. Decide how you want to be remembered by your friends and family and live everyday like it's the only one they'll remember. Be kind, be honest, be brave, and let that be your compass. Tell him there is nothing you can hold in this world that is more important than the love of your friends and family.

Love,

Dad

I couldn't have been more shocked if he had told me he was president of the Irish-American Leprechaun Union. There was so much to unpack that I didn't really know where to begin—literally my mind went blank and I spent several minutes staring into empty space. To start, he was a three-dimensional person with feelings and observations that were totally divorced from The Local Four. Feelings and observations about *me, specifically.* And, oh yeah, he had been a fucking bookie for the past thirty years and there was a pile of tax-free dirty money hidden in the basement.

I decided to put off thinking about anything else until I found the cracker tin. I wasn't sure what to think or believe in that moment, but finding that tin would at least help me know that this wasn't all a dream.

* * *

It was after 1 a.m. by the time I got back to my mother's house. The lights were out except for the ones in the bathroom. She lit the way to the toilet in case I got too drunk to find it in the dark. The door to the basement was in the sunporch and it was left unlocked. Maybe my father left it open for me, or maybe he just didn't care about the money. Or he was the most powerful gangster in New Bedford and people knew not to steal from him. There were hundreds of dollars' worth of tools on his workbench—maybe he thought if anyone went down there they'd steal those and not care about the eighty-year-old cracker tin stuffed with cash. I stood at the top of the basement stairs with my back hunched in anticipation of the cramped descent. I had so many questions, and I wished my father were there to answer them all.

I tiptoed down the stairs. They were solidly built and there was nary a squeak as I descended. I used the light on my iPhone to find the pull-string for the naked bulb that hung over the workbench. The musty cellar smell and cool humid air brought back a rush of childhood memories, times I'd watch my dad fix things on his bench: toasters, a lawnmower engine, he even restitched my baseball glove here. I thought he was magical. He seemed to know how every household gadget worked and had all the right tools to put them back together. *I just throw things away and buy new ones and I don't even have a pile of cash in my basement,* I thought as my eyes adjusted to the light.

It took almost no effort to find the saltine tin. It was between the bench and the ingenious wooden shelf my father had installed to hold fasteners and screws of all types. The bottom of the shelf had jelly-jar lids screwed to it and the glass jars were suspended by their caps. The hanging jars blocked the tin like some basic security measure. It took me few minutes to unscrew enough jars to remove the tin. I popped the lid, caught the unmistakable smell of money—ink and everything else the bills had touched clinging to cotton-and-linen parchment—and there was a lot of parchment. Fifty grand in rolls of twenties and fifties. I hadn't seen a fifty-dollar bill in years and there I was holding fifty of them in each hand—five grand rolled up like tiny hay bales that were held in place with rubber bands.

Everything is different than I believed, I thought, and it wasn't necessarily about the money. Holding this cash was proof that I knew very little about my father. I didn't have a clue as to what made his clock tick, until now. *He didn't do this for the money,* I thought. *He did this for his family. He did it to ensure that we'd be okay. He did what he had to do to make sure we'd have what we needed.* I wondered if I would do the same for Ben, and if so, would I tell him? *Would I be able to keep a secret like this from him for my whole life?*

My mind jumped from thought to thought, but my immediate dilemma was what to do with the money. I couldn't conceive of an outcome that didn't involve keeping it. Fifty grand in cash solves a lot of problems. I was still drunk and trying to sort out all this complicated shit. *How would I even get it through TSA? Sleep on it,* I thought. *I need to get some rest. But what do I do with the money, tonight?*

The cash had been safe where it was for God knows how long—it would likely as not be safe there for a few more days. I put the money in the tin, slid it back under the shelf, and screwed the jars back into their caps. Even in the dim light of the single bulb I could see the place on the bench where dust had been disturbed. If someone knew what was written in that letter and came looking for the money, then I'd essentially marked the spot with an X. I found a rag resting atop a bottle of turpentine and used it to wipe down the bench and everything that rested on it. Realizing that it made the bench look conspicuously clean, I wiped the rag against boxes of Christmas decorations, then yard tools, then old sporting goods. The dust that hung in the air became heavy with the smell of turpentine—it caused me to sneeze three times in quick succession. My work was done. I pulled the string to douse the light. In the darkness, I realized that someone had turned on the lights in the kitchen. *How long have they been on?*

I walked as quietly as I could, not knowing what to expect. I felt like a spy or a gangster. My heart was in my throat. I assumed it had to be my mother, but thought for a moment about getting a monkey wrench to use as a weapon just in case it wasn't. As I got near the top of the stairs, I heard a teacup being placed on its saucer. I'm not sure how different I would have felt if I'd heard the hammer of a gun being cocked.

My mother stood by the counter near the sink wearing the threadbare flannel robe that Derrick gave her for Christmas when we were teenagers. Her face was shiny from whatever lotions she'd applied before bed. Without makeup she looked different, older—the lack of it ampli-fied the intensity of her eyes. They stood out now that they weren't competing with eyeshadow and rouge. She stood in a familiar posture signaling her disapproval: her hips were cocked in the same direction that her head was tilted. She waited for me to talk first, to bear my soul and confess my sins as if I were kneeling before St. Peter. But I felt a deep need to deny her that.

"You're up," I said.

"Odd place to end up in the middle of the night," she replied. "W'ah you too drunk to find ya room?"

"The cellar?" I said, hating myself for getting sucked into this carnival game. It was an enterprise without merit or winners. I'd like to say we played for the spirit of competi-tion, but really we played out of habit, or probably spite. The best possible outcome was the emotional equivalent of a teddy bear that smelled like cigarette smoke and was packed so hard with Styrofoam that it brought no comfort. In the end, both sides came away feeling cheated and depleted of resources, and yet we persisted.

"What might somebody be trying to find in the basement at two in the morning?" She asked, over-pronouncing all her syllables, as if she were a character from one of the PBS mystery series she so loved.

"Could we not do this, please?" I'd like to think I was searching for higher ground, but really I was just too tired for this game. I suspected she knew exactly why I was in the basement.

"And what, may I ask, is *this*?"

"This," I said, making a general motion. "This charade we play, were we pretend one of us is suddenly going to be open and emotionally honest even though we know it's never going to happen."

"Is that what yuppies say now, 'emotionally honest'?"

"Yes, mother, that's what we say, but I'm not sure anyone says 'yuppies' anymore."

"'Ah you drunk?" she inquired before sipping her tea. "Men are always brav'ah when ya drunk."

"I suspect I am, yes," I snapped. "Honesty and directness are also a type of bravery, Mother. So, why don't you just ask me what you want to know before my bravery metabolizes into a hangover?"

"What's going on with you, anyway?"

"Mum." My patience was as threadbare as her robe. My

parents had lied to me my whole life. Certainly, she knew about the gambling. I wanted to know what she knew, but more than that I wanted to know why no one told me. I wanted to believe she'd share more with me in that moment, but our history suggested otherwise. I didn't want to be lied to again. "I just want to know the truth."

Her shoulders slumped and her head bobbed as she rehearsed in her mind what she was going to say. Her lips fluttered as if she was already speaking. She was caught between worlds again and it seemed clear she felt comfortable in neither of them.

"Secrets and lies," she finally muttered. "That's all we have. That's what 'ah family is, secrets and lies. What did Joe tell you at the ba'ah tonight? Did he make up some story about ya fath'ah being Robin Hood or something?"

"Joe didn't tell me anything," I said. "He gave me a letter from Dad. It told me he was a bookie and that he left me some money. The letter told me where to find it. I came home to look for it, because I couldn't believe it was true."

"Well, it is true," she confirmed, her voice thick with disgust. "But you know that by now."

"Yeah, I found the money. There's a lot of it, and if that's what you're worried about, I can leave it right where it is."

She laughed, maybe out of disgust, or maybe out of disbelief. It was hard to tell. "The'ah's a lot more money than's in that crack'ah tin," she said, matter-of-fact. "The real money's in a safety deposit box."

"The *real* money." I stared blankly at her.

"Yes, the *real* money," she shot back. "The money he won betting on the Red Sox. That wasn't in ya lett'ah?"

"No ..." *What in the mother fucking hell is going on?* "So, was he or wasn't he a bookie?"

"The name you give these things doesn't really matt'ah, Mike. It's all sin in the eyes of God. It's all ill-gotten gains."

"It matters to me, Mum," I said. My guard was down. I was too tired for pretense. "Can't you just tell me the truth about Dad, Mum? I want to feel like I know him before we put him in the ground."

She paused, lost in thought.

"I mean he is my father, right?" I joked. "Or was I payment on a bet with the Kochers? Is that it? Dad won his firstborn son betting on a Muhammad Ali fight?"

She laughed, and it felt like the first genuine emotion we'd shared since I came home. She went to the cupboard and took down another saucer and cup, turned on the flame to warm the kettle, took a teabag out of a jar, and sat before she talked again.

"Why don't you let me read the lett'ah, and then at least I'll have a place to begin."

I gave her the letter and waited by the stove for the pot to boil. Eventually I removed the kettle from the heat as the steam whistle turned shrill. I topped off my mother's cup, and tried and failed to read her stoic expression. I sat and let my tea steep.

"That's a beautiful lett'ah," she finally said in a tone that made it clear that this was not the whole truth. "I can't tell you anything that's going to make you feel bett'ah than what he wrote."

"I want to know the truth, Mum. Even if it hurts."

"I can only tell you what I know, Michael, and the'ah's a lot I don't know," she sighed. Her voice had softened. "I can tell you what I've been told, and I don't know wheth'ah that's the truth or not."

"I can accept that."

"I can tell you that he loved you," she began. "That I know. Nothing else changes that."

I agreed. I felt more connected to my mother than I ever had. Her face contorted with anguish. *This is going to be harder for her to say than for me to hear,* I thought as she searched for the right place to begin.

"'The truth doesn't betray anyone,'" I said to ease her way. "That's what my editor said when I told her I wasn't sure I wanted to run the story I wrote about the politician who lied about his background. I knew it would end his career, and I felt bad."

"All of them lie," she replied with a disgusted sigh.

"I felt really bad about what that story did to him. I felt responsible for his collapse, but my editor assured me that he had done it to himself. 'Our allegiance is to the truth,' she told me. 'Never apologize for that.'"

"I don't feel like I'm betraying him, Michael. I feel like

I'm betraying you."

"You know, Mum, for a very long time now, I feel like I've been trying to grasp something that's just out of my reach. That's how I felt when I was with Sarah. I felt like," I laughed because it had finally dawned on me just then, "you know when you think you have all the down answers in a crossword puzzle but then you get the across answer that makes them all wrong? That's what my marriage felt like. I was the down answers and Sarah was the across answer that always made everything wrong. I made her perfect in my mind and I struggled for our whole relationship to become the right answer. I always thought that made me lose who I was, but the truth is, Mum, that I didn't lose myself, because I never knew who I was. After Derrick was born, I never felt like I belonged. This letter and that stupid compass he gave me when I was a kid are all I have. I'm still struggling to understand who I am, Mum. I'm just trying to find something real that I can build from. So, no matter how bad it is, it's better than not knowing."

She reached her hand across the table and smiled at me. "All you need to know is that he loved you," she said again, more for herself than for me. "You 'ah a sensitive boy, Michael. The'ah was a time I thought you might be gay."

"For God's sake, Mum, just tell me what happened," I snapped.

"Alright, I'll tell you about the money and then I'm going to bed. Do you rememb'ah the time you came home to watch the Red Sox? You and Derrick, and everybody went with him to Sully's? I nev'ah understood why you flew all the way he'ah to watch a baseball game on TV, but anyway."

"Yeah, 2004," I said.

"He'd been putting money in that tin since you w'ah a boy. He wanted me to know whe'ah it was just in case something happened to him. I had no idea how much was in the'ah. I thought maybe a thousand, maybe a few thousand." She shrugged. "He always said it was for a rainy day, or if one of you boys got in trouble, then we'd have money to help you out, but I always hated the feeling of having that money in the basement. You boys went off and we w'ah getting old'ah and I wanted that sinful money gone. I felt like it was a curse. He told me the'ah is only one way to get rid of betting money and that's to bet it. The idiot. So, I don't really know how it all works—this betting thing—I just know the Red Sox had to do something that no one had ev'ah done and win the World Series, which he said was impossible. And you know the rest."

"So, he made this bet while I was here?" I asked.

"No. It was befo'ah that. They w'ah playing the Yankees. He said it was impossible to win—that they had to win all the games and no team had ev'ah done it."

"Okay, so when the Sox were down three games to none in the American League Championship Series, he bet fifty grand on them to beat New York and then to sweep the

World Series?" I laughed at the ridiculousness of it. "Does that sound right?"

"Had any team ev'ah done that?" she pressed, annoyed at my persistence.

"No!"

"Then, yes, it does," she said, and finished her tea. "I wanted that sinful money gone. 'The'ah's only one way to get rid of it,' he says, and then he made a deal with the Russian devils he was working f'ah. They'ah Godless men, those people."

"Jesus ..."

"Michael!"

"He was working for the Russian mob?" I asked.

"Yes."

"Okay," I said, trying to clear my head. "This is all real. We're talking about Dad, right? Does Derrick know all this?"

"Yes."

"I had no clue!"

"What do we ev'ah really know?" she murmured as she tipped her cup above her lips to drink the last drop of tea. "This tea is good, isn't it? They sell it at the Ma'ket Basket. You should bring some home. It's only $3.25. It's a good deal."

"They sell tea in Portland, Mum," I said. "That must have been like 20-to-1 odds. Is there like a million dollars hiding in that safety deposit box?"

"No, ya fath'ah was afraid the Russians would kill him

befo'ah they'd pay him, so he talked them down, maybe to nothing," she explained. "I don't really know. He didn't want me to worry. He always told me the less I knew the bett'ah off I was."

My brain was spinning and rattling like a carnival ride. The excess of booze, honesty, perfumed tea, and betrayal had me on the verge of vomiting. My sinuses were filled with dust and my hands smelled of turpentine. I closed my eyes, searching for some peace, but it only exacerbated the spinning sensation.

"'Ah you going to be sick?" my mother asked.

"I think so," I managed.

"Well, why don't you go do that in the bathroom and then go get some rest?" she proposed matter-of-factly. "Sarah and Ben are going to be here early, and you don't want to look and smell like a hobo."

"Wait. What? Sarah's coming?"

"She called the house tonight while you w'ah at the ba'ah," she explained, giving me a pat on the back as she walked by on her way to her bedroom. It was a rare show of affection.

I didn't know what to think, and I was less sure what to believe. I felt the need to write it all down—craft it, rearrange it, find the threads that ran deep through my life. It was the only way I could make it all seem normal. Saliva began to well in my mouth and I rushed to the bathroom.

10

#10 JOSEPH "JO JO" WHITE, POINT GUARD, BOSTON CELTICS

I was suspended between sleep and waking. For an unreasonably brief moment, I felt wonderful. I was untethered from the responsibility of my desires. The voice that nagged, prodded, questioned, judged, and second-guessed my every motivation was either asleep or still drunk from the night before. I was free from the burden of being Michael Quinn. I teetered along the fissure between realities until gravity pulled me into consciousness. I landed with a thump and my thoughts began to move like Jell-O through cheesecloth. Pressure swelled at the backs of my eyes and my ears rang with an electric hum. My joints ached—my gut twisted. I thought about lifting my head from the pillow, but I couldn't find the courage. It was the morning of my father's wake, and like a good Irish Catholic, I was hungover—it was the only part of the catechism I ever fully embraced.

My son and ex-wife were in an airplane somewhere closer to the Hudson than the Mississippi as I lumbered out of bed. Sarah's last-minute decision to accompany Ben had my brain in a knot. She wasn't coming to be supportive. She had some other motive, and it would be wise for me to figure out what it was. I anticipated the areas of conflict and began formulating counterarguments. I prepared for attacks on all fronts. I didn't know what kind of fight I was in for, I just knew that before noon, Sarah would make my father's death about her and demand some recompense.

Sarah always knew what she wanted and had a plan to acquire it. During our marriage, she got pregnant and then told me she wanted kids. When we lived in D.C., she accepted a job in Oregon, resigned as a congressional staffer, and then "asked me" if I wanted to move. When we got to Portland, she carried on a year-long affair and then told me she wanted a divorce on the same day she told me she was moving in with her lover. The world existed to give Sarah what she wanted. If she wanted the same thing as you, life could be grand, but during our relationship those coincidences were extraordinarily rare.

Ben was in Pre-K in Washington D.C. during 9/11. One of his classmates lost his mother during the attack on the Pentagon and since then, he associated flying with great loss. He got very nervous whenever Sarah or I went on trips.

Oddly, he had no fear of being in a plane himself—he only got scared when Sarah or I traveled alone. I would call as soon as the plane arrived to let him know I landed safely. After smartphones became ubiquitous, I started texting him goofy selfies with something iconic from my destination: a Dunkin' Donuts in Boston, a monument in D.C., and when we returned to PDX I'd send a picture of the famous '80s teal carpet that replaced the neon White Stag sign as Portland's kitschy icon. I realized I had forgotten to send a text when I landed this time, and I felt awful. I wondered if Ben would text me after his redeye landed at Logan.

My breath smelled like a dragon shat in my mouth, my eyes were bloodshot, and I was so dehydrated I thought I may have turned to a pillar of salt in my sleep. I was already feeling embarrassed imagining what Ben would think of me. He was brought up Jewish on the West Coast and was never indoctrinated into the rites and rituals of being an East Coast Irish Catholic. I was worried he'd mistake my obligation to get Viking-drunk in honor of my father with being irresponsible.

Sarah always took the Southeast Expressway and would get to New Bedford an hour after they picked up their bags and their rental. That meant I had less than two hours to cure my hangover.

I decided jogging might help me sweat out some of the nasty bile that was flowing through my system. I changed into basketball shorts, sneakers, and a cotton t-shirt. When

I bent over to tie my shoes my head felt like a balloon being pulled underwater. The humidity was dense and the heat was rising. I was sweating before I reached the sidewalk in front of the house. *It will be cooler by the ocean,* I thought, and started in that direction.

Each footfall reverberated with regret, but as my heart rate increased the pain became more tolerable. It didn't take long for me to reach the shore. The ocean was calm, the waves softly rippling across the breakers and gently kissing the seawall. The cool sea air made me realize how much I missed living by the Atlantic. It made me want to sail beyond the horizon and try to touch the sun. The urge felt so primal that I wondered if it was connected to the impulse that led the first sea creature to clamber up on land.

New Bedford was still a working port and jogging past the men toiling on the docks made me feel soft. It was ingrained in me as a boy that a man's work demanded courage and a strong back. I thought I abandoned all my prosaic ideas about manliness in college, but they lingered. My adolescent-self questioned my complacency—he didn't seem to understand that people aren't forever teeming with energy, optimism, and the confidence that accompanies having nothing to lose.

My mind chased every random thought as I continued jogging along the seashore. I thought about my brother and how different we were. I wondered if we'd be closer if I'd never left New Bedford, or if he'd followed me to Emerson. I loved growing up in New Bedford. It was comfortable and predictable. *I could have stayed and found a way to make a living, maybe coaching basketball, and been just as happy, maybe more,* I thought, but I was so determined to get out and see what else I could become.

I was always worried Derrick and my parents thought I was running from them. They had no sympathy for the stigma I felt being one of the poor kids at college. I learned how to fit in at Emerson, but I'd forgotten how to fit in in New Beige, and after a while I didn't feel accepted anywhere. At college, I always felt like someone who'd snuck into the theater without a ticket, and at home I felt like the guy who got caught pissing in a public swimming pool.

There was so much to figure out, about my father, Mary, Ben, and the money—all that money! But as I jogged along the docks, I skipped past all those things to wonder what would have happened if I'd never left New Bedford, if I'd stayed and married a neighborhood girl (I always had crushes on Laurie Whitmore and Susan Maguire—Susan and I would have made lots of freckled redheaded children) and put down roots where my people were buried. I'd still have the accent I worked so hard to lose. Quinns had lived in New Bedford since Fredrick Douglas still walked the streets and lamps were fueled by whale oil. I romanticized our maritime heritage even though my grandfather was the last to work on a boat over 60-years ago. The vocational continuity bonded generations. Fisherman were born into a fraternity. There was a sense of belonging and purpose. It gave life a solid foundation, and

I mourned its loss. I felt nostalgia for a life I'd never known.

I missed the struggle of being a New Bedford kid. I missed the feeling that it was me against the world. I missed knowing nobody gave me a chance at succeeding. It fueled my need to prove that I deserved a place at society's grown-up table. I fought like hell to overcome class barriers and reinvented myself as a newspaperman. When I delivered the *Globes* and *Heralds* through all kinds of weather, I imagined one day my byline would be on the stories everyone wanted to read. But the thing I didn't anticipate was that the prodding voice always telling you that you're not good enough never goes away. I still felt like I had to prove I belonged in a world that valued clicks over quality, and speed over accuracy, and where writers were replaced by "content specialists." I was still a columnist, but how long would it be before I became an "opinion specialist" and my job was to scan the incoherent ramblings in comment sections of stories and stitch the wisdom of Sparky99 and UncleChester into something that resembled intelligent human thought?

Maybe my father was right. Maybe figuring out how you want to be remembered is more important than what you do for a living. I wanted to stop second-guessing my own motives and privilege. I wanted to just be me, but it had been a long time since I knew who that was.

So how do I want to be? I thought as I turned around and headed back toward my parents' house. *How do I want to be remembered?*

* * *

I could smell bacon cooking before I walked down the driveway. *Glorious!* As I came into the kitchen through the sunporch, the scent of bacon was joined with that of frying potatoes and brewing coffee. My mother was clearly making a regal breakfast in anticipation of her grandson's arrival. She was excited to see Ben. We didn't need to be at McMahon's Funeral Parlor until 3:00 p.m., but she was already dressed and ready to go. She was wearing the Red Sox apron that my father used to wear whenever he grilled, and I caught her just as she was sprinkling Old Bay and garlic powder on the eggs, her secret ingredients. There was a sizzle-pop as the bacon grease spattered from the pan, catching my mother's wrist and making her jerk it away from the heat. As she turned, she saw me and jumped again. She was clearly also nervous to see Sarah.

"I'm making Ben his favorite breakfast," she said, quickly stuffing the Old Bay back in the cupboard and shutting the door. "He's always loved when I make him eggs. Will he still not eat you'ahs? I didn't have any rye bread or bagels, so I hope white toast will be okay for Sarah."

I wasn't sure what to address first, her jab at my cooking or her blatant Jewish stereotyping. I decided to address neither. It was the day of my father's wake and I needed to carve out space for us to mourn. *I guess this is how she copes,* I thought, *with slights and small aggressions.*

"I usually scramble them for him," I replied as I gently

rubbed her back in circles. "No one can fry an egg like you, Mum."

"'Ah you going to be okay with seeing Sarah today?"

The question took me by surprise. It was the first time since the divorce that she'd asked about my emotions regarding Sarah.

"Oh, I'll be fine," I assured her. "You know we still see each other all the time, when we're picking up and dropping off, and at Ben's events. We still like each other well enough."

"Just not enough to stay faithful," she countered.

And there it is, I thought. *She's like Ali! That was the classic Rope-A-Dope. Make them think you've gone soft, get them to let down their guard, and then hammer them with a straight right to the chin. Well played, Mum.*

"Yeah, something like that," I sighed. I wondered why we'd fallen back into our typical dysfunctional roles. *Why were we able to have an almost normal conversation the night before? Was it because I was drunk? Was she drunk, too?* I suddenly felt the overwhelming urge to talk with Mary. I wanted to know there was a place for me in the world where I could let my guard down and not suffer for it. I didn't know what time she was flying back, but I really wanted to hear her voice. I wanted to see my son. I wanted my life to be different, and I wanted it to start in that moment.

I went upstairs to take a quick shower, then came back downstairs to find my mother plating food as Ben and Sarah knocked at the back door.

Ben was wearing the Ted Williams replica Red Sox jersey my father sent him for his last birthday. It had only been weeks since I saw him last, but he seemed older. I was somehow expecting a younger version of him to walk through the door. His once curly hair was now wavy and neatly combed. He was taller and thinner, and his baby face was now marked with high cheekbones and a strong chin. Sarah looked as beautiful as she always did, but her beauty no longer affected me. What I once saw as a magical talisman promising happiness was now recognized as a failed experiment.

My mother shut off the stove with a loud click of the knob and took off her apron as she rushed to her grandson. "Oh, look at you!" she cooed. "You 'ah all grown up. Come give me a hug."

Ben shuffled toward my mother as she draped her apron over a kitchen chair. She promptly hugged him and kissed his cheek. I wanted to hug him, too, but his body language told me not to try, so I just put my hand on his shoulder. "Hey, bud. Did you get any sleep on the plane?"

"Some," he said.

My mother rushed back to the stove where four plates of food were getting cold. Sarah stood in the doorway, looking a bit cold herself. I turned to her after greeting Ben. She was waiting to be invited in, but that was a formality that didn't exist at my parents' house. The back door was always open to friends, and ex-wives were a subcategory.

"Well," she finally said as she stepped into the kitchen, "it's good to see you, Adeline. I'm sorry it's under these circumstances."

My mother put the breakfast plates on the kitchen table and forced what she thought would pass for a polite smile. I'm sure Sarah just read it as gas pain, if she noticed at all. I extended my arms to hug Sarah and immediately realized she was stepping toward the table, not me. She grimaced and leaned her shoulder into my chest for an awkward, uncomfortable hug.

"Thanks for dropping everything and bringing Ben out like this," I said.

"I wanted to do something," she said. "Your father was always so kind to me, and Ben, of course, adored him, so yeah, I'm glad it could work out."

"Sit down and eat," my mother insisted. "You must be famished aft'ah flying all night."

Ben and Sarah exchanged awkward glances. "Oh, we were, so we went through a drive-through on the way here," Sarah said. "Had I known you were cooking us such a wonderful breakfast I would have spared us the agony of eating fast food."

"It would have been good to know that you ate," Mum muttered, looking at me as if I was complicit in their plot to trick her into making bacon, eggs, and potatoes. "Did you know?"

I shook my head.

"I certainly won't let it go to waste," I finally said, trying to lighten the mood. My mother began to clear the plates off the table just as I pulled out a chair to sit down. "Mum, what are you doing?"

"Well, they've already agonized ov'ah take-out food," she said as she stacked the plates on top of each other.

Sarah sighed. "Look, Adeline, Ben was hungry—"

"And you didn't have the common courtesy to call and let us know you w'ah eating when you knew we w'ah waiting for you!"

Sarah squared her shoulders to my mother, the way she did when she was getting ready for a fight.

"Adeline, you're obviously under a lot of stress," she began.

"That's right. I am. All the more reason for common courtesy, but like usual all you can think about is ya own needs," my mother snapped, then quickly looked away.

"This was a mistake," said Sarah. "I'll just go."

"Stop this immediately, both of you!" I shouted. It surprised everyone in the room, including me. I very seldom raised my voice, and it felt good.

Ben pulled up a chair at the table to watch the rest of his family act like children. I took the plates from my mother and put them back on the table in their proper places. I scraped food from Sarah's plate onto mine and put her plate in the sink. "Sarah, would you like some coffee?"

"No, thank you." She folded her arms and continued to pout.

"Mother, sit down, please, and get caught up with Ben," I demanded, and for the first time in my life, she capitulated.

"Ben, would you like something to drink?"

He seemed very confused. "No, thank you," he said.

"Did you have enough to eat?" I asked. "Grammie made your favorite eggs."

"I could eat a little more," he admitted.

"Attaboy," I said. "Now, we're all going to sit here and start this over, because life is hard enough without seeking out needless misery. And please, let's remember that we are here to bury my father. Your husband. So, let's just put aside whatever baggage we're dealing with until he's in the ground."

I wasn't really sure where that came from, but I felt my father was somewhere smiling in agreement. I looked around the table, toward the eastern and western fronts, waiting for my outburst to come ricocheting back at me, but there was nothing. Ben took a bite of egg.

"These are good eggs, Grandmum," he said with a smile that was returned by everyone at the table.

"See, we can do this," I chimed in.

"Do you want to bet on that?" my mother deadpanned, which caused me to belly laugh. She flashed me a death stare and I realized her joke was inadvertent. As soon as she figured out why I was laughing, she rolled her eyes and one corner of her mouth slightly lifted into something that resembled a smile. Sarah and Ben were completely confused, and I couldn't explain the joke to them, so I just ate. We sat for a while in this relative state of peaceful discomfort. I devoured every morsel on my plate as Ben and my mother picked at their food and made small talk.

There was a lot of tension in the room, but I was okay with that.

"Are you exhausted, buddy?" I asked Ben.

"Not too bad," he replied.

"When we're done here, I'll give you a quick tour of the neighborhood and then we'll get you settled in my old room so you can rest before the wake," I said. "Sound good?"

Ben stiffened and looked to Sarah. "Mom got a big place on Airbnb on the other side of town," he explained, "so, I was going to stay there with her."

"It's very roomy, and he also needs to get some school-work done while he's here," Sarah added.

"And he's a big boy, Sarah," I said, trying to not show my anger, but some seeped through. I really wanted to spend more time with my son. I wanted him to see me in my natural habitat in hopes that it would help him understand me better. "He can speak for himself."

I used my toast to wipe the last of the bacon grease and egg off my plate—it looked clean enough to put back on the shelf. As I collected the other dishes, I noticed a familiar look in Sarah's eye. I felt like a sea captain staring into a red sky at morning. It was an old look, a trigger that reminded me why I'd been preparing for a fight. I could try to sail around the storm, or I could batten down the hatches and ride it out, but no matter what a storm was coming.

"So, Ben showed me Jake's obituary," she commented, looking at my mother. "He found it online."

My mother nodded and made a dismissive grunting sound. Ben seemed worried, which worried me. I hadn't yet read it and had no idea if we were headed for a summer shower or a category five hurricane.

"I didn't see it—was it in the *Standard Times*?" I asked.

"I don't know," Sarah said dismissively as she plowed forward. Her eyes fixed on my mother. "All I know is that it listed us as if we were still married. Do you know how something like that could have happened?"

"Oh." I rolled my eyes and went back to cleaning dishes. My worst-case scenario was the last line of the obituary reading something like, "The gambling bastard will eventually be joined in Hell by his heathen son and Jewish ex-daughter-in-law." I was fine with just about every alternative.

"I was also listed as Sarah *Quinn*," Sarah snapped. "Which has never been my name. Ever."

"The report'ah, or whatev'ah they 'ah called, asked if my son mah'ried," my mother replied calmly. "I said yes, Sarah, she spells it with an "h," and they have a son, Benjamin. It's reasonable to assume a wife would take the husband's name. A decent one, anyway."

"Did they ask?"

"He may have. I don't rememb'ah," Mum said and then looked to me. "Let me do this. I'll finish the dishes. You take Ben on ya c'ah ride."

"This is not okay!" Sarah exclaimed.

"Look!" my mother barked. "I invited you into my home. Stop being selfish! It's not ya husband who died, or whoev'ah ya living with now. So, stop demanding attention—we can all see you!"

"How is it being selfish for me to be upset that you took it upon yourself to not only say I'm still married to someone other than my current husband, but that I have also decided to change my name?!"

"Sarah, please," I began. "It's the fucking local paper— it's not the Sunday *Times*. No one you know is going to read it."

"It's on the Internet," she snapped. "I have a right to know why she thinks that's okay."

"You have a *right*?" My mother had an Old Testament look in her eye. It was officially on. "That's what *you* think. 'Ah you the only one with rights?"

I had to try to stop this somehow, but I knew the attempt would be futile. "Mum, please stop, please. If not for Dad, then please, for Ben's sake. Don't let this go any further."

"Why don't you tell *her* to stop?!" my mother raged. "Why don't you ev'ah ask Ben's moth'ah to do what's best for Ben?! Or for you?! Maybe you would still be mah'ried if you ev'ah stood up for ya'self!"

"Is *that* what this is this about?" Sarah demanded.

"I-I don't know," I stuttered, and it was true. I didn't.

"You don't know?!" my mother shouted at me. "When has she ev'ah made a decision that wasn't solely about what she wanted? Tell me that! 'I don't know!' Maybe if you made her take ya name then you'd still be mah'ried!"

"Enough with the 'you'd still be married' nonsense! 'Maybe if you chained her to a pole in the basement you'd still be married!'" I mocked. "Wouldn't *that* make everybody happy?"

Ben laughed nervously.

"Everything's a joke to you," my mother said curtly. "Religion, ya mah'riage, everything."

"How did this become about me?"

"Right, because nothing is ever your fault," Sarah piled on. "You're always the victim."

"Are we really doing this now, Sarah? Is this the opportunity you've been waiting for to tally up the score? You *won* the marriage. You *won* the divorce. Is that why you came here without telling me? Winning isn't enough? You needed fly across the country to kick me in the nuts while I'm down? In front of my mother and son, no less!"

Sarah dug in her heels. "Is that what you think? That our marriage was a competition?"

"Yes, Sarah, it *was* a competition to you!"

"Where is this coming from? Why is this the first time

I'm hearing this?"

"Maybe it's the first time you've actually heard it, Sarah, but it's not the first time anyone's said it. Dr. Bashir said it, so we stopped seeing her, and then Dr. Rock said it, so you looked for another couples therapist to sell your story to—"

"How dare you!" Sarah roared. "That is not fair! What kind of monster acts like this in front of his son on the day of his father's wake!?"

My mother looked over at me with a small, wicked smile. Sarah started the argument, my mother baited me into it, and now it was all mine. I'd fallen for it completely, and I was ashamed that Ben had to witness it.

I took a deep breath and calmed myself as much as I could. "It wasn't fair. You're right. I played by the rules. Rules you created. It was never about fairness to you. It was about winning." Guess I didn't calm down very much. "I'm sorry you forced my hand in front of our son. It was unfortunate and unnecessary, and nothing I said was untrue."

That made my mother's vindictive smile widen, which only made me angrier that I'd fallen into this carefully set trap.

"Do you seriously believe that?" Sarah asked me, folding her arms. "You think our relationship was a competition to me?"

"Yes, Sarah, I do and stop asking me if I believe the things I say. If I say it, I believe it. We couldn't settle these issues in therapy, but now you think we're going to work them out in front of our son, and my mother? Is that it?"

"Right," she said. "Make me the bad guy in front of everyone."

"Sarah, you didn't need any help with that today."

"Oh, please, enlighten me!"

"You walked through the door on the day of my father's wake, at the last minute, without letting me know, and made this all about you. There's no other way to see this. That's exactly what happened."

"I don't need to sit here and take this," Sarah growled. "Ben, come with me, we're leaving."

I straightened my spine until it popped. "Ben and I are going on a tour of New Bedford. Text him the address and I'll drop him off when we are good and fucking ready."

Ben was watching this drama unfold like a researcher observing his lab rats. He seemed unfazed by the biting sarcasm and general nastiness, but I knew it couldn't be easy to see us all like this. I took a deep breath and once again tried to find higher ground.

"Look, this is a difficult time for all of us." I stared at my mother, who I knew would escalate this all over again any chance she got. "Let's put this, all of it, in the past and move forward. Okay? This weekend is going to be hard enough without us bickering."

"That's so like you to want to move on without finding a resolution," Sarah muttered.

"She's right," my mother agreed. "If you weren't so

afraid of conflict, maybe you two would still be mah'ried."

"Good, great. You guys have found some common ground. That's fantastic. Now, Ben and I are going for a ride and I'm going to let you two very well-adjusted and non-conflict-averse women stay here and build on what you've started. Okay? Okay. Trashing me is great bonding material for the two of you, so just go ahead. Go nuts! Have at it!"

Ben sought some sign of approval from his mother, which he got in the form of raised eyebrows and rolling eyes. My mother hugged Ben as he stood. "Don't you mind any of this," she said to him as we headed toward the door. "This is just old people blowing off steam."

"Don't keep him too long. Have him back to the Airbnb before he gets too tired," Sarah called after us.

I waited until we were some distance away before turning to talk to my son at long last. "I love them both," I said to him. "At least, I kind of do. And I've never understood why."

"Yeah," Ben replied quietly. "I don't know what just happened. I thought mom was mad at Grammie, but then it got real weird. Sorry that I showed mom the obituary."

"Buddy, you don't have to apologize for that," I insisted as I put my arm around his shoulder. "In no way, shape, or form was any of that your fault. In fact, you were the only one in that room who kept their head. The rest of us should be ashamed of ourselves, and I am. I'm sorry. I really am."

"It's alright," he said. "It makes me feel more like a

grownup when you do it in front of me. It's definitely better than when you thought I couldn't hear you."

"Yeah, I guess we liked to pretend we were sheltering you from all that."

"Yeah, you weren't," he quipped as we got to the curb.

"Well, I don't like the way I just behaved. I want to be a positive role model, not a cautionary tale." I wanted to add, "but it was your mother's fault anyway!" but I thought better of it. Instead, we hugged, and even laughed a little at the absurdity of it all. Things already felt different with Ben. Better. Maybe being on my home turf helped us jump out of our old routine. As I reached for my keys, I realized they were still hanging from the hook on the sunporch doorframe. I let out a big sigh. Ben volunteered to get them, but I insisted on being a grownup and getting them myself.

As I walked back past the kitchen window, I saw my mother and Sarah acting in a way that confused me. I squinted and leaned closer to be sure I wasn't witnessing a crime, but it looked like their hands were gently and carefully placed on each other's backs. They were comforting each other, and it warmed my heart to see it. *They really can be human when they think no one's watching,* I thought. As far as I could hear, they were silent. I was able to get the keys completely undetected.

I let their moment of warmth and vulnerability be their secret.

* * *

Ben asked if I'd become a Republican as he climbed into the SUV for our neighborhood tour. It was a reference to the run-up to the 2004 elections when he observed that all the trucks in the Costco parking lot had Bush bumper stickers and all the Priuses had Kerry stickers. He asked if Democrats were allowed to drive trucks and Sarah and I told him, "no." It remained a family joke.

We drove to the docks where my father worked when I was really young, and then to the Market Basket where he was a butcher. I explained that my father taught me how to drive a stick shift in that parking lot when the Blue Laws kept stores closed on Sundays. I showed him my elementary school, and the porch of Susan Maguire's childhood home where, on the last day of fifth grade, I'd had my first kiss. "My face was redder than her hair when she told me how much she'd miss seeing me every day at school. We saw each other almost every day at the park instead." I got so giddy as I told him about it that he suggested I look her up, which made us both laugh.

I didn't really have a lot of memories to share that involved my dad, but I tried my best to tell Ben what I could. "'Quinn men don't complain,' your grandpa would tell me, 'they provide.' I suspect that Quinn aphorism has been passed down for generations. I think somewhere along the line, though, complaining and conversation became synonymous. The saying seems to have evolved into something like, 'Quinn men don't talk, unless it's about sports.'"

"That's weird. If everyone else was so quiet, how do you think you became a writer?" Ben asked. "Or do you think that's why you became a writer?"

"Yeah, good question. I never really thought about it in that context," I replied. "When I got into journalism it was much more of a quest for truth than being driven to write. Growing up post-Watergate we all understood the importance of the Fourth Estate—journalism literally saved the country. What made you think of that?"

"We're learning about oral histories in my sociology class," Ben explained. "The professor said that for most of human history that's how people passed information from one generation to another. She explained it in a way that made telling stories seem like part of our DNA."

"Yeah, I've been thinking about that a lot these past few days," I agreed. "Well, about stories anyway, and how they keep us connected to our past and tie us to a region, especially the stories we tell ourselves."

"And they help us make sense of our world, and shape our identities, and teach us how to conform to social norms," he added.

"Are you taking this class or teaching it?" I joked.

"It's an interesting class," he said. "It's just getting started, obviously, but it seems like it's going to be more about the role of storytelling in society and who gets to choose the narrative. But it made me think of you and how you got interested in journalism."

"Yeah?" I wasn't sure if I should be flattered or if I was about to learn my son thought I was a narcissist or a manipulator. "What did you come up with?"

"Just questions, really. We've talked about it before, but then I was wondering what came first. I know you really liked that columnist from New York, the author …"

"Jimmy Breslin."

"Right, Breslin. Did you like, idolize him and then decide you wanted to be a journalist, or did you want to be a journalist and then become a fan of his, or …?"

"Journalism came first. I started my paper route in the fifth grade and it made me want to know more about how it was made, who made it, and all that. I knew the newspaper business was important in the grand scheme of things and it was important to me because it provided me with money, plus in the '70s, journalists were cultural heroes. It was Post-Vietnam and the Pentagon Papers had exposed all the lies we were being told about how the war was going. Then there was Watergate and Woodward and Bernstein. They were huge. There was a movie about them, and they were played by the two biggest movie stars in the world. Right. So, yeah, I understood the importance of journalism, and I understood the role of the journalist, they were heroes, but then I found Breslin and he championed causes for the average person. So, yes, he wrote this great book on Watergate, but he also seemed to be looking out for people like me and my family. So, I was definitely interested in journalism and then he really, um, I don't know, showed me what was possible with it."

"So, did you want to be a hero, or did you want to serve the people?" Ben asked.

"To me, a hero was someone who served the people," I answered.

"And gets movies made about them," he joked.

"I was definitely influenced by the movies, and things I saw on TV, and the celebrity journalists. I won't lie. The most watched TV show of the era was *60 Minutes*. Growing up poor and always feeling like an outsider, there's no question that I was looking for that kind of respect, that authority."

"Do you think you would have become a journalist if you were born when I was?" he asked.

"God, that's a great question," I said. "I still believe in journalism. I believe it's more important now than ever, but the media landscape is so fractured that it's just hard to get people to pay attention to what's important. There are a lot of organizations out there profiting from misinforming the public. It's a scary time for democracy."

"But I guess I'm more interested to know if what drew you into journalism is strong enough that you'd do it over again if you had to start today," he said. "What drove you to want to be a journalist?"

"I guess it's true that popular culture influenced me," I

responded slowly, digging deep. I wanted to say yes without hesitation, that I would have been a journalist no matter when I was choosing my career, but I wasn't sure if that would actually be honest. "Um, I was driven by a quest for the truth, and honestly, as corny as this is going to sound, a love for my country. I felt like I was doing my country a service. It really felt like it was a calling for me, like how people are called to religious service."

"But where do you think that came from?"

"My desire to know the truth," I said because that's what I always said, but then took a moment to reflect. "You know, I always felt like an outsider, even in my own family, if I'm being totally honest. I just felt kind of adrift in the world. I felt like knowing more—the things important people knew—would make me feel like I belonged somewhere."

"Did it work?" Ben asked.

"No," I said. "The first time I felt like I belonged some-where was on the day you were born. Being your dad is where I belong." My voice cracked as I spoke. We looked at each other, smiled, sat in comfortable silence for a bit as we drove.

I parked the SUV in front of Sarah's Airbnb. "I'm pretty sure this was a brothel when I was a kid. I knew your mother was trying to corrupt you," I said with a wink. We laughed. It felt so good to laugh with my son.

II

#II DREW BLEDSOE, QUARTERBACK, NEW ENGLAND PATRIOTS

I stood before my father's casket and realized it had been almost a year since I'd last seen him. He was wearing the clothes he bought for Ben's Bar Mitzvah, a blue suit with a red-and-white striped tie. His Red Sox logo pin was tacked to his lapel. His thick white hair was neatly groomed, and the makeup gave him a simulated healthy glow. He also looked irreconcilably different from the man I knew. My father had left his husk behind. The corpse was without kindness or virtue. *Where do those things go, and where do they originate?* Whatever it was that I loved, and was frustrated by, and was so damn confused by, it was no longer there. What remained was compost, and the mystery of it all.

Ben had never been to a wake with an open casket. I

wanted him there with me as I greeted my dad's mourners, but Sarah thought it was too much to ask. She convinced me that he should just come to the second viewing. Derrick hadn't arrived and my mother was in the foyer talking with Jimmy McMahon, the funeral home director. It's hard to know what to do when you're alone with the body. I imagined most people prayed, but that didn't feel right to me.

I was angry that I didn't have answers to the things that were knowable. "You make a fifty-thousand-dollar bet on the Sox and you don't even tell me?" I whispered to the tranquil man in the casket. "Not to mention leaving me with the moral and practical dilemma of what to do with fifty grand of dirty cash. What, I move out of the neighborhood and you think it makes me a snitch?"

The smell of lilies stifled my anger. There was nothing that reminded me of death more than lilies and the perfumed scent of holy water. I stopped fidgeting and tried to focus on something else, admiring the deep finish and workmanship of the oak casket with its brass fittings. For the first time, I noticed there were more than a dozen flower arrangements placed behind the casket, most notably a reproduction of the Irish flag arranged in green, white, and orange carnations sent by Sully's Tab and Bite. I thought I felt a presence, someone entering the room, but I turned and found only empty chairs that would soon be filled with mourners, and the finality of it all hit me again. This was it, game over. A tear fell on the lapel of my black suit jacket.

"I'm sorry, Dad," I said as a blanket apology for all the things I'd done and hadn't done. I sat in the front row and wept. My tears felt like hope leaving my body.

I shouldn't have drunk so much last night, I thought. *Or maybe I should have never sobered up.*

* * *

The doors to McMahon's Funeral Home opened at 3:00 p.m. and the parlor was full by 3:10. Derrick showed up at 3:15, smelling of booze. Some people came in and found seats right away, while others waited in line to pay their respects, which is the custom. Some prayed alone at the kneeler before the casket, others in pairs, and when they were done they made the sign of the cross by tapping on their forehead, chest, left shoulder and then right with the fingers of their right hand. They would look at my father one last time, then come to my mother, Derrick, and me to share their condolences. "Sorry for your loss," they always began, followed by some version of "He was a great man and he'll be missed." Some would then tell us a personal anecdote, usually about how they knew him. Bill Kosher stood close enough to us that people started to confuse him for a family member. My mother begrudged him the privilege of standing with us, as she told me in a private moment, "The silv'ah lining in this dark cloud will be finally having to spend less time with that old man-child."

It was life-affirming to see so many people take time

out of their day to say goodbye. *Little gestures mean a lot,* I thought after hearing so many stories from people for whom he had done small favors. "Every Friday, payday, my husband wanted steak," said Mrs. Costello, who was in her sixties. "And every Friday he'd have it ready for me when I got to the butch'ah's count'ah. Even if there were twenty people in line, he'd say, 'Here's Frank's steak, Mrs. Costello.' Who does that anymo'e? No one, that's who, just ya fath'ah."

There were dozens of similar stories of bringing ticket stubs and programs to collectors, shoveling stairs and walkways for the elderly, some of whom that were younger than him. There also seemed to be a peculiarly large number of stories involving kindness to widows that made me wonder what else I might not know about him.

My mother was impervious to kindness. I'd felt it my whole life, but it was striking to observe it in her interactions with the parade of mourners. "Thank you," and "that's kind of you to say," she would tell them curtly, adding nothing else. She barely made eye contact with anyone for the full two hours. Her face never changed expression. The people who knew her best said the least. They steeled themselves as they walked from the casket. "Sorry, Adeline," they'd say and continue walking. *What opposites my parents were,* I thought. *My father was so connected to the souls of this world while my mother only cared about hers in the next.*

What I did not anticipate was the high school reunion portion of the wake. Everyone who'd stayed in New Bedford came by to pay their respects. It was great to see so many old friends, some of whom I had forgotten, and others who I couldn't believe I'd lost touch with, like my best friend growing up, Joe "Vinny" Ventola. As kids, we were like brothers. We did everything together, but we were mostly known in the neighborhood for playing basketball together in the same backcourt from the fifth grade though our senior year of high school.

Vinny was a solid guy, as we used to say in the neighborhood. That was a recognition earned by a special few. There were guys you liked and trusted because they were friends, but a solid guy was someone everyone respected and trusted whether you were friends or not. He became a paratrooper out of high school and fell in love with Army life, the routine, the travel. He rotated out a few years after Desert Storm and got an impressively high score on the civil service exam, became a New Bedford cop, made detective, and moved into his parents' old house. He looked his age, graying around the temples of his regulation haircut, but he also looked fit enough to crush stone with his fists. We shook hands like we did as ballplayers and we hugged tight.

"Look at you!" I said. "You look like you could go out and drain forty on Durfee tonight!" It felt like no time had passed. We laughed like the old friends we were, but this was louder than decorum allowed, and my mother lets us know it.

"Some things nev'ah change," she whispered after she hushed us.

Vinny passed along condolences from Bruce Toby and Matt Donovan, two other guys from our high school team that were on the police force and couldn't make it. "The guys who stayed all became cops or cons," he said as a joke, but it was partially true. Two of our other teammates served time, and one, Richard Dunham, was shot dead during a drug deal. There weren't a lot of paths out of the neighborhood, and unfortunately crime was an oft traveled one. We made plans to meet at Sully's that night for a beer. I was excited to catch up.

Ben and Sarah came to the funeral home between the afternoon and evening viewings. Ben's only other experience at a funeral came when he was in middle school. An older student he didn't know very well died in a car accident. They weren't close, but it still deeply bothered him for a long time. Ben was close with my dad, and I knew seeing his grandfather in the casket was going to be hard for him. This was one of the few times in my life when I yearned for the structure and security of religion. It would have given me a script for providing Ben with some comfort, which might have been nice for both of us. Instead, I clumsily blathered on about what a nice job the funeral home did making him look so natural.

Sarah and I walked on either side of Ben as we approached the casket. Sarah draped her arm over his shoulder and rubbed his back. "This is just his body," Sarah told him. "I don't pretend to know what happens after we die, but I know he lives on somewhere, even if it's just in our memories. It's impossible for me to believe that this is all there is."

Ben nodded and I was infinitely grateful that Sarah came up with the words that I could not. She was a good mother to Ben and that was all that mattered now. All I could manage was a smile and more tears. Ben hugged me and I told him I loved him for the second time that day.

The three of us, our modern family, sat quietly in the mourners' chairs until Ben told us it was time to go.

The second viewing went a lot like the first, only there were more younger people that knew my dad from Sully's and the grocery store. They came in small groups, spoke with thick accents, and when talking about my dad they called him "Quinny." There was a true sense of community in the stories they told about him. It made me realize how much that was missing from my life in Portland. I felt a bizarre nostalgia for a trajectory my life never took. *My dad had a good life.*

12

#12 TOM BRADY, QUARTERBACK, NEW ENGLAND PATRIOTS

I got to Sully's before Vinny, ordered a Sam Adams, and watched the Sox with Bill and Sandy Kocher. They sat in their regular spots and talked about how nice the wake was going while making sarcastic observations about neighborhood characters, like Mr. Plotnick and his halitosis, and Mrs. White always inquiring about free food. A little of my beer spilled on my dad's plaque as Sully put the mug on the bar. *And some for our fallen homie,* I thought as I reached for a bar napkin and wiped it clean. The door opened and everyone in the sparse crowd looked to see who was entering. I didn't know him, so I looked back to the TV as the guys at a table by the door called out in unison and threw barbs and friendly insults at the new arrival. As their greetings quieted, a Sox's mid-reliever, whose name I didn't even recognize, let up a home run to tie the game in the sixth.

"Fuckin' can-a-co'n," Bill shouted as his hand slapped the bar. "The st'ah'tin' pitchin' is bad enough, but they need a twelve-fuckin'-run lead to even get to Koji!"

Vinny came through the door as Bill's outrage was subsiding. Everyone turned to see who was entering and the bar got dead quiet. Most patrons looked away, but some exchanged curious or worried glances, including Sully Jr. and Bill. Sully glanced to the end of the bar at Dave Sanderson, who seemed to be trying to turn invisible. He turned his face away from Vinny and hunched his shoulders. He would have been less obvious if he wore a sign that read "Hey, quiet, I'm hiding from the cops!"

The crowd murmured as Vinny came to meet me at the bar. We shook hands as he surveyed the room.

"I ain't here on business," he said to Sully, but loud enough for others to hear. "I'm he'ah to drink to Jake."

"Well, what a' ya drinkin'?"

"Jack and Coke," he said as Sanderson slid off his stool and hurried past Vinny. "And we'll catch up next time, huh, Dave?"

Sanderson didn't answer—he just kept moving toward the door. The noise level quickly went back to normal. Bill stuck out his bear claw of a hand for Vinny to shake.

"How's ya fath'ah? He doin' good?" asked Bill as Sully delivered Vinny's drink in a pint glass.

"Good, thanks. How are you, Sandy?" She lifted her drink and nodded as Vinny reached for his drink. He thanked Sully Jr. with a nod. I tapped my thumb against my chest letting Sully Jr. know to put Vinny's drink on my tab.

"Ya money's no good here," Vinny said as he lifted his glass. "To Jake!"

We drank. Bill and Sandy took off after the Sox dropped another run, and Vinny and I found a table where we could get caught up. We talked about the awkwardness of policing the neighborhood where you grew up. He told me he coached Dave Sanderson in Little League and watched him go from a college prospect to small time drug dealer, to part-time gangster. Sanderson mostly sold dope, but would get dragged into bigger jobs from time to time. "A guy like that always assumes I'm aft'ah him f'ah somethin'. It's a fuckin' tragedy, is what it is," said Vinny. "But that's what I signed up for, I guess. But, how 'bout you, Mr. Big Time Writ'ah! Do I have to worry about being on the record here?"

We laughed and I played it down, more than I usually did. I didn't feel like a big time anything. I was more curious to know how he seamlessly slipped in and out of his accent. He said he lost it in the military because most of his superiors were from the South and he was tired of being called a carpetbagger—he also thought it held him back from promotions. "They hated Northerners," he said with a laugh. "They hated a lot of things, but they sure as fuck hated the North and were freaked out by Catholics."

I talked about Ben and my divorce. He talked about his wife, Francesca, and their three daughters. We talked about when we were eleven and got ejected from a Christian Youth Organization basketball game, two minutes after tipoff, for brawling with the team from St. John's. He caught me up on ancient gossip about people I forgot I knew, told me about affairs, sicknesses, crimes, and misdemeanors. The time passed quickly and the drinks went down easily. Eventually the conversation found its way to my father.

"He was a good guy," Vinny said. "He did everything right."

"You must know, right?" I said, curious to see if my suspicion was correct. "The whole thing with Sully and him?"

He looked like I asked him if he peed sitting down. "Everyone knew about that, Mike."

"Everybody but me."

"'Ah you fuckin' with me right now, or what?"

"I'm totally serious. I found out two days ago in a letter that he wrote me before he died," I said.

Vinny was flabbergasted. He struggled to find something to say.

"You look like how I felt when I got the letter," I continued. "Not only did I not know, but I didn't even suspect anything. Nothing. Seriously, I was totally blindsided."

"Wow," he said as he sat upright and regained his composure. "That must'a been a kick in the pants, huh? Come home and find out somethin' like that."

"Yeah, you know, it makes you wonder about every-thing," I said. "What else don't I know, or what do I believe that's total bullshit?"

"Yeah," Vinny let out a cynical laugh, "try being a cop, kid. It takes a lot to surprise me anymore, but you just did it! If you don't want to tell me I get that, but what did the lett'ah say? You know, I'm just kinda fascinated."

"It more or less said he kept it from me because he didn't want his choices to effect my life."

"That was it?"

"I mean in a nutshell," I elaborated. "It was more like, 'Here's some things I wish I told you while I was alive, and, oh, by the way, I was also a bookie for twenty fucking years.'"

"Like I said, everyone knew about your dad," Vinny began. "Him and Sully kept it small and under the radar. By the late '90s there was so much shit happening online with these offshore betting sites. By the time I got back here and got on the force, it felt like cracking down on the nuns for Bingo—nobody fuckin' cared. But then the Russians moved in and it became a different story. These weren't guys makin' a buck on the side—these guys were sendin' people to the hospital over a hundred bucks and ... Anyway, I got worried for ya dad, but you know, he worked somethin' out. Those fuckin' guys, though, the shit they do to people would send you back to church. Scary fucking people with long memories and violent tempers."

"So, we're just talking here, right?" I posed and waited

for his expression to see if I should go on. "Old friends …?"

"Just two old friends talkin'," he confirmed with a smirk.

"Let's say we knew a guy, and he came into some money, cash money, and he didn't know what to do with it," I started and Vinny cut me off.

"How much money 'ah we talkin' about here?" he asked. "Are you talking about The Bet?"

"The World Series bet? No. That wasn't even in the letter. My mother said something about it, but she didn't know a lot."

"So, that's not the money we're talkin' about here, right?" Vinny asked.

"No. I think it's the money he used to make that bet," I explained. "Which makes me think The Bet isn't even real."

"I'd tell that guy that he was a lucky son-of-a bitch," he responded with a smile, "and to keep his fucking mouth shut about where that money is and where it came from, because if he don't, people will start asking questions that nobody wants answered. Nobody. If you know what I mean."

"I feel like I just walked into a Dennis Lehane novel," I laughed, but the reference seemed lost on Vinny.

"You need to take this shit serious, kid," he said. "People go missing around here over a couple grand, and there's a lot of bad people who know about The Bet. There's a lot of people who think *you* probably know about The Bet and it won't be easy to persuade them otherwise."

Fear welled in my stomach and clawed its way into my

chest, making it difficult to breathe. I knew little about my father, but I knew less about his world. Growing up, I knew there were guys who were involved "in the life." I knew there were good cops and bad cops, but that was all I knew. It was all a game to me. A game other people played. Up until that moment, I was only worried about what my father's secrets meant to our relationship, but it was bigger than that.

"Do I gotta be worried here?"

"Yeah." Vinny nodded his head and took a sip of his drink. "You should be very fuckin' worried. And get the fuck out-a town right after the funeral."

"If The Bet is real, I was standing right fucking there when he won that money." I pointed to my father's usual spot at the bar. "He hugged Bill, Sandy, and Derrick, and then patted me on the shoulder and said, 'I'm glad you could be here,' and he never fucking told me."

"It's real. He won a lot of money from some very bad people," Vinny said. "I can't tell you how we know exactly, but we heard they gave him 25-to-1. He tried to talk them down, but from what I heard from my source, who I trust, they thought it would be bad for business. Nikolai Andrianov said—he's the boss—he said, 'Make sure people understand they only get hurt when they don't pay us.' He protected ya father. He respected him, but there's a lot of people who know that story, including some of the people who were in this bar tonight. Andrianov owns this bar now and uses it as a drop."

"A drop?" I asked. "Like a place to launder money?"

"Um, not really," Vinny said. "Look, that doesn't really matt'ah, but that's why everyone went quiet when I came in tonight."

"This is all too much to deal with. I wish I wasn't so drunk," I sighed. "Can I just ask a couple questions here?"

Vinny nodded.

"How fucking involved was my father—*really*—with these Russian guys?"

"Well, there's a plaque with his name on it in a bar they own," he answered quietly. "That should give you a clue, but the real answer is that we don't know exactly. We just know he was under Andrianov's protection, and that's very rare. *Very fuckin' rare!*"

"Okay." I didn't let that sink in—I just moved on to the next question. "It's just starting to register, 25-to-1. You think my dad won something like $1,250,000?"

"That's what our source tells us."

"Is your source my brother?" I shot back.

"No. And it's probably better we leave him out of this," he said. "This is a lot of money, even for these guys. For them to have to cover a bet like that would be a big deal. The fact your dad was under their protection makes me think Andrianov still thinks of that money as being his. We think ya dad cut some kind of deal, but nobody really knows."

"Why would you agree to meet me here?" I couldn't make sense of any of it. "Are you wearing a wire? Am I going to jail or gonna be killed because people think I know more than I do? I didn't even know about The Bet until yesterday, and …"

"I wanted you to see everyone's reaction when I walked in here, so when I told you that I was a good cop, you'd believe me," he explained. "Ya dad asked me, a long time ago, two or three years ago, to help keep you out of trouble after he died. You know, to guide you a little bit."

"To keep me alive?" I clarified bluntly.

"Yeah. That was part of it," he said. "That's what I'm doin'."

My life had become a fever dream. Had Vinny told me in that moment that Sarah married me to create Ben as a KGB sleeper cell, I would have believed him without batting an eye. *I'm gonna die before I get back to Portland,* I thought. I had no choice but to believe Vinny. I needed to trust someone.

"So, what do I do?" I asked as Vinny's phone made a chirping sound.

"Don't trust anyone but me. No one," he answered without hesitation before he looked at his phone. He jumped up and started toward the door. "We gotta go— Bruce Toby just got a call to your mother's house. She called it in, so that's a good sign."

I jumped up and followed behind Vinny. "I'll get the tab tomorrow," I said to Sully Jr. on my way by.

"Don't worry about it," he called after us, and waited

until Vinny was out the door to finish his sentence. "I'll send it to Vinny at the police station, oth'ahwise he'll nev'ah find it." Everyone laughed as the sound of sirens grew louder.

The sirens eventually quieted but the cruiser lights still cut into the thin fog that had crept in off the ocean. Flashes of blue, red, and white light created eerie shadows that directed us to my parents' house. There was a cruiser parked in the driveway and two others on the street. They beat us there by minutes. The cop who called Vinny, Bruce Toby, was the first on the scene. He played basketball with us through junior high and high school. He'd been to my house a hundred times and knew exactly where to go. It was comforting to know that he was the first one through the door. Bruce was six-foot-four and had to weigh 260 pounds, but he had the face of a cherub. His high school nickname was "Toddlernator" because of his Terminator-like body and baby face. He hadn't changed much.

My mother was already making tea by the time I got inside. I patted Bruce on the shoulder and he put his hand on mine as I walked over to my mother. Her stoic expression revealed nothing of the night's events. Had the flashing police lights not made the kitchen look like a disco, it would be hard to tell anything had happened at all.

"I'm gonna check the rest of the house," Bruce said. "Just to be sure nothing else was disturbed."

"Check if you want, but they knew whe'ah they w'ah going," my mother said as she turned to see her kitchen fill with police. There seemed to be relief on her face. "They got what they wanted. They won't be back."

Loaded expressions flashed across everyone's faces. They all assumed she was talking about The Bet. Vinny asked Bruce to stay with us in the kitchen and sent the other cops off to do other cop things. The flashers were doused. Vinny, Bruce, and I stood on one side of the kitchen sharing the same concern for my mother. Her stony face softened at the sight of us. "I've imagined this moment before," she said with a kind smile. "All you boys standing here as grown men. It's nice to see you all turned out so well."

We smiled. I'd also imagined it, but I could no longer remember why I would have found it appealing. I just wanted to get back to my life in Portland. I wanted to be a father to my son, and to explore my relationship with Mary. At one time, Bruce, Vinny, and I were like brothers, but that was decades before we were standing at a crime scene. Now, I wasn't sure I knew them at all.

"What happened, Mum? Are you okay?"

"I heard glass breaking in the basement. I came to the back do'ah and called down to see if it was you. The'ah was more noise and I heard talking. Then they ran up the stairs, screaming and shinning a light in my eyes. They pointed a gun at me—they held it in front of a flashlight. That's all I could see: the gun and the light." Her hands began to shake and her eyes became glassy. I moved toward her and she stiffened, cleared her throat, and continued. "That was it. All I saw was the gun. They ran out the do'ah and I called 9-1-1."

"Did they say anything?" Bruce asked.

"No," she said abruptly. "And I don't know who they we'ah. I didn't recognize them."

"I know they held the light in you'ah eyes, Mrs. Quinn, but did you see *anything*, what they w'ah wearing, how tall they might have been, if they w'ah wearing a watch or a ring, or some kind of jewelry?"

"The light and the gun. That's all I saw," she insisted. "I didn't recognize the voices."

"Was there any exchange between you and them?" Bruce continued, pressing on. "I know this is stressful, but anything could help."

My mother paused. She seemed ashamed. "I told them they w'ah sinn'ahs and to rot in Hell," she admitted.

We all tried to suppress our laughter, but Bruce couldn't help letting out a chuckle. "That seems like the right thing to say to me," he told her.

"Bruce, stay with Mrs. Quinn while me and Mike check the basement," Vinny said, and he led me through the sunporch.

The thieves did know exactly where they were going. Only the workbench had been disturbed. There was a monkey wrench resting amid shattered glass below the missing jars from the shelf where the tin had been hidden. As we got closer, Vinny noticed some bloody skin tissue on a shard of glass that jutted from a jelly jar lid. Drops of blood dotted the bench and made a path to the stairs that we missed on the walk over. Vinny leaned in to get a closer look at the skin.

"At least one of them was Caucasian," he observed.

"Can we get DNA?"

Vinny raised his eyebrows at me. "I'm New Bedford P.D., not Miami C.S.I. Is this where the money was?"

"Yeah," I said. "The money that he told me about."

"Okay. This is a good break. You need to listen to me carefully, okay?" He stepped closer and lowered his voice. "This is good for you. My report's going to say this was a failed incident of breaking and entering, but the rumor on the street's gonna be that they got all the money. Okay? All of it! The whole bet. You understandin' me?"

I nodded that I did, but I wasn't sure why that was so great for me.

"And not a word about this to anybody." Vinny put his hand on my cheek and stared at me until my eyes met his. "Do you understand what I'm saying here, kid? Not Bill, or Joe, or your son, or your priest, or your shrink, and definitely not Derrick. Okay? This is important. Whoev'ah did this is gonna have to answ'ah to Andrianov. This is as real as it gets. People will likely die over what happened here tonight and I don't want it to be you."

"How do you know it wasn't Andrianov himself?" I asked.

"Who did this? Yeah, no," Vinny said immediately, and

I felt naive. "Mikey, ya wading in over ya boots he'ah and you just need to trust me. Okay? Everyone knew Andrianov protected ya dad. Whoev'ah did this has a death wish. No matt'ah who it turns out to be, nobody can protect them. Nobody. Not you. Not me. Not the FBI. Not God."

"I feel like you know who did this."

"I've got some ideas."

"Is it safe here for Ben and Sarah, for my mother?"

"You'll be safer as long as everybody thinks the money's gone," Vinny said. "I'll keep my ear to the ground and my eyes open. Okay?"

"That's not enough," I insisted. "If my family's in danger, Vinny, I need to protect them and I'm willing to do whatever I have to. I'm not afraid of any of these fucking people."

"Don't be dumb, Mike. You should be very, very fuckin' afraid," Vinny said. I felt patronized. "You're not really a player in this, Mike. You're not a threat here, and that's a good thing, so don't become one. That's what will make you safe. But if somebody thinks you know where the money is, or that you knew who took it, or that you're looking for who took it, that becomes very dangerous for you. Okay? That's what I'm trying to tell you. This is life or death shit that's happening, right now. These people don't fuck around and neither should you. Okay?"

"Okay," I confirmed.

"The good news is, right now, you're in a lot less danger than whoever did this. They did you a favor. You know what I mean? All you really need to do right now is keep quiet and let this thing play out while you go back to that weird fucking town where you live."

We went back upstairs. Bruce was having tea with my mother. They were talking about Father Francis, her favorite subject, which seemed to put her totally at ease. Tea, rosary beads, and the good Father were all she needed to keep her universe tied together. Vinny went straight outside from the basement. I walked into the kitchen and stood by the open window. My mother and Bruce stopped talking to see what was going on. About a dozen neighbors had gathered on the sidewalk by the driveway. All conversation stopped as they saw Vinny approach the other cops. A distant foghorn broke the silence. The crowd inched closer, hoping they'd hear Vinny confirm their wildest predictions. They wanted to be first to learn The Bet was stolen. "I was there," they'd say for years to come as the story was told and retold.

The cop who questioned the neighbors told Vinny nobody saw anything. Crime was prevalent in New Bedford, but witnesses were not. Vinny huddled with the other officers and the neighbors surrounded them. I couldn't make out the words through the kitchen window, but I could clearly see the surprised reactions. Vinny turned and before he took his first step back toward the house the whispers escalated to excited chatter. There were big eyes, dropping jaws, hands over mouths, and then came the flashing lights of smartphone screens. By the next morning everyone who'd ever heard about The Bet would think the money was gone.

I didn't lament the loss of the money. Maybe it was the adrenaline, but I felt like I had reached a pivotal moment. For the first time in a long time, I felt like I was in charge of my life instead of passively observing it.

Vinny came back into the kitchen, his expression resolute after a job well done. He announced that it was time to wrap it up. I asked him to stay with my mother for a few more minutes while I went out to the backyard and called Mary. I walked into the night air and dialed her number as I stood under the apple tree my father planted before I was born. It was 1:43 a.m. in New Bedford, 10:43 p.m. in Portland, and I didn't want another minute to go by without Mary knowing that I loved her.

"Hey," Mary greeted with surprised delight.

"Hey," I said.

"I'm so glad it's you."

"Were you expecting someone else?"

"I thought it might be my father making sure I got home okay," she explained. "Are you calling to make sure I got home okay?"

"Not exactly, but I'm glad you did. Hey, here's the deal. I'm still pretty drunk, and my life is totally chaotic. Things are going on right now that are evidently normal in New Bedford, but I'm having a super hard time believing any of it's real."

"Like what?"

"That's not why I called. I'm not sure how to say this, exactly, but you're the best thing in my life and I really don't want to screw this up." The words tumbled out of my mouth so quickly they blended together.

"Well, maybe you should stop there and call again after you've sobered up," she teased.

"I really want to be totally honest with you. Always, about everything," I added.

"Okay, you're kinda scaring me right now, Michael."

"Don't be scared," I blurted. "This is all good. I just. So, I'm just going to say this. Um, we had that whole thing that happened online, the Missed Connections thing. That was you, right?"

"Yeah, I was going to say something about that," she replied. "The timing was off and I—"

"I'm really glad it happened, but I'm also sorry that it happened the way that it did. Um, what I'm trying to say is that I want to be totally honest with you, right now, and hopefully for the rest of our lives. I didn't know it was you when I answered that ad. I lent another woman a book, a woman from work that I barely know, and she's young, probably too young for me, and I'm not even sure I like her anyway—"

"How much have you had to drink?"

"A lot. And I'm also coming down from an adrenaline high, which is suddenly making me feel more drunk, but here's the thing, I was thrilled that someone wanted me, someone who was pretty and had good posture and a good resume, and that was going to be good enough. But it's not good enough. And I know this because when you showed up at my door here in New Bedford, it all became so clear. For my whole life, I never really liked the person I was, so I've been looking for someone who would fall in love with the person I was trying to become. I'm not sure I'm making sense, but what I'm trying to say is that I never believed that I deserved to be happy—happiness was this thing that could only happen after I reached all my goals and became worthy. The thing is, that it's taken me half my life, but I think I'm starting to figure out that I like myself. What I'm trying to say is that I had to be able to see *me* clearly before I could see *you* clearly. And now that I can, I see that you're all I've ever wanted. I didn't want another minute to go by without telling you how much you mean to me."

There was a short, wonderous pause. "Um, that was a lot of words and some of them were very nice," Mary finally said with an incredulous laugh.

"It's not the booze talking," I insisted. "At least not for the good parts, that was all straight from my heart. The babbling stuff, that was the booze."

"I guess I'm flattered and happy, but also a little confused by all this," she replied. "Who is this other younger woman with good posture?"

"That's not the important part," I said. "And you also have good posture."

"But you kinda made it the important part by talking about her at two in the morning," she said in that cutesy voice that made me imagine her doing the nose-crinkle thing.

"Yeah. That was dumb. I'm sorry, I thought this would go better. I just want to be totally honest with you, like 100 percent, and so maybe I'm overcompensating a little bit. But what I'm trying to say is that I love you, and I've loved you for as long as I can remember. And I've been slow to realize this because I'm only just now learning how to love myself. I've never felt like I deserved to be loved by someone like you."

"Okay. That was much better. You should have said that first. You're forgiven," she laughed. "You've always been my guy, Quinn. I never knew how to get through to you and the Missed Connections thing was an act of desperation."

"It was an act of hope," I countered. "Maybe destiny, maybe I'm starting to believe in that a little bit too, but I'm the real me when I'm with you and I hope you feel the same way."

"That's beautiful, Michael. I do. Maybe we're peaking at the same time," she said. "For much of my life there were guys who liked me for the bands I liked, or because I dressed a certain way, or they thought I was cute, but I always felt like you saw more in me than I saw in myself. You saw me as a whole person and that shouldn't be rare, but it is. It's really rare. I remember driving back to school and we were talking about something you wrote in the *Beacon* about The Cure, or some other band, and you talked about how odd it was that people could become so one-dimensional based on a musical interest. I think that's exactly the phrase you used, and I definitely saw myself as one of those people, but you saw me as more than that. You talked about things that I didn't think you would ever remember about me: that I crewed my freshman year, and that I loved Kurt Vonnegut, and that I painted in watercolors, and that I liked to ride horses, and that I played field hockey in high school, and then you talked about a poem that I wrote for the *Review*. You asked me what I thought about things. Anyway, that drive, that night, was life changing for me. After that, I gave myself permission to just be me. You know? So yeah, I think I get what you're saying. And I love you, too, Quinn, and I have for a really long time."

"That's beautiful," I said and maybe slurred a little. "Let's always be us and be honest with each other. Okay?"

"Are you giving me permission to call you on your bullshit Quinn?" she joked.

"You've never needed permission to call bullshit on me, Russell," I joked right back.

"Well seriously, Quinn, are you okay?" she asked. "You said your life was chaotic, and I know about your dad, but. It sounds like there's a lot going on."

"It's all going to be fine," I said. "It's just all kinds of crazy here right now. It's just hardcore New Bedford shit. It will all stay here. It's just making me want to come home."

"Are you being totally honest with me?" she asked.

"I hope so," I answered. "My mother's probably waiting up for me, so I should go."

"Okay. But don't think that just because I said I love you that you're off the hook for having to explain about this younger woman," she said with a chuckle.

"She's a minor leaguer," I insisted.

"And by 'minor leaguer,' do you mean 'a minor'?"

"She was in diapers when we were in college!"

"We're *definitely* gonna talk about this when you get back," she confirmed. "Now go check on your mother before you say more stupid things."

"Okay. I love you."

I walked in on my mother and Vinny talking about Penance and Reconciliation and hoped it was in regard to his daughter's First Confession. Two of his girls were at Holy Family Holy Name Catholic School, but his oldest daughter was in public high school. My mother was presenting Vinny with the supposition that the lack of formal Catholic training was the cause of all social deterioration in the world, but especially in countries that combined lots of non-Catholics with public education. Even though my mother was assuring Vinny that at least two-thirds of his daughters were part of the solution, he was more than happy with my interruption.

13

#13 BAD LUCK

It was the morning of my father's funeral and the finality of his death hit me all over again. I'd become used to getting blindsided by grief. Several times a day, unexpected events made me contemplate life without him—local TV sportscasts, young families, old families, kids playing in the fields, and hearing songs from the *Goodfellas* soundtrack. I wondered about the relationship we might have had if we were more honest with each other.

In the few days I'd been in New Bedford, my reality had morphed into that of a dime novel. That morning, I was faced with the unshakable and irreversible reality that my father's body would be in the ground by sundown. There were no more tomorrows to put off reconciling that truth.

I sat on the lumpy mattress in my old bedroom and looked out the windows to the east. The sun rose over the Figueroas' house and the sky filled with oranges, reds, and yellows. The clouds were lined with veins of sliver and lavender. Birds chirped and the engines of work trucks hummed. Life was moving on without my father. That thought loosed all the tears I'd forgotten to shed these past few days.

Those precious few moments I did share with my father flickered through my mind, evoking feelings of giddy joy and innocence, feelings I had forgotten. My thoughts skipped from Fenway Park to the plush forests of the White Mountains and fishing under the covered bridge on the Kancamagus Highway. There were memories of car rides, dinners, fireworks, playing catch in the front yard, free-throw contests, watching games on TV, stern words, and encouragement. I felt his presence in the room with me. *This is what love looks like*, I imagined him saying as I remembered his laughter and his proud smile as he watched me play basketball as a boy. *These are the moments that are most important.*

This moment is the only one that matters. This thought came into my mind like a voice that reaches into your dreams, waking you from a deep sleep. *This moment is the only one that matters.* It landed in my brain with the force of a meteor hitting the Earth. I shivered with the concern that I'd been wasting my life. *I've always just endured 'this moment' in service of some future imagined moment when my life would be perfect and happy,* I realized.

An existential crisis was hardly what I was hoping for as I prepared for my father's funeral, so I shook it off and headed to the shower.

Well, this could change my eulogy, I thought as I got ready for the difficult day ahead.

* * *

When I got downstairs Derrick was sitting at the kitchen table with my mother wearing an ill-fitting black suit. There were coffees and unwrapped egg-and-sausage sandwiches from Dunkin' Donuts in the middle of the table. The kettle was warming on the stovetop. Sunlight streamed through the open window, casting harsh shadows on the west wall. A cool morning breeze rolled in off the Atlantic and rattled the old wooden window frames. As if on cue, the mourning doves that were perched above the window on the cable wires cooed in greeting. My family didn't coo, or make any other noise for that matter. Derrick looked angry, but I could barely remember a time when he looked any different. My mother turned her back to me as she stood and walked to the kettle. "Derrick brought coffee and egg sandwiches," she announced.

I nodded to the back of her head and looked at Derrick. He seemed strung-out, like he hadn't slept since I saw him at Sully's. I was still concerned that he was using coke or meth. I'd been so drunk and amped on adrenaline the previous night that it only occurred to me right then, as I stood there sober and reasonably clear-headed, that he didn't come to the house the night before.

"Why didn't you call me?" he snapped as my eyes lingered on his.

"Where were you?" I asked as I looked for fresh wounds on the backs of his hands and wrists. "Every other New Bedford cop was here."

My mother maintained her stoic demeanor while she waited for Derrick's response.

"What the fuck 'ah you accusin' me of?" he seethed.

"Did I accuse you of something?" I countered politely.

"Boys," my mother said as she returned to the table with her steeping tea. When we were younger her stern voice would have been enough to quiet us, but we were no longer young.

"I'm a cop, you fuckin' douchebag," he said.

"And?"

"Bein' a cop means something in New Bedford," he continued. "But you ain't from he'ah no mo'ah. So, you wouldn't know about that."

"And I'm a reporter. That means I know a badge doesn't prevent anyone from breaking the law."

Derrick stood so abruptly that his chair flew backwards off its legs. He swung his right arm around his hip, brushing his jacket away from his body, exposing the service revolver on his belt-clip holster. With his knuckles turning white around the grip, he slid the gun up far enough to expose most of the barrel. His index finger pressed into the trigger guard and I thought my life might be hurtling toward its end. There was a better than even chance that the last thing I would ever see was the business end of his gun. It happened so fast and I was so filled with horror and denial that I didn't even flinch. I couldn't believe my own brother would move on me like that.

My mother screamed and Derrick took his finger off the trigger and slid the gun back into its holster.

"What the fuck?!" I shouted. My liver and adrenal gland had been overtaxed since getting back to New Bedford. I wasn't sure how much more abuse they could take.

"Don't you fuckin' call me a bad cop!" Derrick roared.

"I didn't call you a bad cop, but you're sure as fuck acting like one! Do good cops pull their guns on people who ask them questions?"

"Sometimes ..." Derrick muttered.

"Jesus, Mary, and Joseph, what have I done in this world to deserve these two as sons?" my mother shouted at the celling. "The two of you are my penance for my allowing ya fath'ah to live the way he did!"

"Nothing but love in this house," I scoffed.

"Fuck you," Derrick said as he bent down to right his chair.

"The two of you stop this right now!" my mother demanded.

"The two of us?" I said. "I didn't pull a gun on anyone."

"I didn't pull my gun on you," Derrick snapped. "Don't stah't spreadin' that ru'mah."

"Rumor?!"

"If I pulled my gun on you, you'd be dead, okay?"

"Derrick!" My mother slammed her open hand on the table hard enough to make her teacup jump in its saucer. "Enough is enough. Now just stop this! The both of you!"

"Just let this play out, Mum," I said calmly. "I'm really interested in knowing what else my brother thinks of me."

"I don't think you really want that," he growled.

"I give up," my mother sighed as she unwrapped an egg-and-sausage sandwich only to stare at it in disgust.

"You just want everyone to tell you how fuckin' wond'ahful you 'ah," Derrick continued, refusing to let up. "That's all you ev'ah wanted. You don't wanna know the truth about anythin'."

"Yeah? Enlighten me."

"You don't know five fuckin' people at Sully's, but you wrote that fuckin' piece a' shit in the newspap'ah callin' it ya home. It's not ya fuckin' home. It's my fuckin' home. It was Dad's home. You live three thousand miles from he'ah. You chose a different life, but when it's convenient, when it can make you look fuckin' no'mal, when you could profit from it, you swoop in and steal it, like I've just been holdin' it for ya, until it became worth enough for you to come back and take it. Well, fuck that and fuck you. That's what I think of you."

"Yeah," I said as I shook my head and rolled my eyes to give myself time to search for the weakest part of his argument, but it was all pretty solid. It wasn't my home anymore. It's the job of a columnist to present a specific viewpoint, but just because I could present a slice of life with some authenticity that didn't make it mine. *But fuck him, it didn't make it his either.* "Sorry, I didn't know you owned the rights to hometown nostalgia. Yeah, I followed my dreams and went where life took me. I took risks—"

"You took *off*," Derrick interrupted. "You w'ah nev'ah one of us."

"Yeah, maybe that's true," I conceded. "I certainly never felt like I belonged."

"What do you mean by that?" my mother chimed in.

Derrick raised his eyebrows and flashed a shitty grin.

I sighed. "C'mon, Mum, Derrick was always the favorite. Dad favored him because he was a better athlete and he was someone you could pray with, and pray for."

"You don't know a fuckin' thing," Derrick growled.

"I loved you boys equally, and prayed f'ah you equally, except during times of need," my mother declared. It was hard to tell if she was feeling guilty, angry, or remorseful. "And God knows the'ah have been plenty of times of need f'ah the both of you! And I will not stand he'ah and listen to this sad sack talk from eith'ah of you! We will put on a good face through this day and show this town we 'ah a prop'ah family! And so help me God, if eith'ah of you makes a scene!"

"So, don't shoot me in front of Mum's rosary group," I jabbed.

"Fuck you," Derrick hissed.

"Okay, I guess it's time to go," I said with a small smile. "We have a show to put on."

"You really are an asshole," Derrick mumbled as he stood.

"Let that be the end of that!" my mother exclaimed.

We gave her the last word.

#14 JIM RICE, OUTFIELD, BOSTON RED SOX

My mother and I got to the funeral home before Derrick, who took his own car, and his own sweet time. Father Francis was there to greet us and run through the order of things for the Requiem Mass, which was good because it's hard enough to remember when the Catholics stand, sit, and kneel. Moments after Father Frank stopped talking, my mother made a theatrical exit to "go check her face before the mourners arrived." Her "face check" happened to leave me alone for one last time with Father Francis, likely a clever calculation on her part to give the good priest one last shot at leading me down the path of salvation. We stood before my father in silence.

"He's holding up well," I commented when the silence seemed to stretch a bit too long.

"Excuse me?"

"My father," I explained. "He wouldn't have tolerated all this fuss when he was alive, but he seems to be taking it in stride now."

"It's good that you can use humor as a coping mechanism, Michael," Father Francis said with a grimace. "But it's also alright to fully experience your grief. It's healthy and expected."

"Yeah, well," I said, "there hasn't been very much this week that's fallen under the category of 'healthy' or 'expected.'"

"How so?"

"Oh, I don't know, Father. There's been lots of booze, fried foods, and other surprises," I answered vaguely.

"Do you mean the money that was stolen?"

I chuckled, surprised a priest would be in the know about such activities. "You really have your finger on the town's pulse, Father."

"One hears things in my position," he conceded. "The young people who work in the rectory keep me connected to the goings on in New Beige."

"Well, I'm impressed, but it's probably not the right time to get into all that," I said.

"This is the only moment we have, Michael," he replied, and a chill crawled up my spine. Hearing almost the exact phrase aloud that spontaneously rattled though my brain that morning gave me goosebumps. I smiled and my eyes welled with tears that did not spill over. "Maybe you could say a bit more about that, Father," I prompted.

"About what, exactly?" he asked.

"You said, 'now is the only time we ever have,' or something similar," I repeated. "That phrase sort of just popped into my head this morning while I was thinking about my father."

"Oh, it's just an axiom," he said to my great disappointment. "Why, was there something more you were wondering?"

"No," I said with a defeated chuckle. "I was just chasing a wild thought. The way it came to me this morning is hard to explain."

"We find meaning through God, Michael. If there's something you'd like to ask, you should ask it whether you think it's wild or not, whether you think it was God or not."

"You know, Father, I'm a non-believer …"

"That's been well documented by your mother, yes," he responded with a kind smile.

"The thought came to me like it wasn't my own—it came to me like I was dreaming but I was definitely awake. I'm sure the psychiatric and spiritual communities have different explanations for what that might mean, but um, you brought up the phrase or at least something close and I gave it more meaning than it probably deserved," I said.

"I'm not going to pretend to know what happened to you this morning, but there's another axiom which is, 'God works in mysterious ways,'" Father Francis began with a mischievous smile. "I know, I know, but just stick with me for a minute. There are a lot of reasons not to believe in the purity of The Church or even in religion in general. I get that. I don't blame anyone for being cynical. But corruption by men is inconsequential to me when contrasted with the question of what is love and where does it come from. It's a great mystery, and for me, it's the only question worth asking. I've dedicated my life to trying to understand it. If it turns out that life is just a hamster wheel, I'll have no regrets because mine will have been filled with love and purpose, and was dedicated to helping others. To answer to your question, Michael, maybe you drank too much. Maybe your experience was nothing more than a temporary chemical imbalance, or maybe you tapped into something bigger that we can't fully understand. Faith is believing in something bigger—something unprovable, mystical, maybe even nonsensical. I believe in love and I believe love has a source. Finding that source is what motivates me."

"Thank you, Father, that's not even within the realm of what I thought was possible for you to say. I can't imagine that's what my mother asked you to say to me," I replied with a wink and a smile.

"It's true that your mother asked me to talk to you. Her faith is very meaningful to her and you should try to respect that more."

"So, wait, did she send you to convert me or to scold me?" I asked.

"A little bit of both, I suppose, but more of the latter. It upsets her when you call me a wizard," he said.

I thought I might laugh hard enough to wake my father, but I was able to suppress my outburst to a slight cough. "I'm sorry, Father. I really am. It's not personal. I'm sure you realize that," I said.

He laughed unapologetically. "To be honest, I kind of like it. If the kids thought I was more like Harry Potter, there'd be more butts in pews on Sundays."

"You're a hot shit, Father," I said, realizing it might not be the most appropriate thing to say a priest, even though it was considered high praise in the neighborhood.

He didn't seem fazed in the least. "Thank you," he chuckled.

"I'm sure my approval means a lot to you," I said ironically. "Probably, more than anything."

"Um, Michael," he said with a sigh and a serious look. "I've enjoyed our chat, and I'm not sure how to broach this, so I'll just say it. I'm just as concerned for your physical safety. Your father was involved with serious and dangerous people. After I heard about what happened last night, I felt the need to warn you of that. I don't know if you're thinking about taking some action to retrieve the money, but if you are, it would be a mistake, and possibly a fatal one. Your mother didn't know a lot about your father's associates but from what she told me, and what I've heard from others, they are far more brutal than I could ever imagine anyone could be."

"Thank you, Father. Yeah, I'm just looking forward to getting back to Portland, alive. I have no plans on confronting whoever took the money."

"That's good. You should keep to that plan no matter who it turns out to be," he urged, patting me on the shoulder.

Does he suspect Derrick, I wondered?

Ben and Sarah arrived at the funeral home just before the final viewing. Ben was wearing a new black suit, and to pay homage to my dad, black Chuck Taylors. It was an old school New Bedford look, and it made me happy. Sarah wore a simple black dress with pearls I gave her for our tenth anniversary. She looked like old New England money. She would have fit in perfectly anywhere in the region except for my father's funeral. She came, gave me a hug, and said her final goodbyes to my dad. It was truly sweet of her.

"I like the kicks," I commented as I looked at Ben's shoes. "Grandpa would have liked that. I'm less sure about Grammie, but that's alright."

"Maybe we could throw them over the telephone wires after the funeral," he said. "You know, for like, a tribute to Grandpa."

"Maybe," I agreed as I hugged him. He held me tight, like he did when he was little. I felt no doubt in that moment about my place in his life. Sarah joined us in time to give me a Kleenex and tell me not to cry. We both bore the contemptuously fake smiles of people who wondered if they could have ever loved each other, yet there we were.

Vinny was among the first to arrive for the final viewing. My mother asked him to be a pallbearer and he recruited Bruce Toby and Matt Donovan to join him, all three guys from my high school basketball team who went on to be cops. They joined Bill Kocher, Joe Staid, and Sully Jr. It was a motley crew that perfectly represented the dichotomy of my dad's life.

We were there to mourn my father, but all I could think about was the break-in and Derrick reaching for his gun.

Vinny told me I was lucky the $50,000 was stolen, but I wasn't so sure. If Nikolai Andrianov thought the money was gone, it seemed like an open invitation for anyone who knew the truth to steal The Bet. *Is this a mistake, or a lie, or am I overthinking this?*

Ben stood by my side, my mother next to him, and Derrick next to her as the crowd began to arrive. I liked having Ben next to me, but it felt a little reckless given the potential threats. My mind jumped from suspect to suspect. *Was it my brother? Was it Andrianov's henchmen? Was Vinny somehow involved?*

"Thanks for being here," I said to Ben. "Having you here makes all of this a lot easier. Are you doing okay?"

"I am. Are you okay?" he asked with deep concern.

I told him I was and gave him a quick hug. I looked to my father, resting peacefully in his coffin, and I wondered what he would be thinking. *I don't know if you'd be worried shitless or laughing your ass off right now,* I smiled, imagining he could somehow hear my thoughts.

There was a steady crowd coming in to pay their last respects. Everyone wore their dark dresses and freshly pressed suits. They all knew the routine. Vinny lingered near the foyer waiting for Bruce and Matt to arrive before saying his final prayers and coming through the condolence line. The three old teammates huddled before coming forward. Bruce and Vinny hugged me and told me they were sorry. I thanked them for being there for my mother the night before. Matt fumbled to find the right words. It had been too long since we'd last seen each other. We were close once, but now all I knew about him was that he wore a badge. "Matty," I said as I put my hand out. "It's great to see you. Thanks for coming." He looked at my hand and then into my eyes. He seemed to be trying to read my mind. There was an awkward moment of hesitation before he stepped in and threw his arms around me for a hug. It was odd and abrupt, but welcome.

"I'm so sorry. I really am," he said quietly, and he stepped back, putting his hands in his pockets like he was reaching for something. "My broth'ah sends his condolences. He couldn't get back from the Vineyard."

I introduced the guys to Ben while wondering if Bruce and Matt stole the money. *Bruce was the first one on the scene. It easily could have been these three. Vinny could've gotten me out of the house while these guys robbed it,* I thought and then I tried to stop thinking. *Vinny is a good friend and a good cop.*

"Matt Donovan, Bruce Toby, and Joe "Vinny" Ventola, this is my son, Ben," I said as I gestured to each of them. "Ben, these guys and me were four of the starting five of a slightly better than mediocre high school basketball team."

"But we beat Durfee," noted Bruce, and we all laughed—even Matt forced a smile.

"That makes a winnin' season in my book," Vinny declared.

"It's nice to meet you, Ben," Bruce said, and he patted me on the shoulder. "Take care of this guy, okay? Ya old man needs lookin' aft'ah. He's gone soft since he left the neighb'ah'hood."

"I'll try," Ben said with a smile. "Good to meet you all."

The guys hugged my mother and told her to reach out to them if she ever needed help. They seemed slightly cold to Derrick. Bruce and Vinny just nodded and patted him on the shoulder as they passed, but Matt gave Derrick a heartfelt hug, which made him really uncomfortable. There was a bandage on Matt's hand between his thumb and index finger. Derrick saw me notice and tried to cover it with his hands as the hug transitioned into a handshake. *What the fuck is going on here?*

Vinny saw what transpired and threw me a cold look that sent a chill down my spine. *I'm not going to live through the weekend,* I thought. *They're all crooked.* "I wanted you to believe me when I told you I was a good cop," Vinny had said while we were at Sully's. *Last night was all neatly curated for my consumption. They've all got to be in on it.*

Fear surged in my veins. I felt like my emotions had been thrown in a blender. I was barely keeping it together as the other mourners came through the line. My mother, who had almost no ability to detect human emotion, even changed places with Ben so she could check on me.

"'Ah you okay, Michael?" she asked. "I'm relying on you to get through this with me."

"Is Joe an honest cop, Mum?" I questioned her softly. "Vinny, is he an honest cop?"

"Is the'ah such a thing?" she snipped. "Ya fath'ah trusted him, Michael. So, you decide what that means."

I couldn't decide. I scanned through the previous night's events. Bruce could have already been there when we heard the sirens. He could have been waiting out front when my mother made the call. Vinny was the highest-ranking cop at the location and he was the only one to see the crime scene—he called it a failed breaking-and-entering. He let the rumor spread that The Bet was stolen and convinced me it was a lucky break. *Those three bastards pulled off the perfect crime. They were all in on it. Vinny kept me at the bar until they had the money, and then he went and cleaned up the whole fucking thing. No matter how bad Andrianov is, he's not going to kill three, or four, cops. How fucking stupid am I? It was a set up all along.*

I was staring darts into Vinny's head when I saw Bruce react to something in the foyer. It was as if he saw my father sit up in the coffin. Vinny, Bruce, and Matt all looked to the entrance. A short guy with salt-and-pepper hair came into the parlor—he had powerful forearms and shoulders that resembled cannonballs. He was dressed impeccably and moved with purpose. He had an old-world look to him, possibly Mediterranean, or somewhere in the former Soviet Bloc. *It must be Andrianov,* I thought. Sully Jr. and Bill Kocher walked in behind him. If this was a movie, the scene would have unfolded in slow motion, The Rolling Stones blaring on the soundtrack once the bullets started flying. *This can't be my real life,* I thought. I was all the way through the looking glass and regretting ever calling Father Francis a wizard as I imagined him administering my last rights.

"Oh, God," my mother whispered.

"What is it, Mum?" I spoke softly, trying to take deep, calming breaths.

"I can't believe they brought him to ya fath'ah's wake," she sighed.

"Who, Mum? Brought who here?"

"What's going on?" Ben asked.

"Why don't you go sit with your mother for a little bit, Ben?" I suggested, trying not to alarm him.

"What's happening?" he persisted. "Is everything okay?"

"It's all fine, buddy," I said. "Go sit with your mother, please."

"Don't make this big'ah than it has to be," my mother sniped.

Bruce's shocked expression became a sly smile, which worried me more. He had a crazy streak—one that sought out conflict. Ben didn't go sit with Sarah, but insisted to know what was going on, which caused Sarah, and others, to also wonder what was going on.

"Oh, for goodness sake, that's Marco Sapienza! He worked with ya grandfath'ah and he tried to kiss me once at Sully's and Grandpa punched him in the mouth," she said in a loud whisper. "They nev'ah talked again aft'ah that. Okay? Now you know!" She turned from Ben and the others to me. "Now please stop making such a big deal out of this!"

"O-o-o-kay," I gasped like I'd just run a hundred-yard dash.

I was so relieved that it wasn't Andrianov that I didn't pursue the kiss-at-Sully's incident any further, but I did make a mental note of it. I took a few more deep breaths as Marco, Bill, and Sully Jr. made their way around. Marco barely looked at me and completely ignored Ben as he approached my mother.

"He begged me to bring him. So, be nice, would ya, Adeline?" said Bill as my mother stared Marco down like she was a prizefighter waiting for the bell. She was at least three inches taller than him. His brown eyes were deeply set and almost completely hidden beneath a hedge of thick black-and-grey eyebrows. He seemed fixated on something that was not visible to the rest of us. He exuded longing and sadness. He looked so pitiful that I would have kissed him to wipe that expression off his face.

"Ya always causing trouble, Bill. Even today," my mother said, then she looked at Marco. "Tell me ya sorry and be on ya way."

"I am truly sorry, Adeline, for everyt'in', and especially f'ah ya loss," he said with his hands over his heart. "You 'ah a good lady ..."

"Thank you. Very kind. Goodbye," she shot back before leaning over to Sully Jr. and whispering, "You keep him away from the funeral, even if it means breaking his legs. Do you understand me?"

The way Sully Jr. snapped to attention made me wonder if Andrianov was a front, and my mother was the puppet master running New Bedford's underworld. I don't know whether people feared or respected my mother, but they certainly listened to her. She showed no signs of softening with age. As Marco and the boys found seats, she smoothed her dress, looped her rosary beads around her hand, and adjusted her rigid stance to avoid accidentally catching Marco's pathetic gaze. I, on the other hand, was fascinated by his seeming devotion to my mother. I was bewildered by her power over this man. I speculated he was born in a laboratory, wet-nursed by a reptile, and was generally repelled by displays of human kindness. It was the only plausible explanation.

15

#15 TOM HEINSOHN, FORWARD, COACH, BROADCASTER, BOSTON CELTICS

The funeral home cleared out and it was time to seal the casket. Seeing my father in the coffin was hard, but knowing the lid was about to close was agonizing. It seemed merciless to confine someone to a box for all eternity. Forever is unfathomable.

It was irrational to be concerned with a dead man's comfort, but rituals are not for the dead. I would have felt more comfortable putting coins on his eyes to pay the ferryman and setting him atop a funeral pyre. But he was in a box and it was the last place he would ever be.

My mother, Sarah, Ben, Derrick, and I stood in the foyer of the funeral home waiting for the casket to be sealed and loaded into the hearse before the limo brought us the four blocks to St. Anthony's. As we stood in silence, I noticed a placard at the opposite end of the hall directing Timothy Griffin's mourners to another room in the funeral parlor. I turned back to read my father's name one last time, but his placard had been replaced with one for Judith McElroy. His time was over. I wondered about Timothy and Judith and the names that would be on those placards the next day and the day after that. *What were their secrets? What were their regrets? What were their untold stories?*

The funeral director came to escort us to the limo. As we walked outside, he gently took my arm and motioned to a third car behind the hearse and limo. It was a silver Audi A8 with blacked out windows. "The gentleman in the silver Audi wants to pay his respects. He asked if you'd come to the car," said the director.

Well, this is it, I thought.

My family got into the limo and I told them I'd be right back. I hoped I wasn't lying. I looked to Derrick for some sign, but there was none. He just looked down.

"Who is it, Dad?" Ben asked.

"I don't know," I said honestly, but of course I feared it was Andrianov or one of his henchmen. I tried to show my bravest face to Ben, but more than that, I wanted to be brave for myself. *Cowards die a thousand deaths and a brave man only once,* I thought, even though it didn't exactly fit my situation. I had imagined my own death several times since arriving in New Bedford and at least once already that day.

But if it was my time, I needed something to steel my nerves.

I shut the door and ran my left hand along the limo as I walked toward the Audi. There was no grit or dirt on the car—not even pollen. I was surprised by how clean it was. The Audi's rear driver's side door opened, and an older man stepped out. He was unassuming, maybe in his early sixties. He was thin and shorter than average. He was wearing wool slacks and a collared sweater under his suit jacket, which was odd, given the heat and humidity. He had no distinguishing marks. If I saw him in a crowd, I'm not sure I would have notice him at all.

"Do you know who I am?" he inquired as I got close enough to shake his hand. He was deliberate in choosing his words and spoke without an accent.

I shook my head no.

"I'm Nikolai Andrianov," he introduced as he offered me his hand, which I shook. "Do you know who I am now?"

"I do," I said as I nodded and took my hand back.

"Why do you think I'm here?" he questioned. "And no games."

"I was told my father worked for you, and that he also won a lot of money from you," I said, surprised at how calm I was. "I suspect it has something to do with that."

"My people tell me that money has been stolen," he said. "Is that true?"

"Some money's been stolen, but I don't know how much he really won," I said, neither lying nor completely telling the truth.

"But you know some money was stolen, yes?"

"Yes," I said. "It was taken last night."

"Do you know who took it?" he pressed.

I shook my head no, but I thought for a moment about speculating aloud.

"If you find out, you tell me," Andrianov insisted. "Me or Sully. Not the police. Not your brother, and not your friend, the detective. Okay?"

I nodded in agreement.

"Okay. Enough about business. I'm sorry about your father," he continued. "He was a good man, an honest man, someone who could be counted on. Are you such a man?"

"I try to be," I replied, horrified by what I might be "counted on" to do.

"We all try," he said with a small smile. "But I find they are rare, such men as your father. Maybe I don't meet so many good people in my line of work. Maybe newspaper writers only meet honest people."

Andrianov was a charming man. He reminded me of so many of the elected officials I'd known whose platforms I hated, but somehow still found them enjoyable to be around. This paradox made me uneasy. I wanted to hate him. Sweat beaded on his forehead. He saw me noticing and seemed embarrassed, but didn't wipe it.

"I paid the Irish man for the funeral arrangements," he continued. "So, don't let him charge you twice."

"That's very kind Mr. Andrianov, but not necessary," I said.

"It's done," he replied, opening the door to his car. "I like your articles. But don't ever write one about me. Understand?"

I nodded and he turned to get back in his car. There was so much more I wanted to know. "Mr. Andrianov, thank you," I managed to say as he settled into his seat. "Sir, my father kept what he did for you a secret from me. I didn't even know your name before I came home for his funeral. Is there anything you can tell me about him to help me understand that side of him?"

"If he didn't tell you himself then it's not my place," he said. "Jake had integrity. That's all I ever needed to know."

"Is there anything else you can tell me?" I pleaded.

"In my experience, people don't have more than one side. There's only who you are in the moment when you face the devil."

Chills ran though my body like I'd been dunked in ice water. He closed the door and opened his window. I stood, watching, unable to move. "Tell Sully when you find out who took the money and be careful not to talk with anyone else. Understand?"

I nodded as he drove away. I felt like I'd been swallowed by a serpent, but for the first time in days, I also felt safe and secure. As mad as I was at Derrick, Vinny, Bruce, and Matt, or whomever stole the money, I didn't want them dead. I just wanted this nightmare to end. As I walked to the limo, I realized that having met Andrianov gave me a hand to play. My first thought was how I could use this meeting to my advantage. My second thought was, *Just keep your fucking head down and get back to Oregon alive.*

By the time I got back to the limo, I was feeling a different kind of scared. I was too calm for having just looked into the eyes of the devil. In a matter of minutes, I went from wondering who posed the biggest threat to me, to knowing I held people's lives in my hand. *Lives are at stake, and I may be choosing the next person to end up in a casket.* I settled into the limo feeling a deep sense of responsibility.

"Who was that, Dad?" Ben asked.

"It was a guy who worked with Grandpa," I said. "He wanted to pay his respects."

My mother looked out her window, pretending not to hear me as she rubbed her rosary beads. Derrick fixed me with his dark, expressionless eyes. I returned his stare.

"He just wanted to let me know that he was there for me. No matter what I needed."

* * *

When we arrived at St. Anthony's, I scanned the crowd ascending the stairs. Ben was the only person I saw who I fully trusted. I put my hand on his back and told him I loved him. He smiled and nodded.

"Let's never grow apart," I told him. He seemed to

wonder why such a thing needed to be said.

"We'll never grow apart, Dad," he said softly.

My mother took a tissue from her clutch and yanked me from the moment. "Don't cry again and embarrass yourself. You need to talk in front of all these people."

Being judged by "all these people" didn't seem like a compelling reason for me not to cry, but I didn't. I turned my attention to the crooked cops on one side of my father's coffin and then to Sully Jr. and Bill, who were probably just as crooked. Then I wondered about Joe Staid. It perplexed me, how he fit into the group. *The mobsters probably call him "Quiet Joe,"* I thought as I watched the group prepare to carry my father up St. Anthony's granite steps. *Quiet Joe, you nev'ah see 'im commin'.*

The sun was hours away from its apex, but the heat and humidity were already oppressive. Matt Donovan was sweating through his black suit. His pale freckled face was beaded with perspiration. His shirt had lost all its starch and clung to the lumpy shape of his body. He started to loosen his tie until Vinny chided him. The others were uncomfortable, we were all uncomfortable, but Matt looked like the sun had singled him out for punishment—he looked a hot mess. The pallbearers lifted my father onto their shoulders. As they climbed the first set of stairs, the sunlight bounced off the casket's brilliant finish. Each step caused subtle undulations that sent flares of blinding light into the crowd.

St. Anthony's was over a hundred-years old and its

grandeur made me almost believe in heaven. It was among the most beautiful manmade places I'd ever seen. Winged angels stood atop marble pillars that supported Romanesque arches. The church was filled with Byzantine and Italian embellishments: frescoes, reliefs, stained glass, and musical cherubs supporting the organ pipes. Behind the pulpit was a relief of the vision of St. Anthony, the saint kneeling with his arms open to an image of the baby Jesus. I once asked my dad why Jesus appeared to St. Anthony as a baby and not as a man. "I suppose if you appea'ah in anoth'ah man's bedroom in the middle of the night, a baby would cause less concern," he'd posited, and I accepted that.

The casket had been placed on the church truck in the foyer. Father Francis performed some ritual and draped the pall over the casket. The other mourners found their seats. When it was time to roll the casket down the aisle, the organist played, Father Francis led the parade of sinners, and God winced. I didn't know what song was playing on the organ, but it made me wish it was John Kiley, the Boston Garden organist, playing "Lady of Spain" followed by Rene Rancourt singing the National Anthem. I walked down the church aisle behind my ex-wife and my brother (who'd pulled a gun on me that morning) to the empty space before the alter where the casket came to rest. We sat in the front row, which was a first for me. Sarah and Ben had never been to a Catholic mass and they whispered questions to each other that neither of them could answer.

Father Francis said some things in Latin and sprinkled holy water over the casket with an ornate looking contraption that seemed like it might ensconce a genie. Sarah jumped a bit when some of the perfumed water sprinkled on her. She rubbed it from her dress with a handkerchief. I wasn't sure if she was afraid it would stain her clothes or turn her Catholic, but either way, she didn't like it.

When the time came to deliver the eulogy, I was overcome by the feeling that what I'd written was inadequate. I decided to improvise. It was surreal to be standing at the pulpit looking out over rows of crowded pews without knowing what I was going to say. This was the church where I took First Communion and I'd imagined it was where I would be married, but I never imagined myself addressing the congregation—it was the stuff of fever dreams.

"Thank you all for coming today to honor my father. Your being here is a tribute to how many lives he touched. He meant something different to all of us. He *was* something different to all of us. My dad, Jake Quinn, was a complex man, more than I ever gave him credit for. I prepared to talk about all of those complexities for this eulogy, but as I stand here it just doesn't seem adequate." I paused to gather myself before I went on.

"The thing that made my father stand out was that he was a man of integrity. He was a man who kept his word—a man you could trust. I was reminded of that today. People reveal their true nature during times of great temptation, or difficulty. My dad was consistent through it all. He did what he thought was right in every moment and you always knew what to expect from him. How rare is that? We don't always know people's intentions—we only know their actions. I only have my own perspective on my dad's life, the things he taught me. The most important thing I learned from my father is that life is made up of moments, but there is only one moment that matters. There is only one moment in each of our lives when we have the ability to put our ideals, thoughts, and intentions into motion, and that's *this moment.* Life, history, legacy, it's all created in how we respond to the present moment. My father understood what it meant to be present, the importance of being there, and showing up. He was present in my life and he was always trying to teach by example, but I rarely noticed it for what it was. Once, when I was a kid, he took me to the White Mountains up in New Hampshire. He drove me out into the middle of the woods, and he gave me a compass that was inscribed with the words, 'Always move toward your goals.'" I pulled the compass from my pocket and held it up to the congregation.

"He gave me this compass and no map, pushed me out of the car, and told me to find my way to Hidden Falls, this secret swimming hole that I desperately wanted to visit. I'm pretty sure his not giving me a map was a mistake. I don't think his intention was to get me lost, but that's what happened. I was never far off the path, but I felt lost right up to the moment we met up again at the swimming hole. It turned out to be a very valuable lesson. We don't get a map in life that tells us what direction to take, and sometimes we get bad advice. He told me recently that his regret about that day wasn't that he forgot the map, but rather, what he had inscribed on the lid. He told me I should smash this compass to pieces and tell his grandson, Ben, to follow the arrow of his own principles to become the man he wants to be. There is no destination greater than the virtue of the traveler. For my father, the arrow pointed to integrity. No matter how complex his situation became, he always found a way to do what he thought was right. In the end, no goal, no prize, no badge is worth more than staring into that good night and knowing that you raged against the temptation to do what was easy over doing what was right. When I look back over my dad's life, the thing that I see, the common thread, is that he was a beacon we could follow. He was someone we could trust and rely on. His example was there to direct us. He was my compass. Rest in peace, Dad."

I felt acutely alive as I finished the eulogy and stepped down from the pulpit. I strode back toward the pew as if my bones were steel and my skin were Kevlar. *This is the kind of feeling that gets people killed in this neighborhood,* I thought as I glanced at the pallbearers. Vinny looked back at me with a vacant expression. Bruce seemed like he was thinking about cheesesteaks, and Matt continued to melt. The other three all had poker faces. I didn't trust a single one of them, and it made me understand why Andrianov had such affection for my father. It's not something that should have made me proud, but it was.

The pallbearers all knew I could make them disappear by saying their names to Andrianov. The power to instill fear was intoxicating. I looked at my brother and hoped he felt the same horror that I did in the kitchen that morning, and then I immediately felt sick to my stomach. *This feeling is why people carry guns. This isn't strength, it's a sickness. The weakness to yield is all it takes to end a life,* I thought.

I sat next to Ben, embarrassed by my thoughts. I was comforted by the innocence in his eyes. "Good job, Dad," he said, and he patted my shoulder. There was nothing else I needed in that moment.

"Thanks, buddy," I said. Sarah smiled, unaware of the danger that surrounded us. Derrick looked over at me with a contemptuous grin, and my mother seemed weary for having carried the weight of all our sins.

* * *

We waited by the hearse on Acushnet Avenue, across from the pawn shop, and watched the pallbearers carry my father's casket out of the old gothic church. The heat and humidity were still rising and with them, the aroma of urban decay. The heat bugs screeched, pigeons cooed, and mourners thanked me for my eulogy. I was feeling hungry and lightheaded, regretful that I didn't eat one of the breakfast sandwiches Derrick brought to my parents' house that morning. My phone vibrated. It was a text from the *Portland Daily's* publisher that read "Check your email."

Derrick and Sarah stood close enough to each other that they looked like a couple. The meanest part of me wished that on them. They looked to me with disbelief as I checked my phone. I made an incredulous face and mouthed the words "It's the publisher." Sarah rolled her eyes and Derrick whispered something to her that merited her approval. I got into the limo so I could use my phone out of sight of the other mourners. Patricia had forwarded me an email from the corporate office letting her know that my articles about my father received more web traffic than the special series on the missing elementary school kid. They wanted me to increase the frequency of my columns.

I forwarded the email to Paul with the message "The Suits are asking me to increase the rate of my suffering so they can more efficiently monetize my pain!" I closed my email and tried to forget what I'd read. I returned Patricia's text ("Can't now. Graveside.") and then turned off my phone.

My father's coffin was being pushed into the hearse as I remerged from the limo. Sarah asked me what they wanted.

"A pound of flesh," I replied, shaking my head in disgust.

People went back to their lives after that, and the few of us who were headed to the graveyard got into our cars and followed the hearse. We rode in silence for a while, which allowed us to feel a bit like a normal family. It felt nice. I briefly held my mother's hand for the first time in many decades. She smiled. "Ya dad would have been proud of you today," she said. The kind words even seemed to shock her, and she immediately pulled her hand away.

I looked across the car at Sarah. Derrick was sitting next to her and stared at me until I caught his eye. As soon as he knew I would see it, he patted Sarah on the thigh and grinned at me. That he thought touching Sarah would bother me was the only thing that really bothered me about his gesture. Sarah looked to his hand, then to his gaze. She flashed him a smarmy look and curt smile. *I remember that look,* I thought, looking away.

"I could get used to being driven around like this," I said to Ben.

"Me too," he agreed.

I thought again about the gall of the corporate asshats. *If they want more, they need to give me more,* I thought. "Hey, let's stick around for a few extra days and go up to the White Mountains. We'll go camping, fishing, and we'll see if we can find the same path I took to Hidden Falls. When we get there, we'll smash the crap out of the compass just like Grandpa said. My work will pay for it. It'll be great."

Ben's face lit up. Then he saw Sarah's look of disapproval.

"He's already missed enough school," she said. "I don't want him to fall behind this early into his freshman year."

"Yeah, well, another class or two this early in the semester isn't going to make or break his academic career," I replied.

"All my assignments are online," Ben chimed in quickly, "and I can email my professors. It'll be fine."

My heart swelled in my chest. "Alright, done. We'll go to the Covered Bridge campsite on the Kancamagus Highway."

For a brief moment, my life felt normal again.

16 - 0, UNDEFEATED REGULAR SEASON, 2007 NEW ENGLAND PATRIOTS

The flowers were brought from the funeral home and displayed in a row behind the gravesite. Sully's Irish flag carnation arrangement was prominently displayed near the head of the casket. I wondered if I should thank Sully Jr. or charge him an advertising fee.

The polyester bunting intended to hide the casket stand had pulled away from the brass frame exposing the grave beneath. A few feet away, Astroturf enshrouded the pile of freshly dug earth that would soon cover the coffin, and the backhoe used to dig the hole was parked in plain sight just a dozen yards away. Everything intended to obscure the fact that my father was returning to the earth in fact brought more attention to it.

For the first time since returning to New Bedford, I saw my mother cry. She pulled a tissue from her clutch and blotted her eyes and nose. I tried to hug her, but she stiffened and put her hand against my chest. "Don't, don't," she said. "I don't want my makeup to run. I'll be alright in a minute."

"You don't need to be alright, Mum," I told her with as much care as I could muster. "You're at your husband's funeral. It's okay to cry."

She turned to Sarah and asked if her makeup was still intact. Sarah took the tissue from my mother's hand, licked it, and cleaned some mascara from the corners of my mother's eyes. The two sat down next to each other on the plastic and aluminum folding chairs and waited in silence.

The others arrived a few at a time. Father Francis was among the first and he approached to console my mother. I didn't want to sit. I felt an overwhelming desire to throw around a baseball with my father one last time. Instead I read the cards attached to the flower arrangements. As I made my way down the line, I felt a hand on my shoulder and turned to see Vinny. I wanted to take a swing at him, but I also wanted a friend.

"Don't you think my father would have rather been cremated and spread around the infield at Fenway?" I asked.

"Catholics don't get cremated," he said without pause. "What did Andrianov say to you?"

"He thinks I know who took the money," I replied, "and

so do I."

"But what did you tell him?"

"I didn't tell him anything. He told me to tell Sully when I knew who took it."

Vinny cupped his hand and put it out for me to shake. I took it and he pulled me in tight for a bro-hug. There was a key in his hand—he pressed it into mine. He spoke softly as he patted my back. "This is from ya fath'ah. Now keep ya fuckin' mouth shut, because you don't know anything. Okay? First Citizens' Federal. The box numb'ah is on the key. Don't tell anyone. No one."

I wanted to throw the key in the grave and be done with it all. I wanted to spend time with my son. I wanted to hold Mary in my arms, and I wanted to be home. *My father's life has infected me like a virus.*

I wiped my eye with the back of my hand, reached into my pocket, dropped the key in, and retrieved a tissue. *I'm pretty good at this. Maybe it's heredity,* I thought as I made my way through the rows of mourners to sit next to my mother with her still-perfect makeup. Father Francis said some more things, and it was over.

We left. They lowered my father into the ground and carved his name in stone.

The drive to my mother's was quiet. We would soon go back to our own lives and feel less compelled to be nice to one another. It was a relief that my mother was still in good health and we didn't need to worry yet about her living on her own. I was struck one last time by another deeper sense of loss. *My mother, Derrick, and I will never feel closer than we do right now,* I thought. I wondered if Derick and I would ever talk again. I didn't miss being married to Sarah, but I longed for the things we never had, all the missed opportunities for kindness, the chance to accumulate a lifetime of memories together with our son.

We went to Sully's one last time and watched as the mourners transformed back into drinkers. I stayed long into the night and laughed endlessly as people retold their favorite stories about my father. It felt good to laugh, but I could not drink away the weight of my reality.

17

#17 JOHN "HONDO" HAVLICEK, SHOOTING GUARD, SMALL FORWARD, BOSTON CELTICS

My throat was raw from having talked over the din at Sully's Irish Catholic après-death party. My head throbbed in time with my heartbeat and my eyes felt swollen shut as they strained to meet the day. I stayed at Sully's much later than I'd intended and didn't remember going home. I was half surprised and completely relieved to see I was in my mother's house. My lips were chapped, and my entire body was itchy. I felt like a worm that had crawled onto a Las Vegas sidewalk, dry and brittle with a patina of sin. I had spent a week macerated in alcohol and bingeing on Dunkin' Dounuts and fried clams. It would take quarts of Gatorade, a mound of greasy food, and days of lethargy just to make me feel like I had a normal hangover.

I tried desperately to remember coming home and getting in bed, but I couldn't. Fear welled in my stomach. *What did I say? I couldn't have been so drunk that I blabbed about The Bet, or worse. What would be worse? Probably nothing ...*

I didn't remember where I put the key Vinny gave me. I scanned the room for the pants I wore the night before until I realized I was still in them. *Jesus, how drunk was I?* The pockets were empty, but I saw wadded-up cash on the desk where I did my homework as a kid. It hurt to stand. I had to pause and wait for my eyes to readjust after a surge of pressure tried to push them from their sockets. The key had been separated from the money. The number 521 was etched on its bow. *That's how many home runs Ted Williams hit during his career,* I thought. *That would be the perfect irony. I'm going to risk my life to find Ted Williams's cryogenically frozen head in the deposit box.*

I held the key in my hand and wondered what I would really find at First Citizens'. *What would I even do if there was over a million dollars in cash in there? Will Vinny and the guys be waiting for me after I get it?* The anxiety was exhausting, constantly having to sort friends from enemies.

I needed to file another column, but I had already strip-mined all the sentimental gold from my personal Mt. Nostalgia—all that remained was the toxic heap of tailings that needed to be cleaned up, and nobody wanted to read about that.

The assignment forced me to look more critically at my

life than I wanted to that morning. I'd become a stranger in my childhood home, an unwilling interloper. *Maybe the truth doesn't matter,* I thought. *Maybe I don't possess insight. Maybe I just have the ability to make delusions seem credible—I have a gift for fabricating optimism.*

Mary's name appeared on my caller ID. Suddenly the feeling of caterpillars writhing in my gut turned to butterflies. *The metamorphosis of love,* I thought, and snickered at myself. I put down the key and grabbed the phone. The sound of her voice put me immediately at ease. *Maybe the place I belong is not a place at all,* I thought. I was too old to believe in soul mates. I wasn't even sure I believed in the soul, but Mary and I shared something that I was having a hard time understanding—in a good way.

"Hey," I said.

"Hey," she replied in the caring voice I was so desperate to hear. "Are you doing okay?"

"My body's rebelling from a diet of diuretics and mollusks cooked in lard," I explained wryly.

"You should market that," she suggested after she was done laughing. "Do you have a name for it? The Tower Beach Diet?"

"Maybe the Clam-Up and Shit Your Life Away Diet, or the Suicide Diet, or maybe just the New England Diet."

We laughed and then paused to make room for the pain. "Are you up for talking?" she posed, tentative.

"Yeah, I really am," I assured her. "I wish you were here."

"You'll be back soon," she said. "I can't wait to see you. Do you want to talk about what's going on? I've been worried about you."

"Thank you. I do, but I don't. There's just so much that I don't know how to explain it all. When I start unwinding it in my mind, I feel like I'm going crazy."

"Well, maybe just start with your emotions."

"I feel unhinged."

"Give me a little more than that."

"I'm scared. I'm disillusioned. I'm becoming paranoid. I'm feeling like I never knew my family. But on a positive note, I feel like I've been learning a lot about myself, and I feel like the past few days have brought me closer with Ben. But in the process, I've uncovered things about my family that make me question everything I thought I knew."

"Things about your father, or more than that?"

"My father had a lot of secrets. It turns out that I never really knew him. All I knew was the façade he created. I used to come back to New Bedford to ground myself in what I thought was real, but it was all a lie."

"What do you mean by that exactly?"

"Everybody knew things about my father that I didn't. Um, I haven't said this out loud yet, and I'm having trouble finding the words. It turns out he was pretty well connected in the mob ..."

"Is that a joke?"

"No. A crime boss paid for his funeral. And there's a

plaque with his name on it in the bar the mobster owns and uses to launder money, or some such thing that I don't really understand."

"That's, um, stunning, Michael. I'm sorry. I'm sure that's, well, shocking. I'm shocked," she stammered.

"I don't know what to do with it. I mean seriously, I feel like it makes my whole life a lie."

"But it's not your life. It's his. What your father did for a living, or didn't tell you he did for a living, doesn't make *your* life a lie."

"It kind of does. People treated me differently my whole life and I never really realized that. I grew up in a tough neighborhood, but I never felt threatened. I'd go to the bakery and the owners would always give me free pastry. I just thought that was how life worked. I thought they just liked me. I never realized I was being treated differently because of who my father was. It's no wonder I always felt so confident here. It's because I was being protected by the mob and I didn't even know it."

"God, my head is spinning just thinking about it. I mean, your brother's a cop."

"Yeah, I don't think he's a good cop, and by that I mean I don't think he's an honest cop. No one seems to trust him. *No one.* I thought he just had problems with me, but he seems to have problems with the entire world."

"I'm starting to see," she conceded, and took a deep breath. "God, Michael, that's a lot. I'm sorry."

"Yeah, and you know, I don't want to believe any of it, but here I am."

"I know this is hard, but still, I just need to reiterate that it doesn't change who you are. You're still the same guy I'm falling in love with."

"Am I though? Are you trying to convince yourself or me? Because, I'm honestly struggling with it."

"Your father hiding his other life doesn't make you a different person. It changes your perception of him, but it doesn't change you. Knowing about it can help you understand your upbringing better, I guess. And I'm not trying to belittle how you feel. It's got to be really hard to learn something like this. I'm sure your father wasn't trying to hurt you by keeping that part of his life a secret. I'm sure it came from a place of love."

"I guess. And, you know, thank you, but I'm not sure you're right. If I'm given this protection, or authority, or position, or whatever you want to call it, that I never earned but have always possessed, what does that make me?"

"A white man in America."

I laughed. She caught me off guard. "So, in addition to my white male privilege, I just got a little extra privilege boost from the Mob. Well, that pretty much sums it up. You've just saved me years of therapy."

"Look, I don't mean to belittle your pain or your accomplishments, but yeah," she laughed. "I mean, some people treated you differently in New Bedford as a result of your father, but it's not like you're George W. Bush or Mitt Romney trying to say you're a self-made man when your father was the president or a governor, right? I mean, your privilege didn't carry outside of New Bedford."

"Yeah. I get it, but I'm talking about New Bedford. I'm talking about the foundation of who I am."

"I'm just trying to say, are any of us who we thought we were as kids, or teens, or even when we were in our twenties? Are any of our parents who we thought they were?"

"But, if we're not our experiences, then what are we?"

"We are *all* of our experiences. Even the things we never counted as being important. All of it matters."

I knew there was truth in what Mary said, like I knew there's beauty in a sunrise. I appreciated both, but I couldn't say I understood the meaning of either. We talked for a while longer before we said "I love you" to each other as our goodbye.

* * *

I had three major things left to accomplish that morning: write a column, acquire camping gear, and check the box at First Citizens' Federal Credit Union for a million dollars. I learned that having a key to a treasure chest makes it really hard to concentrate on anything else, especially writing a column. The bank, however, didn't open until 10 a.m., so I broke out my laptop.

I felt resentful toward the *Daily* for pushing me to

write about the loss of my father. Of course, I also felt a deep sense of irony, because I was being asked to do what newspapers usually do—what I usually do—find empathetic victims, colorful perpetrators, and interesting events and use them to tell our collective story. We tally up the dead and tell the stories of survivors. I just wasn't used to being the empathetic victim.

I sat at the desk in my childhood bedroom where I had struggled with mathematics in all its forms and stared at the blinking cursor. The blank page had always represented new beginnings and infinite possibilities, but to me in that moment the empty page represented the abject fear that I had no self-awareness, and therefore, nothing left to write.

Everything I know about myself is already on the page, I thought. I felt eager to give in to despair. *Trying is hard.* I looked around the room for some kind of inspiration, for some toehold that would give my column a starting point. On the wall by the door were a handful of ancient trophies topped with basketball players taking hooks and two-handed-set shots. I should have thrown those relics away long ago, but they were still resting on the shelf my father built sturdy enough to hold a lot more hardware. Next to the shelf was a framed team picture of the 1978 Red Sox taken in the outfield in front of the Green Monster at Fenway Park. The headline I cut from the *Boston Globe,* now yellowed and brittle, still clung to the frame. It read: "The Boston Massacre." I remembered cutting that out the morning after Bucky "Fucking" Dent hit the go-ahead home run—only his fifth of the year—to catapult the Yankees past the Sox to win the pennant. That game made me believe that the Sox were indeed inflicted by the Curse of the Bambino. *There might be some material there,* I thought. *Eh, nah. Too cliché.*

I turned in my chair to look behind me and saw the picture of my high school basketball team sitting on a bookshelf. There we all were, the whole team: Vinny, Matt, Bruce, Dexter, Jack, the Davids and the Kevins, Pete, and me. We were so young, and thin, and we all had hair. It was hard to imagine the boys in that photo having a life beyond New Bedford, and many of us didn't. Four of us went to college, all firsts in our families, but only two graduated. More guys from our team went to jail than earned bachelor's degrees. There was a column in that, but it wasn't the one the Suits from Staten Island wanted. More frustrated than before, I turned my chair back around and let out a big sigh. The words "Always move toward your goals" were sitting on the desk in front of me. I'd come to hate that phrase and the compass on which it was etched. It represented all the lies I'd swallowed to feed my ambition. *Well, the Suits aren't going to get exactly what they want this time,* I thought.

There was a line from my father's letter that I couldn't remember precisely, so I unpacked it from my bag and reread it. It was pithier in my memory than it was in my father's handwriting, but the sentiment remained. "Decide how you want to be remembered by your friends and family and live everyday like it's the only one they'll remember. Be kind, be honest, be brave, and let that be your compass."

So, I began to write. It was time for me to be kind, brave, and honest with myself and my readers.

I have always spent more time preparing for the life I wanted than I have enjoying the life I'm living. I spent a lot of time goal-setting, thinking proactively, envisioning my perfect future, and working toward it. All that preparation and forethought—along with a healthy dose of luck and privilege—landed me exactly where I am today. I always wanted to be a columnist for a major metropolitan newspaper, and here I am. My problem is that I don't really like the person I became to get here.

Regular readers know my father died recently. Yesterday mourners packed the church, went to the graveyard, and then to Sully's neighborhood bar. We drank and told stories late into the night. It was a true Irish wake. It was a great sendoff for my father and a tribute to what he meant to his community. I've thought and written a lot in the past week about family, memories, loss, and how to cope with living a continent away from the place your family calls home.

To anyone who has read my columns since my father died, I apologize. I've been misleading you, or more accurately, I've been misleading myself and I dragged you along with me. I created an illusory past that helped me project a romanticized version of myself into the world. The last few weeks, I've been writing about a history that was only partially real.

The way I kept my love for my hometown alive was to remember a place more idealized than the one I left. Did I really not see the truth that was so obvious to everyone else, or did I simply choose to believe a story I liked better? This is the question that has been on loop in my mind the past few days. I wanted to believe in the things that I wrote but wanting doesn't make them true. Turning my beliefs, my wishes, my desires into words gave me a sense of power over my life. It helped me create a world in which I truly belonged. When I felt adrift, I could always return in my mind to the place I was from, but that place, as it turns out, only existed in my mind's eye.

My father arranged for me to get a letter after he died. It was a message that divulged secrets and regrets about his life, while making a few observations about mine. In sum, his letter said I had become too big for my britches. He was kinder in his assessment, more subtle at least, but that was the takeaway. He told me I spent too much time working to become my job. I didn't expend as much energy on becoming a good person, husband, or father.

When I was a kid, my dad gave me a compass etched with the words "Always move toward your goals." I took those words pretty seriously. That hunk of metal was one of my most prized possessions, but in the end it was something my father, and now I, came to believe was a symbol of poor advice. His parting words to me were "There is nothing you can hold in this world that is more important than the love of your friends and family."

My dad didn't care what he did for a living. He cared about supporting his family. He cared about being a man of integrity, a man of his word. Faced with my father's circumstances, I suspect I would have made different choices, but perhaps it is exactly because of my father's choices that I never had to face his circumstances.

After my father lost his union job in the '80s, my brother and I got free lunches at school, and our family lived on government assistance while he looked for another steady job. He found work as a butcher and swore he'd never again put his hand out in need, and he never did. That was a humbling period in our lives, but it never hardened his soul. He remained a kind, thoughtful, and generous man until his very last breath. He always remembered those times and it made him grateful for what he had. I, on the other hand, worked hard to distance myself from all of it and forget.

My father didn't want me to know everything about him. I saw only what he wanted me to see. It only occurred to me as I sat down to write this article that his hiding himself from me was an act of love. My father and I were alike in many ways, but different in that my father knew he was keeping secrets—I, on the other hand, was living a lie. My father knew himself, but I only knew what I wanted to become. My father understood his environment and found a way to be successful within it. I have been struggling my whole life to change my surroundings to suit my vision of a perfect life. My father was wise. I have been a fool.

It was enough for my father to know his own sacrifices. He wanted no fanfare or recognition. He only wanted a better life for his family. I don't know if the word "irony" is big enough to encapsulate the fact that it took his death for me to know how much he cared about me in life. He had a remarkable and bizarrely simple existence. And he died a quiet death that left a tangle of complicated emotions to unwind. I feel closer to him now than I did while he was alive. His death has taught me what's important in my life. I will spend more time in the present moment appreciating the life I've been given and less time imagining a future that will always be out of my reach.

After all these years of trying, I think my father finally helped give my life direction.

I uploaded the column into the queue, not caring at all what a single person would think of it. It was 9:35 a.m. and I needed to get ready to go to the bank before I went camping on the Kancamagus Highway with my son.

#18 DAVE COWENS, CENTER, COACH, BOSTON CELTICS

The whaling museum was just a few blocks from the credit union. I pondered bringing Ben there after clearing out the safety deposit box. It was weird, how normal it all felt. *I'll just grab the piles the ill-gotten cash and then do a little sightseeing,* I joked to myself to calm my nerves. The fact that gambling was now advertised on TV didn't make my father's money legal, and I didn't know who to trust less: Andrianov, Vinny, or Derrick. As far as I knew, they were all on the same team. *I just need to see what's in the box and then get the fuck out of town*, I thought as I turned onto Union Street and looked for a place to park.

I found a spot a block away and shifted the SUV into park. I sat for a few minutes surveying my surroundings. I scanned for conspicuous people milling about, talking into their sleeves or pressing on their ear and talking to no one. I really had no idea what I was hoping to see. The only context I had for situations like this were from TV thrillers and '50s noir movies. I opened the car door, looked over at the passenger seat, and imagined an oilskin hat seated there, waiting for me to tug it over my brow. There was nothing that said "I'm ready for business" like squaring your shoulders and pulling down the brim of a fedora. *This is why I'm gonna get killed,* I thought, trying to keep my anxious inner monologue lighthearted to keep from throwing up.

Cars passed, but there was no one walking on Union Street. The credit union had only been open for a few minutes but there was already a line for the tellers. I didn't recognize anyone, and no one seemed to recognize me. I ambled by the desks of loan writers with eager eyes hoping to snag someone's attention. A chipper young man with gelled hair and a gold tie chain asked me if I needed help. Unprompted, he told me it was his first month on the job, his name was Victor, and he was a graduate of Westfield State College. He went there to study criminal justice but changed majors during his second semester after learning how much of law enforcement was administrative and boring. He'd like to start a family one day and hoped "that the banking world would provide the stability a young family needs." He didn't want to be like other young people who rushed into things and needed the assistance of their families or, God forbid, the government.

Victor had a lot to say. He also smelled like the Father's Day gift counter at CVS. I took advantage of his first breath to ask for someone who could bring me to the safety deposit boxes. I was not surprised when he responded by reciting bank policy verbatim. I stood at the ready, anticipating my next chance to interject. If I wasn't quick enough, I feared he'd start to quote from the Dodd-Frank Act.

"Victor." I felt I knew him well enough to use the familiar without asking permission. "Could you then, please, get the bank manager, or the vice president, or one of their proxies, to assist me? I'm in a bit of a hurry."

After several dozen words about how he would proceed to find one of those people, the bank manager happened to find us, thank goodness. I recognized her immediately, Irene Downey. We were high school classmates. She had barely aged. "Irene?" I asked to be sure. She put out her arms.

"Michael!" she exclaimed as she hugged me. "I'm so sorry about your father."

"Oh, thank you," I said. She was still holding on as I tried to pull away.

"I feel terrible that I didn't get to go to the funeral," she said. "We rented a house on the Vineyard and couldn't get out of it on short notice. He was a wonderful man. He was always so kind to everyone here at First Citizens'."

Victor continued to stand close by, presumably in case we needed him to explain the distinction between cumulus and altocumulus clouds, or something of equal importance. I was becoming fearful he would speak again and suck all the oxygen out of the room. "Victor has been a wonderful help," I mentioned to Irene while glancing briefly toward him.

"Thank you, Victor," Irene said pointedly, but Victor continued to stand there. "I'll take it from here," she finally insisted, taking me by the arm and walking me away from him.

"These millennials want a gold star every time they manage not to shit their pants," she muttered loud enough for only us to hear. "I feel like I'm running a daycare half the time."

"God, I miss the East Coast," I added. "In Portland we'd set up an intergovernmental commission to decide the best way to get Victor his gold star to prevent a pants-shitting epidemic."

"Sorry," she said. "I shouldn't complain like that, but my God, he's exhausting."

"No worries," I assured her. "It's refreshing."

"I've been reading your articles," she said as we walked into her office. "Everyone's been posting them to Facebook. The house on the Vineyard had Wi-Fi. They're really wonderful."

"Oh. That's nice of you to say," I replied, thinking to myself, *She's really proud of her trip to the Vineyard.* "Thank you."

"No, I mean it," she said as she walked around her desk,

unlocked the top drawer, and pulled out another set of keys. "You are here for the safety deposit box, I assume? You and your dad are the only ones with access, so I assumed I'd see you."

That made me a little nervous. *How does she know that?* She must have read the confusion on my face and she rushed to clarify.

"Um, I was eavesdropping on Victor before I recognized it was you," she explained. "He's only been here a few weeks, but we've had complaints from customers, and staff, and a few service dogs, about his, um, inability to get to the point. Sorry."

I smiled, relieved. "No worries," I said, suddenly realizing I didn't bring a bag to carry the money in. "Yes, that's why I'm here. And I just realized that, well, I don't know what's in there exactly, but I also didn't bring anything to carry it."

It was Irene's turn to look oddly at me. "We have plastic bags we give to people when they open checking accounts. I can get you a few of those, if you'd like?"

"That would be great. Thank you," I said, and she left the room. Her office was spotless, like an operating room. It even smelled sterile. There were no personal effects on her desk or the walls. There were only two framed pictures atop a row of filing cabinets that lined the wall behind her desk. One was a wedding picture that looked recent—her husband was tall, heavy and balding—looked familiar. The other was taken on a Disney cruise ship …*Holy fuck, that's Michael Donovan,* I thought. My mind immediately rushed to his brother Matthew at the wake, and his bandaged hand. Michael didn't show up to the funeral, which I didn't question as he was always the black sheep of his family, and people get busy, and some of them rent houses on the Vineyard, but sometimes they also need alibis.

I frantically tried to piece together all the combinations of people who could have been in on the basement robbery at my parents' house. My mother said there were two guys. They had guns. They obviously knew the house. Matt had a bandaged hand and a guilty conscience—he was a cop and came to the wake with two other cops that entered the house that night. Michael had been a hood rat his whole life and easily could have been his brother's accomplice. He was one of those guys who was always trying to convince you he was connected. I never believed it, but it started to feel possible. *The fucking Donovan brothers stole the money, but did they do it alone? They know everyone I know. The potential conspirators are everyone I know in New Bedford.*

The fear was becoming overwhelming. The calculations were too complex, and the stakes were too high to get it wrong. No matter who else was in on it, Irene was likely off letting them know I was at the bank. I had no one to trust, no one to call. I took out my phone and texted Ben, thinking to myself, *This is the most fatalistic thing I've ever done.* The message read "Hey, buddy, I love you and am so proud of you! Always know that. I wish we were already camping."

After flying in from three times zones away and being up late the night before, I assumed Ben was still asleep. *I might be dead by the time he sees this,* I thought. My heart raced and my hands got clammy. I tried to take a deep breath but couldn't get it to catch. I felt like I was drowning. The reality had caught up to me. I was trapped and in way over my head.

Fight or flight were my only options. *I have to know what's in that box,* I thought. *I can leave it there, but I have to know. These motherfuckers may have guns or whatever, but they aren't smarter than me. They're not more determined than me. And fuck them if they think I'm just going to lie down and let this happen.*

Irene came back with the plastic bags. "Sorry that took so long," she said as she noticed I was looking at the picture of her and the hood rat.

"Are you married to Michael Donovan?" I asked with only a hint of cynicism.

"Can you believe that?" she said, her face turning a pale shade of red.

"I have to admit that it came as a bit of a shock," I said.

"Yeah, it's funny how time has a way of wearing down your defenses," she chuckled. It was clearly a line she had used many times before. "People change."

"That's something I often wonder about. Well, let's head

back," I said before she could speak again.

She led me into the vault and went to the box etched with the number 521. She put her key into one of two locks on the face of the box and left the vault. I put the key in the second lock. All my other concerns faded away as I heard the mechanical sound of the tumblers falling and the cylinder turning. Those sounds became my entire world. My heart pounded faster and faster and my face became hot. I could feel sweat beading at my hairline. I pulled the key and the drawer slid open. It was smaller than I imagined it would need to be to hold over a million dollars. *Maybe it's in Krugerrands, or bonds, or a bank check,* I speculated.

I opened the lid and saw nothing.

The box was empty.

Someone got here before me, I thought, *but that doesn't make sense—why would Vinny give me the key if he knew the box was empty? It would have to be him who stole it.* Then I saw something small and white in the box. I crouched and contorted my neck to see inside. There was a single scrap of paper, no, a cocktail napkin with Sully's logo on it. I laughed—I didn't know why, but I couldn't stop laughing. I pulled out the napkin. On the back was written "I.O.U. $1.25 million" with no names, signatures, or dates. Just "I.O.U $1.25 million."

Why am I even surprised?

"He got this from a Nigerian prince, no doubt," I said aloud as if my father could hear me. "Well, fuck, at least

I'm gonna live." I just stood there for a few minutes trying to understand who I was mad at and why. All I knew was that I was mad.

I put the napkin in my pocket and headed out of the vault. Irene was waiting for me. I handed her the empty plastic bags she had given me. "I won't be needing these," I said and kept walking. I was too confused and angry for pleasantries.

Seriously, I thought, *is my life a fucking practical joke?*

Blinded by anger, I stormed out of First Citizens'. I headed back toward the SUV. The other pedestrians were inconsequential to me, shapeless blobs of motion and color.

A big guy banged into me and grabbed me by the arm. The collision jerked me back to reality. It took me a second to recognize him as human. He was taller than me and outweighed me by at least 40 pounds. His doughy features matched those of the man in the picture in Irene's office. Michael Donovan. He was holding a handgun in his right hand.

He thrust his massive arm toward my throat and grabbed the collar of my undershirt, knocking me on my heels and slamming me against the wall of the bank. My shirt seam dug into the back of my neck. Michael Donovan pulled me forward, then sideways, then tossed me back against the wall two or three times, just to prove how easily he could.

"Give me the fuckin' money," he said.

And this is where my story began. These where the

events that lead to a guy I'd known my whole life shooting me in the chest over a cocktail napkin.

I saw Vinny leaning over me, felt his fingers against my neck, checking for my pulse. "Ya gonna be okay!" he said as I was beginning to drown in my own blood as I lay dying on the streets of New Bedford. "You 'ah a tough son of a bitch! Don't fo'get that!"

There was one more gunshot. It was the last thing I remembered before going unconscious. The noise from the street all went away, and I felt at peace. I felt connected to everything. I had absolutely no worries.

My heart stopped. I died in the ambulance on the way to the hospital.

I don't know how the timeline of these events match up with my memories, because time lost all its meaning to me. The bullet didn't go through my heart, but it collapsed my lungs and filled them with blood. I couldn't breathe and I flatlined. All the things I had heard and read and never believed came true. I left my body and watched EMTs working to bring me back to life. They frantically tried to resuscitate me. One of the EMTs radioed the hospital saying they weren't getting any vital signs. I realized they were talking about *my* vital signs, that it was *me* who was dead.

Upon this realization, I appeared in what I assumed was a different plane of existence, a dream maybe. I was alone but did not feel alone. There was only light and darkness until I made that observation and then there was beauty everywhere. It was a kind of beauty that I could not adequately describe. It was so subjective and bizarrely constructed that it had to be of my own making. It was every awe-inspiring moment I had ever experienced or wished that I had experienced stitched together in a breathtaking pastiche. It was like traveling through a two-dimensional world, but wherever I focused my attention, I suddenly appeared. Not only did the space become three-dimensional, but I became a part of it. There was no me. There was no "Michael Quinn." There was just beauty and love and appreciation of being part of something so magnificent, so much bigger than a single being.

No matter where I was in this grand dreamscape, off in the periphery was the light, that light that everyone who comes back from the dead talks about. It was the one constant on that plane. It followed me everywhere and called to me like the sea calls to a sailor. Everything flowed into the light. The more I focused on it, the more desirable it became, and eventually I could not resist it. I knew the light was beyond my senses and beyond my ability to comprehend. As I looked into it, I felt as if I was standing before the origin of all creation.

When I arrived at the event horizon, the point at which I would enter the light, everything else vanished. There was light, and there was void. The light was everything that has ever been and everything there ever will be.

Suddenly, my father was standing next to me, but there

was no me. There was no him. I had no form, just a powerful awareness of our being there. "It's not your time," he
said with more kindness than I had ever experienced. He
knew I would be disappointed, and I felt engulfed by his
love. It went far beyond any explanation or apology for the
things that happened during our lifetime, a lifetime that
now felt like a teardrop that had fallen into an ocean.

I could feel his smile. Everything shifted and we regained
our form. We were traveling along the path I took as a boy
to get to Hidden Falls. It was more beautiful than I remembered. We were experiencing the forest from all perspectives
at once, the squirrels and the birds, the flowers and the dew,
the trees and the sun, we were part of it all. We got to the
point where, as a boy, I realized I had gone too far east, but
this time we didn't turn around. We continued toward the
sound of the powerful rapids.

"There's so much I want to know," I said, but I was no
longer talking about him, or his life, or our time together on
Earth. Time had become irrelevant. The moment we were
in was infinite. It would always be there, just as it was, in all
of its perfection. We made our way through the forest with
no effort. My father said nothing, but he didn't need to. I
felt his presence and his love and there was nothing more
that needed to be communicated.

The path took a switchback and brought us down a
steep hillside where we lost sight of the water, but we could
hear it and feel its power. The ground vibrated. The sunlight

refracted against the mist that hung in the air. The smell of damp earth, pine sap, and wildflowers swirled in gusts of wind that raced through stands of old pines. I had never seen pines so thick and tall. They were quiet and majestic amid the roar of the water that demanded our attention as we came through the trees. We had found Hidden Falls. The real Hidden Falls.

Above us were spires of granite that had been patiently carved by the water's flow. The river leapt from the granite's edge, thundering downward to crash and then rest in a tranquil pool that stretched out before us. The water was as I remembered it when my father and I fished beneath the covered bridge all those years before, the color of weak tea. I felt no nostalgia, or loss, or longing, but rather an immeasurable sense of gratitude for having lived. *Human existence is so improbable in the universe and that it should be surrounded by such love and beauty is truly a miracle. We are all one thing. I'm not separate from any of this. I'm a part of it all*, I thought. I could feel my father's happiness. He was filled with caring, goodness, warmth, and hope.

"You're ready," he said. "Let them know they already possess what it is they seek."

And then he was gone, and everything went black.

I felt a sense of purpose and urgency. I was heavy, uncomfortable. Alive. My perspective was again limited to that of my own senses—I could feel my body around me, cumbersome. I much preferred feeling light and effervescent, but I was still so happy. My first thoughts were of Ben. I hoped he wasn't too scared. Slowly, I could feel my strength returning. I could hear the unmistakable beep of a heart monitor. *I'm in a hospital*, I thought, and my brilliant observation made me smile.

"Dad!" I heard Ben call out. Like Scrooge on Christmas morning, I feared that I had been gone too long and missed too much. I struggled to open my eyes, partially from weakness and partially from fear that Ben would be fully grown. I still felt connected to the light. *Don't lose that*, I thought.

Ben gradually came into view, and he was still as I remembered him. I smiled wider. My mother was there by his side. "It's a miracle," she said. "God has given us a miracle."

"We are the miracle," I tried to say, but my lungs gave me no fuel to propel my words. The relief and joy in Ben's eyes as they flowed with tears was the most motivating sight of my life. All I wanted was to get better and enjoy all the time I had left with my son. *Let them know they possess what it is they seek*, I remembered, but from where? *Where was I? What happened to me?*

I looked to Ben and thought, *I can be whatever I need to be for him. It's not about what I do. It's about who I am.*

"Can you hear me, Dad?" he asked.

I just kept smiling—it was all I could manage to do. He put his head on my chest and it hurt like a bastard, but it also felt wonderful. I was alive and everything was possible.

The doctor rushed in and asked Ben to move so he could listen to my heartbeat and feel my pulse. Then he talked to me slow and loud like he was teaching me a new language.

"You have been unconscious for a few days," he said. "Do not try to talk or get out of bed just yet. Okay? Your body is still healing. We're taking good care of you. You have really beaten the odds, but you're not entirely out of the woods. Keep up the good work."

Interesting mix of metaphors, I thought. I looked at Ben, hoping he could see the love in my eyes. I had never felt so weak and frail. I didn't even have the energy to be frightened. I wanted to reach for him, but lifting my arm seemed as impossible as flying. I looked at my right hand and lifted my index finger up and down until it caught Ben's eye. He saw it and took my hand in his. I wanted to tell him that it was impossible for us to ever be apart, even in death I would be a part of him. We shared the same essence. We would be together even after the sun stopped rising and the Earth turned to dust. But all I could do was gently squeeze his hand. A tear rolled down my cheek.

"We really need to let him rest and regain his strength," the doctor insisted. I held Ben's hand tighter for a moment, then let it go. I didn't know what time it was, or what day it was, and that bothered me. I wondered if Mary knew I had been shot. I thought about the experience of being dead. *I'm sure if I just tell everyone about it, they'll all believe me, and we'll finally achieve world peace.* I let myself slowly fall to sleep aided by an increased dosage to my morphine drip and the lukewarm comfort of my own cynicism.

The next time I woke, I was alone and in a different room. My bed faced west toward a row of windows. The sun rose from the other side of the hospital. Outside my window I saw only sky. It was a dazzling mix of lavender, blue, and orange. I wondered how much time had passed since I was last awake. *Compared to death, all other obligations are trivial.*

I stared out the window until my eyes regained their focus. A seagull flew into view—*I don't see them in Portland.* I never paid much attention to seagulls other than to think of them as common and dirty birds, but they are really muscular and agile. It glided on the wind and hovered in place for a moment on a thermal gust. It looked around, I suppose for prey or predators, but I wanted to imagine it was just enjoying the view. *A few million years ago you were a dinosaur—now you're flying around looking for french fries. Evolution doesn't care what you are, it just cares that life continues. There's probably a column in that.*

A nurse came into the room. He shined like a dim bulb, literally. I assumed it was the morphine playing tricks with my eyes, but he looked as if he were radiating light. "Good morning," he greeted. "How are you feeling?"

I was surprised that he was asking me a question because the doctor told me not to talk. I took a shallow breath and my lungs stung like I was breathing frigid arctic air. I coughed and it hurt. I sucked in a few more shallow breaths and tried out my voice. "How long?" was all I could get out. It took me a few more breaths to ask how long I'd been in the hospital. The nurse kindly explained that I had been out for almost six weeks. After I saw Ben, my lungs became infected and the doctor decided to induce a coma and filter my blood through a machine that cleaned it and enriched it with oxygen. I was stabilized in New Bedford, then mede-vacked to Mass General Hospital in Boston.

"You've become pretty famous," the nurse, Raymond, added. "The *Globe* reprinted the articles you wrote about your father. There's been a lot of speculation on talk radio about why you got shot. Some people think it was random and others think it was ... well, that it wasn't. What do you think?"

I grimaced and managed a tiny shrug. All I wanted was to see my son and Mary. But Raymond's query didn't seem like a casual question. I may have been groggy, but I was still a journalist and I didn't want Raymond to become "a source close to the investigation." But he raised a salient issue. What was I going to say to the cops? I hadn't done anything illegal, so the truth was certainly an option, but probably only in moderation.

"I'll get you the newspapers," said Raymond. "We've been keeping them at the nurses' station for you."

"Thank you," I croaked. It would be neat to see my byline in the *Globe*, but really I wanted to know what had been printed about my situation before talking with the cops. I hoped it would all be pinned on Matthew and Michael Donovan—that would make it neat and tidy. I feared seeing Derrick, Vinny, or Bruce's names in the paper, because that would be heartbreaking after all this. I'd only been among the living for an hour and already the bullshit was bringing me down.

I'm happy to be alive, I thought. *But I wish life were different.*

Raymond didn't bring me whole newspapers—he just brought the clippings of my articles. I wondered if the omission of the news was ordered by the police who wouldn't want my response to their questioning to be influenced by what I read. My speculation was reinforced the next morning when my first visitors were Detectives Combs and Maguire from the Massachusetts State Police Department.

Combs had a distinct seriousness about her, and Maguire looked like a TV cop. Combs carried the weight of the badge, and Maguire appeared to spend all his time at the barber shop and in front of the mirror practicing his furrowed brow. Combs made the introductions and let me know they were there to investigate my "situation." She was careful not to say my "shooting," and I noticed her deliberate phrasing cast a wide net. "What can you tell us about what happened around the time of the incident outside of First Citizens'?" she asked. "Tell us everything you can remember even if you think it might be unrelated."

"What happened to Donovan?" I whispered, my lungs

still tender and weak. The cops seemed surprised by my question, but maybe they were just surprised that someone from New Bedford would be willing to talk at all.

"Which Donovan?" asked Combs.

"Mike," I said, realizing Matthew must have also been involved. "The shooter."

"So, you did know the shooter, Michael Donovan?" Combs clarified.

"We grew up together," I explained.

"And obviously, you also know his brother, Matthew?"

I nodded.

"Do you know why Matthew may have gone missing on the day you got shot?"

I shook my head no. But I certainly had my thoughts.

Combs held up a clear evidence bag containing the I.O.U. that I took from the bank. One quarter of the napkin had been saturated with blood and was stiff, red, and crusty. The sight of it brought flashes of violence to mind. It gave me chills to see my blood being held in front of me. My breathing became shallow and I began to sweat.

"Mr. Quinn, we found this on your person the day you were shot," Combs began. "Could you explain what this is?"

"An I.O.U. for 1.25 million dollars," I answered with a weak smirk, trying maintain my composure. "Can't believe you haven't cashed it."

"Is this what was in the safety deposit box at First Citizens'?"

I nodded.

"Do you know how it got there?"

"I don't," I rasped.

"Was there anything else in the box?"

"No."

"There was no money in the box?"

"No."

"Do you have any speculation as to who may have written the note in the box?"

I shook my head no.

"How are you connected to Nikolai Andrianov?" Maguire asked, despite the blatant disapproval of his partner.

They knew who shot me and I'm sure they knew why. I had been unconscious for over a month and their investigation must have gone cold. *They're here to investigate me.*

"I'd like a lawyer," I said.

"Why would an innocent man need a lawyer, Mr. Quinn?" Maguire asked, confirming my suspicion he really wanted to be a TV cop. "We're just here to ask you a few questions."

"In high-profile cases, sometimes innocent people go to jail," I slowly wheezed.

Combs sighed. She was here on a fishing trip, and here her partner was scaring away all the fish. "Hey Billy, why don't you grab us some coffee?" She didn't talk again until we were alone.

"Look, Mr. Quinn. Two people are dead, and Matthew

Donovan and your brother are missing. There are a lot of unanswered questions, a little over a million of them, if you get what I mean." She paused. "And you're right. This has become a high-profile case and a tabloid sensation. There's a lot of interest at the state, local, and federal levels surrounding the particular events preceding and subsequent to the incident of your having been shot."

"My brother's missing?" I asked.

"Yes, Mr. Quinn, he is. We have reason to believe he was involved in a plot with Michael Donovan to steal whatever you were hoping to retrieve from the credit union."

I nodded once, carefully.

"This doesn't surprise you?"

I gently shook my head.

"So, you and your brother weren't close, I take it?"

"No, we're not."

"Mr. Quinn, I probably should have made this clear from the beginning. My partner and I are from a division of the state police that investigates suspected illegal activities committed by other cops. We were working with Detective Ventola on an investigation of your brother and Matthew Donovan at the time of his death."

"Whose death? You said Derrick and Matthew were missing. Vinny's death?"

"Yes, Mr. Quinn," she said. "I'm sorry. I didn't realize ... I forgot how long you've been out. I apologize to break the news to you this way. Detective Ventola shot Michael

Donovan and probably saved your life. Your brother's report said that Michael Donovan and Detective Ventola got their shots off at each other at the same moment, but the ballistics didn't check out. The gun that killed Detective Ventola hasn't been identified. We haven't seen Matthew Donovan or your brother since they filed that report."

I took my time responding to her. "After I got shot it was all a blur, but I remember Vinny pressing my neck for a pulse. He told me I'd be okay. I heard a gunshot as I was losing consciousness," I said, knowing that if my brother was alive I'd probably just condemned him. "Why were you investigating my brother?"

"I can't really comment on an ongoing investigation, but there was a rumor of two cops extorting money from members of a crime ring," she answered.

"What a waste," I sighed.

"We know from Detective Ventola's surveillance, and our interview with your mother, that you didn't know about your father's association with Nikolai Andrianov."

"Vinny was spying on me?"

"Well, your brother, actually," she clarified. "But, by extension, yes."

"So, like wiretaps and spooks in vans?"

"Something like that," she smiled.

"And you heard all my embarrassing drunken phone calls?"

Her cop façade came down and she smiled in a way that

made me feel really exposed.

"I'm sorry, Mr. Quinn," she said with a playfully sly smile. "But you two seem perfect for each other."

"Thanks, and please call me Michael. I feel like you know me well enough now," my smile widened and I shook my head. "I'm surprised my mother talked with you."

"She was a wreck. She just lost your dad, had one son in a coma, and another missing," Combs paused. "I'm sorry, Michael. That is to say that you're clear. But, look, we don't know if your brother is alive or not. We don't know if he stole the money from the credit union or not. And we don't know if he shot Vinny or not. But until we get some answers, I think he's in a lot of danger, and I also think you're in a lot of danger."

"I don't think The Bet was real, or, I think The Bet was real, but I don't think any money ever exchanged hands," I said.

"Why do you think that?"

"It's a hunch, really. But, Andrianov came to my father's wake and talked a lot about trust and integrity. Everything my father did was a secret, but *everyone* knew about The Bet. Everyone but me. It just doesn't fit. Something about it just feels really wrong, but…"

"But what?"

"But I've been wrong about everything else," I said with a pained chuckle. "My father didn't want the money. He made The Bet to get rid of the illegal cash he had in the basement, and I don't know why else Andrianov would have that kind of affection—admiration—for him unless the whole thing was a hoax or a marketing ploy where everyone hears about this huge bet, but no money changes hands. Why else would the fifty grand still have been in the basement? Right? Nothing else makes sense to me."

"Well, the fact that we haven't found any trace of the money lends credence to your theory. So, look, I'm sorry I was the one who broke all this news to you," said Combs as she pulled a business card from her suit pocket and put it on the stand by my bed. "I've enjoyed reading your articles, especially your last one. If there's anything you want to tell us, my direct line's on that card."

I nodded and began to process everything I'd been told, but it seemed Combs wasn't quite done. She stopped by the door and looked over her shoulder at me.

"And Michael, if you are approached by Mr. Andrianov or any of his men, call that line," she said.

I smiled an incredulous smile and nodded my head yes, but we both knew I was saying no.

* * *

It was my last day in the hospital. I was to be released and sitting on a flight back to Portland the next morning. I had lost 22 pounds and felt weaker than ever, but also clean from the inside out. I had lived for weeks on sustenance from tubes, then eventually steamed veggies, oatmeal, rice, and bland proteins that fed my atrophied muscles. I'd been given a second chance at life. It's a trope, but it was immensely powerful to have survived a near-death experience. Sitting in isolation for so long gave me time to listen to the sound of my own breath and the thoughts that emanated from a place deep within me. I felt gratitude for the miracle of my life.

The fact that machines and medical staff provided so many functions my body could not, challenged my understanding of independence. My continued existence was made possible by a series of medical innovations and people who dedicated their lives to understanding the science of human construction. I owed my life to these people, and the people who taught them, and so on, back to the first shamans and healers. I thought for so long about this chain of dependence it became impossible to find a person with whom my existence shared no thread.

I could barely wait to see Ben and Mary. I felt bad that Ben and I never made it to New Hampshire, but I was happy that I would have opportunities to create more memories with him. There was no shortage of places to explore in the Pacific Northwest.

Ben was going to meet me at PDX. He wanted to fly back to help me with my physical therapy, but Sarah forbid it after reading the *Globe* story: "Two Dead, Cops Missing, One Critical, Over a Cocktail Napkin." The story implied that The Bet was an urban myth, but she felt as if it still had the potential to "bring out the crazies." I didn't know if The

Bet was a myth or not—I just knew I was never going to see the cash. I also didn't think there was anyone crazy enough to push their luck getting involved with the "suspected criminal elements" mentioned in the story.

The reporter didn't speculate as to the whereabouts of Matthew and Derrick, but the comment section was littered with "articulate hypotheses" about their disappearance. The comments claimed they were everywhere from the bottom of Clark's Cove to a beach in Argentina. I was having trouble reconciling my feelings about Derrick. He was my brother and also likely part of a conspiracy to kill me. Every day that went by it seemed less likely he'd be found alive.

The reprints of my articles were so successful that the *Boston Globe* offered me a job as a columnist, and a fancy publishing house in New York offered me an advance to write a book about "the napkin incident." My dream scenario was unfolding before me. I would have to win the lottery to afford a house by Jamaica Pond (my dream neighborhood), but the way things were falling into place, I wasn't yet willing to rule it out. To stack the deck in Boston's favor, the *Portland Daily* was offering buyouts (a.k.a. forced layoffs) to everyone at the paper who made over $55,000 a year. It seemed like the universe was pushing me to take the job at the *Globe*. But Ben and Mary were in Oregon, and being with them was what I wanted most. There would be time to sort it all out, but whatever solution I arrived at would have to include being with the people I loved.

My mother brought my laptop the last time she and Father Francis came to visit. While my brush with death was fresh in my mind, she thought it would be the perfect time to lure me back into the flock. I admired her tenacity, but I had plenty of time to seek explanations of my experience. With my laptop open, I looked inward and wrote things down as they came into my head. For the first time in a long time, I was writing simply because I felt compelled to write.

"I found that happiness and love emanated from a place deep inside me," I began. "I always sought them in other people, goals, and objects, but that search often just led me to a bottle of gin. Perhaps when we find happiness and satisfaction in a task it's like a Geiger counter that helps us understand when we've found the things worth pursuing."

I stopped typing as I noticed my door gently swinging open. It was early, so I assumed it would be the night nurse, Anita, checking on me one last time before she went home. A shoulder came through the door about where her head would have been. It belonged to a big man in work clothes: Timberland boots, Carhartt pants, and a thick blue zippered hoodie. He was carrying a toolbox, but the way it swung around the door made it clear that it was too light to be carrying tools. *Something's wrong about this,* I thought, and immediately typed "My killer was dressed like a plumber," desperately hoping I was wrong.

I shut my laptop as the man entered the room. The hood obscured his face, but I knew it was Derrick before he pushed it back from his head. He looked like he'd escaped from the pits of hell. He placed the toolbox on the foot of my bed and opened it. His eyes were dim and bloodshot. There was no sign from him that he saw me as another human, let alone his brother. He reeked of neglect and stale cigarettes. He looked completely fried.

"There are a lot of people looking for you, Derrick," I whispered.

He nodded as he pulled a handgun and a silencer out of the toolbox. He still hadn't looked at me as he screwed the silencer onto the barrel. He stared at his hands as he spoke. "It wasn't personal before, Mikey. It was about the money. But now I want to kill you."

"I thought you were dead," I said.

"Pretty much," he conceded, looking at me for the first time. His eyes were red with anguish.

"Derrick, it's me," I pleaded as the repetitive sound of metal turning on metal marked my moments left. "I'm your brother. Don't do this."

"I nev'ah had a broth'ah, Mike. Ma and Dad had an example that I nev'ah lived up to," he said, calmly tightening the silencer in place. "You weren't gonna share that money with me and ya know it. It doesn't matt'ah what you say now."

"I only knew about the money the day before you stole it."

"That money was mine," he hissed. "The fuck did you

ev'ah do to earn that money? You abandoned us. That's all you ev'ah did. You w'ah nev'ah around to help me with the shit I was goin' through!"

"I'm sorry, Derrick," I said. "But you never reached out to me either. Why didn't you ever say something?"

"Why, so you could tell Ma and Dad?" he snapped.

"No, Derrick," I said. "So I could have helped. How'd you get into such a fucking mess?"

"You don't give a shit," he said with animus. "The'ah ain't nothin' you can say now to save ya life. I'm gonna kill you and it's gonna make me happy. It's gonna feel good to watch you die."

"Fuck you. You never gave a shit about me either. Your life was too fucking easy. The second you had to try at anything you just gave up. What kind of a fuckin' coward points a gun at his own mother?" I shot back. "Nobody owes you a fucking thing in this life."

"I wanted to kill you the night we stole the money," Derrick said coldly. "But Vinny said not until we had The Bet. I gave him that fifty grand in exchange f'ah the key, but he gave it to you instead. I should'a known he was workin' for Andrianov, but I didn't until he gave you that fuckin' key."

"It was you that killed Vinny?"

"We had it all planned out aft'ah that," Derrick said as his eyes glazed and his voice became even more distant. "Matt shoots Vinny with the plant gun. I shoot you for killing Vinny and we plant the gun on you. Then me and the Donovans split the money. But Vinny was working with the fuckin' Staties to get me and Matt."

"You said Vinny was working for Andrianov?"

"You really 'ah fuckin' stupid, huh?" he said. "The Staties and Andrianov both wanted us f'ah the same fuckin' reason. Vinny put the whole fuckin' thing togeth'ah."

"Sounds like we were both setup."

Derrick began to shake—his mind and body seemed completely dissociated. "Matt got too afraid about what they'd do when they found us. He blew his own fuckin' head off. I went to get us food and I came back to find his fuckin' brains on the wall."

"I'm sorry, Derrick."

He pointed the gun at me. I wanted to live. I wanted to be there for the people I loved, but I didn't fear death. "I'm not afraid to die, Derrick," I said, maybe out of kindness. There was so much pain in his eyes that it hurt to look at him. "But think about what you're doin' to Mum and Ben."

His eyes filled with tears. The pain seemed to increase with every word. "You w'ah supposed to have the money. Me and Matt w'ah just gonna leave."

"You don't have to do this, Derrick," I pleaded one last time.

"But, I want to, Mikey. You 'ah supposed to be dead already, not Matt." He broke down as he spoke. "You aint gonna feel a thing, Mike, 'cause I'm filled with fuckin' mercy."

He took aim and I jerked my head to the side, closed my eyes, and waited for the impact. Two shots were fired. I felt searing pain on the left side of my head. I opened my eyes to see Derrick going limp, the gun falling away from his chin as his lifeless body collapsed to the floor. His blood had splattered on the ceiling and everywhere behind him. I was alive. The first bullet had grazed my head above my temple. Blood was spilling down the side of my face and all over the bed.

I dropped my head into a pool of my own blood and fixed my eyes on the ceiling above me. My wound felt like it was on fire. The flowing blood eased the pain. The hospital staff rushed in. There was a lot of yelling. The nurse, Anita, asked me if I was alive. I moved my eyes in her direction and smiled. She yelled for a doctor. "You're going to be fine, sweetie," she said. "You're going to hold on and you're gonna be fine."

That made me smile wider as they rolled my bed toward the operating room. I thought about Ben and felt awash with love and then my thoughts raced to my father. It only took me getting shot twice to understand why he hid everything from me. I finally understood what he was protecting me from. He was a loving man.

My heart was broken. I hoped my brother found peace.

19

#19 MICHAEL QUINN, GUARD, NEW BEDFORD HIGH SCHOOL WHALERS

It rained for eight straight days after I got back to Portland, but eventually a cloudless sky reveled the snowcapped peaks of Mt. Hood and Mt. St. Helens. I took in their magnificence from the balcony of my apartment as I tended to the salmon, potatoes, and asparagus on the grill.

Paul and his family were over for an early dinner. Mary was opening wine. Paul was explaining to Ben and Tia who the ex-football player Brian Bosworth was and why the shaved swath of hair above my ear that exposed my stitches had earned me the nickname "The Boz" when I went to watch the guys at my regular Saturday morning basketball game. They seemed unconvinced that the moniker would stick.

"I understand it," Ben goaded, "but it's just, you know, dumb."

"It's not dumb," Paul insisted. "It's perfect."

"M.C. Hammer is perfect. It's the same haircut," Ben said, and Tia laughed, but not as loud as Renee and Mary.

These moments with my son and the family we constructed were why the universe was created, I decided. An explosion released all the matter in our universe and a few billion years later, sentient beings were able to observe this creation and to see it in each other. *What more purpose do we need in our lives than to understand that love exists and to have someone to share it with?* I felt content.

"But we already got a 'Hammer Time' at basketball," Paul said. "You can't have two guys with the same nickname. It doesn't work that way."

"You could have 'Hammer Time' and '2 Legit 2 Quit,'" said Renee as Mary brought her some wine.

"I don't know about that." Paul was taking this all very seriously. "I know your dad's not exactly a badass, but it's not like he can dance either."

"I'm standing right here, guys. I can hear you," I reminded them. "And I am a badass *and* a badass dancer!"

"Show us your moves!" Mary crowed as she crinkled her nose.

"Et tu, Mary?" I said with a wink, and she kissed my head.

The doorbell rang. I jumped and made a noise like I'd

been punched in the gut, which startled everyone. There was a pause as I regained my composure. I'd been suffering post-traumatic stress since leaving the hospital. Sudden or unexpected noises rattled me to the core. I caught my breath, smiled an embarrassed smile, and apologized. I asked Paul to take over the grill. Everyone was quiet and tentative. It was all new and nobody really knew how to act when that happened.

"I can get the door," Mary said, and the care in her voice and the gesture warmed my heart.

"I've got to get past this," I told her, rubbing her back. "Thank you." My hand was shaking, but the feel of her skin against mine helped me relax. My mind hummed like a live wire had been plugged directly into my brain. I focused on taking one step at a time, but it felt like I was walking along the edge of a cliff. Every day something happened to trigger my fear, a barking dog, a car horn blast, but I just had to face it. I just had to continue to move forward. I looked back to the patio as I got closer to the door to see everyone staring at me. I smiled and everyone looked away as inconspicuously as possible—which is to say, they were all awkward and conspicuous.

I looked through the peephole. It was the FedEx guy. He was familiar, but I didn't know his name. I signed for a box of copier paper that I hadn't ordered. The return address was Providence, Rhode Island, which made me nervous. I carried it into the bedroom, thinking that if it was a bomb or somebody's body parts, I'd spare the others. It was heavy and felt like paper. It was packed tight, weighed what I thought a box of paper should, and there was no rattling or clunkiness. I put it on my bed and opened it slowly. There were indeed reams of paper in it, but on top was a note: "You remind me of your father. When you write your book, name my character after a Russian gymnast. I always wanted to be a gymnast. Make him handsome with no accent." There was no signature.

This is a lot of effort to tell me it's okay to write the book, I thought.

It was all so surreal. I had calmed down almost completely, enough to realize that I had been sweating profusely and needed to change my shirt. I went into the bathroom and toweled off. *Andrianov wouldn't have just sent a box of paper,* I thought as I reapplied deodorant.

I got a new shirt from the closet and looked at the box as I fastened the buttons. I lifted up one of the reams and felt the paper shift around. I tore off the wrapper and saw four stacks of hundred-dollar bills with about a 2.5-inch buffer of copier paper along the edge. There were six reams of paper each containing $200,000. *The crazy son-of-a-bitch sent me $1.2 million in cash through FedEx.*

I put the money back in the box, covered it with the lid, and placed it on the floor by my desk because I didn't know what else to do.

I went back out to the patio and Paul was taking the

food off the grill. "Did you overcook the fish?" I teased.

"Who do you think you're talking to?" he joked. "I'm the king of the grill! I'm the LeBron James of grilling!"

Ben came close and asked me if I was okay. I hugged him and told him I was and kissed him on the head.

"What was the package?" he asked.

"Just some paper," I said and held him a little while longer. "It was from someone wishing me good luck on my book."